Triple
Cross

Triple Cross

A Triad of Chilling Suspense

TSV RAGHAVAN

PARTRIDGE
A Penguin Company

ISBN: Hardcover   978-1-4828-1219-0
               Softcover   978-1-4828-1220-6
               Ebook   978-1-4828-1218-3

Partridge books may be ordered through booksellers or by contacting:

Partridge India
Penguin Books India Pvt.Ltd
11, Community Centre, Panchsheel Park, New Delhi 110017
India
www.partridgepublishing.com
Phone: 000.800.10062.62

Dedicated to my family and friends

CHIKNA

Senior Inspector Jacob Janardhanan sat on his desk reading a file and sipping the piping hot tea that was served to him a few moments earlier. It was his seventh cup from the time when he came to the office last evening. There was one cigarette left in the packet that he had bought on the way to the office. And it was a pack of twenty. '*Too many cigarettes and too many teas*' He thought ruefully. '*I'll have to cut down.*'

This was a resolution he made every day, and broke after a few hours. Nothing had changed in the past twenty years. It was 4 AM and Jacob had finished reading the file. He stretched himself on the chair and then went to the wash room.

"*I am a little tired.*" He told the constable. "*I shall go to the back room and lie down a bit. Don't wake me up unless it is absolutely important.*"

"*Yes Sir!*" The constable replied.

Very tall, very thin with a long face and sharp features, Jacob with his receding hairline and brooding deep set black eyes would have blended perfectly into a college room or a seminar. He was an intellectual and he looked it. He was a voracious reade r and had a gluttonous appetite for knowledge. He had chosen to be a cop not because of the action involved but because he loved to solve mysteries. He had an excellent record and had won several rewards, increments and awards for his devotion, sincerity, and hard work. Meticulousness was a habit with him. He had solved many cases by sheer scientific and logical analysis and was averse to using force.

The phone rang and the constable picked up. Some one was reporting an accident. The constable jotted down the details on a pad and then rang up the patrolling party. The accident had happened at the east coast road near a place called Uthandi some half a kilometer away from the sea.

When Jacob came out at 5 AM, the constable told him about the phone call. Jacob nodded when the constable told him about the action taken. Jacob went to the wash room again and drank a glass of water. The phone rang again. He picked up.

"Pallavakkam police station,"

"Jacob Sir, Chellappa here."

"Tell me."

"Sir I am at the site where the accident occurred."

"Oh!"

"Sir I think its some thing that could interest you."

Jacob's drowsiness vanished. He listened for a moment and then ran out to his bike, shouting instructions to the constable on the way.

The car lay inside a ditch with the front side hitting the ground and the back side hanging obscenely in air. It was a red colored Maruti Zen but in that early morning light, the color wasn't very clear.

There were a lot of police men and a couple of them were standing inside the pit. Jacob parked his bike near the patrol car and walked towards a dark well built man who was talking on the Walkie talkie.

"Hello Chellappa."

The man saluted and Jacob acknowledged the salute.

"Sir, As soon as I got the message from your station I came here."

Jacob nodded.

"*I saw the car in this condition and got down immediately to see if I could save the people inside. But there is only one man and he is dead.*"

Jacob nodded again and went near the pit. Then he peered inside. The police men were careful not to tamper with anything. Chellappa had told them that Mr Jacob was on the way.

"*Informed the ambulance?*"

"*Yes Sir. They are on the way.*"

As if on cue they heard the sound of the fast approaching ambulance. Men got out and laid out the stretcher.

"*Please be careful.*" Chellappa went and told the chief among them. "*This is a police case.*"

Chellappa was one of Jacob's favorite assistants. At thirty five he was ten years younger than Jacob. In the initial stages he had had, an opportunity to work under Jacob and had learnt a lot from the experience. Even after they were posted to different police stations or check posts, Chellappa had kept in touch with his mentor. When ever he came across a case, Chellappa applied his mind to it, the way Jacob had taught him. This had borne the desired results and Chellappa was praised for his style of working on the cases. Where ever he had doubts, Chellappa would not hesitate to contact Jacob who in turn would extend all possible help. And this time too it wasn't different. Chellappa had called Jacob as soon as he had studied the over turned car.

The body was carefully extracted and brought up. Jacob and Chellappa went closer to have a look.

It was that of a remarkably handsome male dressed in a white shirt and dark trousers. The man wore white socks and brown shoes which looked quite expensive. He was obviously well to do. As the body was placed on the stretcher, Jacob peered at it. On the right wrist the dead man wore a golden watch. He also wore expensive rings on the fingers of both his hands. There was a faint smell of perfume from his clothes. The eyes were half open. What intrigued Jacob most was that, except for a few scratch marks the beautiful face was intact. The face was oval, with regular features, a thin clipped moustache, and fleshy lips, the color of mahogany. The man was a smoker.

The ambulance took the body away to the nearest hospital.

Jacob and Chellappa returned to Jacob's office. Jacob called the constable who was on duty at the time when the call came. That man had completed his night duty and was eager to go home. Jacob did not detain him.

"What time did the call come?"

"At 4.40 AM Sir"

"Thanks, you may go now"

Jacob then put a call to the control room. "Please trace the call which came to Pallavakkam police station at 4. 40 AM."

Tea and biscuits arrived.

"Now tell me brother what makes you feel that there is something special about this accident."

Jacob smiled at Chellappa.

"Sir, Yesterday night there was a downpour at east coast road. The car had fallen into the ditch on the side which would be used by a driver while going from Chennai towards Mahabalipuram."

Jacob nodded.

"The way it ended up at the ditch, at such an hour, shows that it was running at quite a speed."

Jacob nodded again.

"Maruti Zen is a small and comparatively light vehicle. The ditch is five feet from the road. This patch of land in between is muddy because of yesterday's rain. If the Maruti had for some reason skidded and gone into the ditch, there would have been lots of marks on the muddy ground. Secondly with the force with which it landed, the front portion of the car would have been completely smashed."

"Fantastic." Jacob smiled and lit a cigarette. *"Go ahead."*

Chellappa smiled happily. *"In that case Sir, the driver in the car would have been a pulpy mess."*

Jacob chuckled.

The phone rang. Jacob picked up. Then he gestured to Chellappa. Chellappa noted down the phone number of the caller who had informed about the accident. It was from a cell phone.

"May I know whose cell it is? Oh! It is registered in the name of Rashmi enterprises. Thank you."

Jacob put down the phone. There were no skid marks on the muddy ground between the road and the ditch. Chellappa was right. There was a possibility that the car had been pushed into the ditch to make it look like an accident.

At 8.00 AM both went to the hospital where the body was kept. As they entered the corridor, Jacob spotted a woman and a young girl sitting outside a particular room.

"The guy's relatives," Jacob whispered to Chellappa who nodded in return.

Jacob entered the room and identified himself. Chellappa stood outside near the women. Without looking at them straight, Chellappa observed the two. The older woman was dressed soberly and was holding the corner of the sari to hide her mouth. She was sobbing softly. The girl was a very pretty looking teenager and bore a striking resemblance to the dead man. She was weeping with her face against the shoulder of the woman. They were obviously mother and daughter. The daughter was dressed in off white jeans and red T shirt. Then Chellappa spotted a man at the corner of the corridor. He was a dark medium built young man of around twenty five. He was dressed in white pant and white trousers. On seeing Chellappa the man made a move towards him. When he approached nearer, the man saluted Chellappa.

"Who are you?"

"Driver Sir!"

The two women looked at them.

"*What is your name?*"

"*Muthu Sir*"

"*You brought them here?*" Chellappa pointed at the women.

"*Yes Sir*"

Jacob peeped out and gestured. Chellappa went in. The body had been kept in an ante room inside. The Doctor was standing by its side.

"*He died because of a blow from a blunt object to his chest.*" The doctor said. *A couple of ribs are broken, and the death was due to sudden and severe asphyxiation leading to cardiac arrest.*"

"*Could it be because the car hit the ground with such sudden force and his chest hit the steering wheel?*" Jacob asked.

"*Could be, I am not sure. But I was told that the accident was reported in the early hours today.*"

"*That is right. At 4.40 AM*"

"*The man died at least three hours before that.*"

Both Jacob and Chellappa kept a poker face. "*Sure?*"

"*Absolutely*"

The family had been informed about the tragedy by the inspector who had accompanied the body to the hospital. His name was Gopinath and he came to Jacob with a puzzled look on his face.

"*Sir, I want to tell you something.*"

Jacob nodded.

"Sir when the doctors checked the belongings of this man, there was a purse containing several credit cards and thousand two hundred rupees in cash. There was also a small leather pouch with his visiting cards, a small packet containing some gem stones, a big perfumed hand kerchief, and a Parker pen."

"So?"

"But Sir there was no cell phone."

Jacob and Chellappa exchanged glances.

"It Could be in the car." Chellappa said.

"No Sir! I checked. The policemen who were there confirmed that neither the cell phone nor the car keys were found. Both are missing."

"Thanks Gopinath! Your information is really vital." Jacob said politely.

The name of the deceased man was Radhey Shyam. He was a very successful businessman and investor mainly dealing in fancy items, artificial jewelry and precious stones. He was the senior partner of a firm called Rashmi Enterprises. He lived in a sprawling bungalow in the northern part of the city called Anna Nagar, with his wife Sarita and daughter Rashmi, on whose name the firm was formed.

Radhey Shyam was on business trips almost twenty days a month. He used to travel by car, whenever his work took him to some place near the city. He drove himself and seldom used a driver except when he had to be dropped at the airport, bus stop, or railway station. Muthu was specifically recruited to drive either Sarita or Rashmi. The family owned a fleet of cars of various makes and Radhey Shyam drove all of them. The Maruthi Zen was taken by him that fateful evening because first the tank was full and secondly, he had to make a short and fast trip.

Radhey shyam, as Jacob would learn later, never ever discussed his business or his movements with any one including his own wife and daughter. This was the first load of information that Jacob collected by evening of the day when the body was found.

Radhey Shyam had fantastic contacts with the local politicians and big wigs. Jacob informed his immediate superior ACP Dhananjayan about the incident. He also told him what he suspected and that he would be interested in investigating the case. Mr Dhananjayan knew Jacob well.

"*Playing the super sleuth as usual*" He quipped.

"*Yes Sir.*" Jacob said.

"*Okay! Go ahead!*"

"*Thank you Sir!*"

"*You need some one to assist you?*"

"*Sir, I have Inspector Chellappa who was the first person on the site.*"

"*Good! As the deceased belongs to Anna Nagar it comes under the jurisdiction of that circle too. I shall inform them to extend you all possible help.*"

"Thank you very much Sir."

Jacob saluted and left. Within half an hour he got the call from the Anna Nagar in charge. Jacob gave him some instructions

"Please post as many persons as possible both men and women in civil dress near the bungalow. They should blend with the crowd, and if necessary, pose as mourners. I shall be there too."

"Okay!"

Jacob had learnt that Radhey Shyam was a big man. But how big, he came to know only when he reached the bungalow. He and Chellappa had gone there dressed in white shirt and light colored pants. Jacob had wanted to pose as a press reporter but Chellappa's build and tough guy appearance gave him second thoughts. Chellappa looked more like a local don than a press photographer. There was a huge crowd out side the house. A long queue waited outside the bungalow to pay the last respects to the departed soul. Radheshyam's body was kept in the hall.

A small group of children led by an elderly man came near the gate. The watch man saw them and asked the people to make way for them. The group went inside. In a moment there was a wailing sound from the hall. This intrigued Jacob and he looked at Chellappa.

"Wonder who these kids are?" Chellappa mused aloud. Some people turned back to look at him.

"They are from the ashram." One man said.

"Aiyya was a great man. He ran the orphanage." Another man ventured.

Chellappa nodded.

Jacob moved away from and Chellappa stood behind the last man in the queue. From his vantage point, Jacob studied the crowd. What he saw, intrigued him.

Radhey Shaym was a north Indian. But the crowd of mourners consisted mostly of south Indians. At first thought, it did not look any thing special. There are cases where a person has more friends outside his family or community than within. But as it was a crime case Jacob filed away this observation at the back of his mind.

Chellappa's turn came too. Using a large kerchief to pretend that he was mopping his perspiring face, Chellappa entered the room. The body, draped in a white cloth, was lying in state in a glass coffin in the center of the hall. People were going near the coffin, paying their respects, placing flowers or wreaths, and going out of the hall through a side door. Some were weeping softly and some touched the coffin, as a mark of respect for the departed soul. The woman and the girl he had seen in the morning were sitting on the other side near the head of the coffin. Every one was saluting them while going out. Some women even touched the girl and the woman to console them.

Chellappa paid his respects and moved away fast.

―――――――◆―――――――

There was a huge crowd in the funeral procession. Jacob would learn later that several shops and establishments in the area remained closed as a mark of respect for the departed soul. Local politicians placed huge wreaths on the body and local news papers published full length features complete with photographs about the great man. It also formed part of the TV news that day.

It was reported that RadheyShayam belonged to a business family in north, and had come to Chennai twenty years back. He had fallen in love with the city and its people and had decided to make it his home. His wife Sarita and daughter Rashmi were wonderful people. Radhey Shayam had taken pains to learn the language here and people loved to hear his accented Tamil. His daughter Rashmi was born and brought up in Chennai and spoke the language fluently. She was studying in a local college and had a lot of friends. Sarita, it was reported was a highly religious lady and loved to go to temples, make donations and give alms.

At 6.30 PM, RadheyShayam's mortal remains were consigned to the flames amidst wails and slogans.

Next day Jacob sat on his desk with a heap of previous day's news papers. Due to his exposure and his wide experience, Jacob could not only speak, but also read and write Hindi. As he went through the reports, he smiled inwardly at his own apt observation. The Tamil newspapers had the Radheyshyam item in the front pages, under bold head lines. The articles were emotionally charged and short of terming the dead man some sort of a demigod, they had praised him and his family sky high.

'His sudden demise is a great loss to the city and many poor people who had benefited from his generosity and large heartedness would feel orphaned.' The reporter had declared. There were photographs of the great man, and opinions from local leaders.

Even the Tamil news channels did not stay behind in reporting the matter in, as colorful a way as possible.

On the contrary, the same news made it only to the third page of the Hindi newspapers and that too as a small item on one corner. The reporter had been matter of fact, and had added a subtle hint that Mr Radhey Shyam found more comfort in the company of local bigwigs, than in interacting with people of his own community.

As per Jacob's request, the suspicion that it was a murder case was not leaked to the press. The police maintained that it was an accident.

Chellappa had reported that, where as some girls including Rashmi were weeping copiously, Sarita just sat there with a blank expression on her face.

'*Probably numb with shock.*' Chellappa opined.

He had also observed that a young man who looked like a north Indian, and a young girl probably in her early twenties, were near the mother and daughter and that they seemed to be quite close to the family.

The finger print and other experts went through the car with a fine toothed comb. Every inch was examined and finger prints dusted. The dash board had the usual car papers and a copy of Radhey Shyam's license. Almost all finger prints matched with that of Radhey Shyam and his driver.

The doctor had said that the victim had died at least three hours before the accident was reported. That meant that Radheyshyam died at around 1.30 AM the previous night. Going by what the driver Muthu said, Radheyshyam had gone to Mahabalipuram. So the possibility was that the death occurred there.

And the person who had reported the accident, who ever he was, had driven the car with the body in it, to the place where he had dumped it. Jacob began thinking in that angle. It was a rainy night. There would not have been much traffic during that period, except the occasional trucks and buses. A Maruthi Zen would have been a rare vehicle at that hour in that route. Jacob contacted the check post.

From them, Jacob learnt that the Zen had passed through the check post and the driver had opened the window and paid the toll tax. There was nothing unusual about it and Jacob was slightly disappointed when he learnt that cars frequently passed through that route at that hour, carrying tourists, or party goers. Jacob met the staff which was on duty that fateful night, and requested them to give him any tip regarding the car and the occupants, that would help Jacob. Then he returned to the city.

The offices of Rashmi enterprises were situated in a commercial complex a kilometer from Radheyshyam's house. The company owned the complete first floor. The name of the young man, who Chellappa had seen that day in Radheyshyam's house, was Mayank Kumar. He was the manager of the company, and the young girl who had accompanied him, was Ragini, Radheyshyam's secretary cum receptionist.

Jacob called Mayank the next day and told him that he was needed at the police station to sign papers for the release of the Maruti Zen. Mayank was in his late twenties, thin, attractive and well dressed. The man was polite and decent. Jacob took him to the garage where the car was kept. As it was in the name of the company, Mayank signed some papers as authorized signatory. The car was junk any way. Later Jacob took him back to his cabin.

"Mr. Mayank, how long have you been in this company?"

"*I joined three years back Sir.*"

"*What is the main line of business for your company?*"

"*We deal in artificial jewellery, gems and precious stones.*"

"*Mr. Mayank please tell me something about your employer, late Radheyshyam.*"

"*I met him in Bangalore, where I had gone to put a stall in an exhibition. Mr Radheyshyam had visited my stall and examined the wares. I am a good salesman. Mr. Radheyshyam saw me talk to the customers and then on the day the exhibition concluded, he came to me. He told me that he was on the look out for someone who could manage his business in Chennai, as he was on tour most of the time. The offer he made was indeed lucrative, a handsome salary, free accommodation, and a percentage in the profits. I accepted the offer and joined the company.*"

"*Mr. Radheyshyam was on tour for at least two weeks in a month. Even when he was in the city he seldom came to the office. We usually talked on the phone. He was doing a lot of charity and he would either be meeting some political bigwig or making the rounds of orphanages, or schools or hospitals that he ran or donated to.*"

"*Quite a high profile man*" Jacob mused aloud.

"*Sir*" Mayank smiled feebly "*On the contrary, he was a man who shunned the lime light.*"

"*Oh! Really*"

"*Yes Sir. Mr Radheyshyam was a very humble person. He would send his wife and his daughter to cultural functions but would* seldom attend them himself. He was so handsome and well groomed, but he always tried to hug the background."

Jacob nodded slowly. "*Tell me Mr. Mayank where did Mr. Radheyshyam go on his frequent business trips?*"

"*All the states in south, sometimes to Mumbai or Kolkata*"

"*How is the business?*"

"*It is running very well Sir! We get good orders from big parties. And because Mr. Radheyshyam spent a lot of it on charity, it is growing at a steady pace thanks to the best wishes of people.*"

"*Hm! Mr. Mayank you are from North?*"

"*Yes Sir! I am from Kota, Rajasthan.*"

"*and Mr. Radheyshyam?*"

"*he is from Gwalior Sir.*"

"*Madhya Pradesh?*" Jacob asked.

"*Yes Sir.*"

"*Thanks Mr. Mayank for your co-operation.*" Jacob shook his hand.

"*Can I disturb you in case I need your help?*"

"*Certainly Sir*" Mayank said.

As soon as Mayank left, Jacob sent a copy of Radheyshyam's finger prints to the main police station at Gwalior, with a request to check it with their records and see whether they matched with any one. Then he busied himself with his routine work. The reply from Gwalior came after twelve hours. Though Jacob suspected it, the report made him wince and smile at the same time.

The Gwalior police informed that the set of prints matched with that of a notorious gangster called Omi Chikna who was killed in a gangland hit twenty years ago.

'Thank god for small mercies' Jacob thought. *'Chellappa deserved a pat on the back. This was indeed a complex case.'*

Kailashnath belonged to a small village near Jabalpur. One of a brood of five children of a farm laborer, he had gone through all the deprivations, and frustrations that a poor rustic child experiences in the villages of India. He dropped out of school at the age of twelve and came to the town looking for a job. After a short struggle, he landed one, as a helper in a grocery shop. Compared, to the endless hungry days and nights that were his lot in the village, this opening seemed like a paradise to him. Kailashnath worked hard and within a few years became a favorite of the owner Radheyshyam. When he was twenty, Kailashnath got married to a girl from his own village. Her name was Bhagwanthi.

Kailashnath's luck picked up after the wedding. Radheyshyam got him a cycle cart. Kailashnath would load fruits and vegetables from his village every morning, and bring it to the city where Radheyshyam would purchase it from him and sell it in the retail market. Kailashnath would in turn, load his cart with grocery items and ride back to his village, and to the nearby villages and sell them at a good price. A few years after this routine grind, Kailashnath was earning a respectable income from this business.

By prudently investing his earnings, Kailashnath grew richer and richer and within a span of twenty years, he was the owner of half a dozen cycle carts, one shop in the village, and one in the town, and a couple of acres of land where he grew the vegetables and fruits that he sold in the town. He gave jobs to his family members, relatives and several young men in the village as cart drivers, farm laborers and shop salesmen. Kailashnath also built a spacious independent house in the village, for his residence.

But In spite of their improved financial status, Kailashnath and Bhagwanthi were deprived of the joys of parenthood. This hurt the wife more than the husband. She was the one to bear the brunt of snide remarks from relatives and neighbors. Bhagwanthi would weep and complain, and Kailashnath would try to calm her down, but the fact remained that Kailashnath was not able to father a child who would enjoy the fruits of his labor.

When Kailashnath was forty years old, Radheyshyam died. Kailashnath was distraught. Radheyshyam was a father figure for him and Kailsahnath could not imagine life without his nice and kind old employer. For weeks Kailashnath wandered about the village like a mad man.

And then it happened. Bhagwanthi conceived and gave birth to an exceptionally beautiful male child. Believing, that his mentor had incarnated as his son, Kailashnath christened the child as Radheyshyam.

However due to respect and reverence for his ex-employer, Kailashnath gave the child another name—Omkarnath.

"How can I, call my son by the name of the person, who is god to me?" Kailashnath reasoned.

With the arrival of his son, Kailashnath got even more prosperous. He purchased a small delivery van, and converted it into a shop on wheels. This van used to tour the villages and towns and sell all house hold items. It turned out to be a fantastic idea, and within years, Kailashnath had a couple of more such delivery vans.

As his father enjoyed a Godfather like status, Omkar grew up being pampered and spoilt silly by his doting mother, and the villagers. Omkar had every thing going in his favor. Light skinned, with wavy long hair, an oval face, big languorous eyes and regular pleasing features, He was the most beautiful child in the locality. Besides that he was a precocious kid of above average intelligence.

When he reached the age of four, Damayanthi got him admitted to a near by school. Even here Omkar was the star attraction. He had an amazing focus towards what ever he did, and he was among the best students in the class. He studied well, had his share of sports activities, and was a favorite with the boys, not because of his talent in sports, but because he was very generous with his toys which he gladly lent to the other not so fortunate kids. The children vied with each other to be close to him.

As he grew up, Omkar realized that he had the inborn qualities of leadership. He was intelligent, tactful, and had the magnetism to attract the other boys. Business acumen came naturally to him. Above all, he had a special fondness for jewelry, and items which looked shiny and beautiful.

At the age of twelve, with the considerable pocket money that he received from his mother, he started a small money lending business in the school. First he indulged the kids with sweetmeats and savories that were sold outside the school compound, and then when the children got used to it he started doling out small sums to them to buy their favorite eatables. The loan was interest free, and the kids were enamored by Omkar's generosity.

Once he realized that the guys were in the bag, Omkar began extracting his pound of flesh. He made the kids run errands for him while he sat in one corner and regulated the activities. Kids were ready to do his bidding and Omkar made the best of it. After they were totally under his spell, Omkar made his first move towards his game plan.

He carefully selected four boys who were more daring than the others, and told them to raid the fancy stores, in the large market a couple of kilometers from their village. On weekends the boys would go there on the pretext of seeing the wares or buying them and then pick some of the items and vanish. Omkar would receive them from the guys and pay them in cash at a price fixed by Omkar. Every one was happy. Omkar had his collection of fake jewellry and the boys had their money. The kids worked with such professional meticulousness that, by the time, their parents and the public realized what they were up to, the boys were already in their mid teens.

One evening, as usual, when the boys were on the job in a store, a salesman spotted them and tipped off the owner. Caution signs and messages were exchanged between the staff, and when the four boys tried to check out of the store, with their pockets bulging, they were nabbed. There was a big hue and cry and the public joined the staff of the shop to administer a sound thrashing to the four guys. They were taken to the police station and grilled. But by prior agreement, the kids did not divulge Omkar's name.

Though the boys saved him from the law, Omkar could not escape Kailsahnath's suspicious glare. Being doting parents, Kailashnath and Bhagwanthi, had looked on helplessly as their only child was going wayward. They loved him too much, and this prevented them from chastising him. They tried to caution him indirectly, but the boy did not bother to listen. His greed for glamour, and quick money was too much to be controlled. Kailashnath knew that, given the chance, Omkar would not hesitate to sell the same fancy items at a far higher price, as genuine jewelry.

The four boys were let out a fortnight later. Omkar discreetly avoided them They had been branded as thieves in the village, and so any one who had an interaction with them, was looked at with suspicion. Omkar limited himself to his studies and helped his father in the business during spare time.

Years of hard work, and Omkar's capers began taking their toll on Kalashnath. One evening he complained of a severe headache. He was in his shop at Jabalpur. The staff took him to the doctor who examined him, gave him some medicines, and advised complete rest. Kailashnath, came home, took the medicines, had his supper and went to bed, never to wake up again. Omkar was Twenty One.

Now Jacob had something to chew on. So, Radheyshyam was a shady character. That explained why he shunned the company of north Indians. He feared that some day some one may recognize him. He was safe in a city which was totally new to him and where the people would neither know nor care to know about his past. Mayank had told him that Radhey Shyam usually toured only the four southern states.

It was now quite evident that this was a murder case and that the killer or killers had planned every move perfectly. They had to be extremely clever to have successfully trapped a criminal like Radhey Shyam. Everything pointed towards a revenge killing probably in retaliation to some double cross.

The three root causes for any animosity are land, money and women. In this case Jacob chose the second one to begin his investigation. Radhey Shyam had been a gangster and so it could be the more likely cause for his death. Some of the answers lay in Mahabalipuram.

Jacob went about his work in the old fashioned plodding manner. He took one of the news papers into confidence and got several copies of Radhey Shyam's mug shot that they had published with his obituary. He then distributed it among the police men and asked them to scour through every hotel, motel and eating place in Mahabalipuram to find out if any one recognized the face.

Then he shifted his gaze towards something nearer home. Years of working as an investigator had taught Jacob to take up more than one lead to solve any complicated problem. The Gwalior police had informed that Omi Chikna ie Radhey Shyam had died twenty years ago. Radhey Shyam's daughter was eighteen. That could mean that his marriage to Sarita was around twenty years old. There were two possibilities. Either, Sarita did not know any thing about Radhey Shyam's past or she was a co-conspirator in her late husband's activities. The two had staged the killing of the gangster Omi Chikna, and eloped with the loot. Jacob chose to believe the other story. More so because of the way she reacted at the wake. She seemed more stoic than shocked.

Four days after the police began the rounds at Mahabalipuram, Jacob got a call from one of the constables that they had a lead. Jacob rushed to the spot. It was a motel situated in the outskirts of Mahabalipuram, on the way to Pondicherry. The manager of the motel, a young man called Balaji had recognized the face.

Balaji told Jacob that the man in the picture had come to the hotel to meet a man who was staying in room number 108. Balaji showed the register in which the names and addresses of the boarders were registered. Though Jacob was positive that the entry was totally fake nevertheless he jotted it own.

Lalit Kumar, 43/49, Bara Mohalla, Near Government Hospital, Itarsi, M.P.

And then Jacob saw the date and stiffened. It was the day before Jacob found Radhey Shyam's body in the ditch. This man, who called himself Lalit Kumar, had checked in at ten in the morning.

"*What time did this man come here?*" Jacob asked pointing at Radhey Shyam's Photograph.

"*Evening Sir, around 7 PM*" Balaji replied.

"*And when did he go back?*"

"*Around half an hour later Sir, both went together in this man's car.*"

"*Can you describe this Lalit Kumar?*"

"*Yes Sir! He was a north Indian. Medium height, medium build, fair skinned, neatly dressed, around forty years of age.*"

"*Anything else you can tell about him?*"

"*Yes Sir. This was the first time he came to our motel. I mean he is not a regular guest. He returned alone and checked out the same day at 10 PM*"

"*Anything else*"

Balaji thought for a moment. Then he called Babu the waiter. Babu was a veteran of around fifty years of age who looked like he had been waiting on people for donkey's years. He was a small man with a 'Fed up to the neck' look.

"*Babu*" Balaji said "*Inspector Sir would like to talk to you.*" Then he turned towards Jacob. "*Sir he is our senior most waiter. He attended to Room No 108.*"

What the bored looking Babu said made more sense than the dope from Balaji. Babu said that Lalit Kumar was talking continuously on his cell phone. Over the years Babu had picked up a smattering of various languages including hindi, and from Lalit's monologue, he could make out that he was waiting to hand over some important parcel to the person on the other side. He also said that the parcel would arrive in the evening.

"*Could you hear the voice from the other end?*" Jacob asked.

"*I could not hear what he was saying but just once when I was a few paces from the guest, I heard the voice. It was very gruff and virile, more like a growl. Our man was very respectful towards the one on the other side of the line.*"

Jacob nodded thoughtfully. He knew that parcel meant "*RadheyShyam*" And that this man who called himself Lalit Kumar was instrumental in handing him over to the "*Growl*" who could be the killer.

The whole village turned up for the funeral. Kailashnath had been a benefactor and Philanthropist and every one missed him. Omkar took charge of his father's business, and developed it. He was an astute business man and he knew how to make money. Slowly, he began diversifying into his favorite line—fancy goods. He sold the delivery vans, the shop in the village, the land that Kailashnath used for growing fruits and vegetables, and shifted to Jabalpur with his mother Bhagwanthi. The village house was also sold to a wealthy business man. With the proceeds of the sale, Omkar purchased a big flat in Jabalpur.

He then converted the Jabalpur shop into a showroom. After managing it for six months, Omkar put a man in charge of the shop and began touring nearby by towns for business.

No one could have imagined that Omkar was using this business as a front for his main profession as a receiver of stolen goods. So devilishly intelligent was he that even at such a young age, he had already made contacts with professional robbers, and burglars and was purchasing stolen jewelry from them and selling them off at lucrative prices, after reshaping them to change their identity. Not only that, he was also the brain behind several such burglaries. Due to his extraordinary IQ, the gangsters came to him to plan the robberies, which they would then execute verbatim.

When Omkar was twenty four, Bhagwanthi who had been mourning the loss of her husband, fell ill and became bed ridden. Omkar employed a female nurse to serve his mother. He was genuinely fond of her and wanted to show that he cared. But all the treatment, medicines and diet were of no avail. Bhagwanthi's health continued to fail and one month after she took to the bed, Bhagwanthi passed away.

With both his parents gone, Omkar was free to do what he wanted. He sold the shop and the flat in Jabalpur and relocated to Gwalior for good.

———————◆———————

Jacob called Chellappa and gave him the necessary instructions. Then he called Mayank to his office.

"*Do you know someone called Lalit Kumar?*" Jacob came straight to the point.

"*Yes. He contacted us a month ago. He is a gem dealer from Mumbai.*"

"Gem dealer?"

"*Yes Sir? He said that he had received an order for export of gems and as he was not so big in the line he wanted to get into a joint venture with us.*"

"*Have you seen him?*"

"*He never came to the office. I have talked to him on phone. Mr Radhey Shyam met him a couple of times in Mumbai.*"

"*As you have talked to him on phone, can you tell me something about his voice or something that you could judge about the man?*"

"*He is very polite and soft spoken. But he is also very businesslike and in spite of several conversations that I have had with him, he has never gone beyond the formal greetings.*"

Jacob smiled slightly.

"Mr. Mayank! You are an intelligent young man. Now listen carefully. I doubt that Mr. Lalit Kumar would ever call you again. But you never know. In case he does, can you record the conversation?"

"Sure Sir."

"Thanks. And keep this absolutely confidential."

"Certainly Sir!" Mayank said and left.

Kairy, Bankey, Gopa, and Kanju were professional burglars. They were based in various locations in and around Gwalior, and had been Omkar's regular associates and clients. Omkar had planned a couple of very successful heists for them and had disposed off the stolen property too. Everyone had prospered and the foursome looked up to Omkar for guidance. When they came to know that he had settled down in Gwalior, they were delighted.

Omkar had grown up into an exceptionally handsome man. He always kept himself well groomed. The foursome learnt dress sense from him and that helped them maintain a respectable façade in the society. Without making things explicit, Omkar took over the leadership of the gang. Being the most intelligent and educated in the gang, his word soon became law. It was his suggestion that they should all lead separate lives and should not recognize each other in public. None should interfere in the privacy of the other. They had to meet only when they had a job to execute. And Omkar was the one to choose the meeting place. There, they would plan the heist, over drinks and dinner and then the four carried out the plan while Omkar arranged for disposing off the loot. They all lived in different localities and that helped in implementing this code of conduct.

Omkar was already a wealthy guy when he landed in Gwalior. He had his own business card printed, and he introduced himself as a dealer in fancy goods and artificial jewelry. Within the gang he was "*Omi Chikna*" ie "*Omi the looker*". To the society he was Omkar Kailashnath. It wasn't difficult for him to rent an apartment in the heart of the city. He employed a fulltime maid who did the cooking, washing and cleaning. In spite of his beauty, Omkar was sober, businesslike and shunned female company. This image was carefully cultivated by him to keep away from inquisitive and indiscreet neighbors. None had any inkling of the other side of the young man who was so good looking and polite.

Meanwhile, Chellappa accosted Muthu, the driver in Radhey Shyam's house hold. Thoughtfully Chellappa had called the guy to the service center where Muthu used to get his cars repaired. Chellappa was in civil dress, but because of his build and his demeanor any one could have known that he was a cop. So Chellappa brought his own car there on the pretext of getting it serviced. As the mechanics took charge of his car, he took Muthu to a side.

"*How are things?*" Chellappa began the conversation.

"*Fine Sir, my work has increased now.*" Muthu said politely.

"*Is it?*"

"*Yes Sir. Previously I was just a driver, but now I have to do other errands too.*"

"*What sort of errands?*"

"Ayya's tenth day and thirteenth day ceremonies are approaching. So I have to do all the running around to make arrangements, purchase groceries and the like."

"Tell me Muthu how long have you been with them?"

"I have been with them from my childhood Sir. I am an orphan. I was brought up in the orphanage that Ayya runs. My father died when I was ten years old, and my mother married another man. That man had me admitted in the Orphanage. Later when I grew up, Ayya brought me to his house, and I became their domestic servant. He had me educated and then sent me to a driving school. Thus I became a driver in the household."

"So you are like a member of the family."

"Yes Sir."

Chellappa nodded thoughtfully.

"Tell me about everyone in the family Muthu."

"Sir, everyone in the family is very good to me. Ayya was always busy and went on tour often. Amma is a very religious person and she mostly goes to temples, and does a lot of charity. Whenever Amma or Rashmi papa goes somewhere, I drive the car."

"Now think carefully and answer my question Muthu." Chellappa said. *"In the past few months, did anything happen in the house hold or around you that was different from what you had been experiencing all these years?"*

Muthu stood staring at the ground for a few moments. When he looked up, Chellappa frowned. Muthu's eyes were moist.

"*Yes Sir!*" He said in a choked voice. "*Amma suddenly changed after meeting that man in the temple.*"

Chellappa stiffened slightly "*Which man?*"

"A few months ago, I don't remember the date, I and Amma went to the big Shiva temple in Thiruvottrivoor. Amma used to go there at least once a month. That day too as usual we had gone to do charity. I parked the car and Amma stepped out. She began walking towards the temple. Mean while I was opening the boot to take out the bundles of clothes that were to be distributed to the beggars there. Suddenly one man came and called Amma by her first name. She stopped, looked at the man, ejaculated and then said

"*Bhaiyya!*" Then she went and touched his feet.

"*Wait!*" Chellappa said "*Tell me what he looked like*"

"*Sir he was a very tall and well built man. Just like you Sir. And he looked like a north indian.*"

"*How old was he?*"

"*He must be around fifty or fifty five. He looked like a retired Police officer.*"

"*What?*" Chellappa smiled.

"*Yes Sir. He looked like a cop. He had that type of short hair, a clipped moustache and a very deep and gravelly voice.*"

Chellappa hid his excitement. Jacob had mentioned about the "*growl*".

"*Hmmmm! then?*"

"*Then the two looked at each other. And the man said something to her and pointed at a direction. Probably he said that he was staying there. Then Amma asked him to wait, called me and we two went to the temple. The man kept standing there. Usually Amma used to stay a long time in the temple and supervise the distribution of the clothes and eatables. But on that day she went straight to the office, asked me to place the clothes there, gave a bundle of notes to the office manager, requested him to distribute the things and came out with me. Then she went to the man and they both sat in the car. Amma asked me to drive to a park that is near the temple. It has a lot of trees with benches under them. Amma asked me to wait in the car and the two went inside the park and sat in a corner. After a few moments the conversation became more and more animated. I could not hear anything but I saw that Amma had suddenly taken the corner of her Sari and placed it on her mouth. The man was evidently excited and angry and I was very scared for Amma. I looked around for help but it was dusk and there weren't many people around. The man's voice was getting louder and thicker but yet as he was talking very fast in Hindi, I could not understand anything. Suddenly Amma got up, hugged the man who was still sitting and then came running towards the car. She was very upset and when she came near me I saw that her face was as red as a tomato. She simply got into the car, and asked me to take her home. As I went towards the car I saw that the man was sitting on the bench and sobbing uncontrollably.*"

Muthu stopped for a moment. Chellappa waited patiently.

"*When we reached home, Amma ran into the pooja room and shut the door. When she came out an hour later, her face was swollen, and she looked totally spent and distressed. It looked like she had been weeping bitterly.*"

"*Where was Ayya?*"

"*He was on tour.*"

"*Then what happened?*"

"*From then on Amma changed completely. She became a Zombie.*"

"*Did the man meet her again?*"

"*Amma stopped going out. She began spending more and more time in the pooja room. For the past few months, I have been taking the clothes, money and things like that to the temples. A couple of times Rashmi Papa also came with me.*"

"*How was Amma's relationship with Ayya?*"

"*Amma and Ayya are both taciturn by nature. But I could make out that after the incident the relationship had cooled down even further.*"

"*Hm! Muthu you have been quite helpful. Don't let anyone know that we met.*"

"*Yes Sir.*"

Chellappa waited till Muthu went away and then he called Jacob

"*I have a ton of information for you.*" He said. "*I want to meet you immediately.*"

———————◆———————

Jacob sat poker faced. Chellappa had just briefed him about whatever Muthu told him.

"*So, my intuition was correct.*" He said at last. "*This guy had made enemies in two different fields.*"

"*Now that we know that the killer is somehow connected with the family, shall we—*"

"*Question the lady?*"

"*Yes!*"

Jacob shook his head in negative. "*No Chellappa. It would be very unwise and foolhardy. From what Muthu has told you, it looks that the man who we suspect as the killer, was not a bad guy. Further he should have been quite close to the woman, for her to address him as her elder brother. And lastly, for all you know, the woman is either accepting our version that Radhey Shyam indeed died in an accident, or she may even suspect that it was a very well planned execution, and we are not aware of it. In both cases, if we go and question her, it may make her shrink further into a shell, and she may even tip off the killer. That would make things more difficult for us. We have to move in very carefully.*"

"*You mean through the Lalit Kumar angle?*"

"*That line is dead. Lalit Kumar would have vanished in thin air. His job is over and he will never ever contact Mayank. I told you, these guys must have carried out the job with extraordinary precision and tact.*"

The two sat quietly for some time. Jacob was thinking hard. After fifteen minutes, Jacob put a call to the Gwalior police station.

"*Hello! Good evening, I am Jacob, from the Chennai Pallavakkam police station. It was I who asked you about the finger print. Can I*" *talk to the in charge of the police station where this Omi Chikna's case was registered? Yes Just a minute—"*

Jacob Gestured to Chellappa to take a paper and pencil.

"Yes please."

Jacob spelt the phone number aloud and Chellappa jotted it down.

"Thank you Sir." Jacob ended the call and then called on the number that Chellappa had jotted down.

"Hello, Inspector Puran Singh?"

Jacob talked to the man for a couple of moments about the Omi Chikna case. Then he casually asked him whether he knew someone answering the description of the growl. What he heard made Jacob sit up bolt upright. Chellappa frowned.

"Mr. Puran Singh, just don't do anything. I would like to meet the man personally. I shall come over there. Thanks. Bye." Jacob put the receiver down.

Jacob and Chellappa were on the train to Gwalior that evening. In the mean time, Jacob had given the necessary instructions to Inspector Puran Singh.

It was around 4 PM, when the jeep, entered the Gwalior police station. Jacob and Chellappa got down and walked through the main door, acknowledging the salutes of the constables. Inspector Puran Singh received them in his cabin. After the pleasantries were over, Puran Singh ordered tea and snacks.

"Our guy will be here any moment." Puran Singh said.

"Thanks inspector." Jacob said.

"I am sorry I still can't make out, what exactly the matter is." Puran Singh said. He was genuinely puzzled.

"Inspector it all depends on what our friend has to say now. Till then I shall reserve my opinion. But I can assure you that if my judgment is right, this could be one of the most interesting and complicated cases you would have ever come across."

"Oh Really!"

"I hope so."

There was a murmur outside the cabin and after a moment, there was a knock at the door.

"Come in" Puran Singh said.

The door opened and a man came in smiling. He looked at Puran Singh and then at Jacob and Chellappa. Instinctively he stiffened and stood rooted to the ground. His face tightened and his eyes dilated. Jacob and Chellappa looked at him.

He was around five foot ten inches tall, approximately fifty years of age and built like an aging commando. He had a long, extremely virile face and a clipped moustache. He was wheatish in complexion and had a dignified and respectable air about him. The man was dressed in a white shirt and dark pants.

'*Every inch a soldier*' Jacob thought

"Hello Mr. Dinesh. Please sit down." Puran Singh said softly.

The man, who Puran Singh addressed as Dinesh, walked stiffly and sat down on a chair facing the three Police Officers. Puran Singh pushed a glass of water towards him. The man grabbed the glass, and drained it to the last drop. Puran Singh then introduced him to Jacob and Chellappa as police officers from Chennai. Dinesh nodded at the two and then shook hands.

Jacob found his grip quite manly. He marveled at the man's self control. It was evident that Dinesh knew the purpose of their visit. Yet he did not drop his guard a bit. The silence in the room for the next few moments was deafening. Jacob broke it.

"*Mr Dinesh we came here in connection with a murder case.*"

"*Culpable homicide*" Dinesh corrected him.

Chellappa winced. The voice as Muthu had mentioned was, deep and gravelly.

Jacob smiled broadly. "*Oh! Yes! I am sorry.*"

"*You came to arrest me?*" Dinesh was disarmingly matter of fact. "*Depends, on what you have to say.*" Jacob replied politely. Dinesh looked at the floor for a couple of moments.

"*I am not sorry that Radhey Shyam died.*" He said in a low voice which sounded like a growl. "*On the contrary I am glad that I was his nemesis. Yet whether you believe it or not, I never intended to kill him. I can prove it. If I had thought of doing so, I would have first smashed his cruel and handsome face.*" Dinesh paused.

Jacob and Puran singh looked at each other. Chellappa stared at the ground.

"You have been so kind to me. Inspector Saab—" Dinesh looked at Puran Singh *"You could have simply dragged me down to the station with handcuffs on. If you permit me I shall give you the complete story. It may look like a tall tale spun out by me, hence I swear on my family, my wife and my children that what I am going to tell you now is the truth, the absolute truth and nothing but the truth."*

Puran Singh looked at Jacob. Jacob nodded.

"My name is Dinesh Kumar. I am an ex army man. I retired from the Border Security Force, and now I days I work as a driver in a transport company. I drive my own truck which I purchased from the Army quota. I am saying this just to give a back ground about me."

(Dinesh had a younger brother. His name was Naresh Kumar. Naresh too wanted to join the forces, but he was too soft and mild for the job. Yet Dinesh never discouraged him because Naresh had the noble intention of serving his mother land. He was a nice hard working young man. Even while appearing for the competitive exams, he was working as a salesman in a jewelry shop.

Those days Dinesh was posted on the Rajasthan Border, and was busy trying to prevent the infiltration and smuggling that was rampant in that area. He used to get correspondence from his home only once a week. It was only when something was very urgent, did he receive phone calls.

On day Dinesh got a message on his walkie talkie that he should call his family as soon as possible. The message unnerved him, because he was the eldest son in the family and he feared the worst. It was late evening when he reached the check post and put a call to my family. He heaved a sigh of relief when his father answered the call. Dinesh asked him if every thing was alright. His father soothed his frayed nerves and then said softly that Naresh was not well.

Dinesh took a deep breath and asked his father to be more clear about the information. By now he could feel butterflies in his stomach. In a sobbing voice his father broke the news that said that Dinesh's kid brother Naresh was no more.)

After saying this Dinesh paused. He then wiped his moist eyes. The atmosphere in the room in the police station turned gloomy. Jacob and Chellappa stared at the ground. A moment later Dinesh resumed his monologue.

At the time of Naresh's death Dinesh was thirty years old, a commando and unlike his younger brother, a tough no nonsense guy. The news of his brother's sudden demise stunned him. His father had said that Naresh suddenly passed away after a short illness.

Dinesh could not make it to the funeral as there was a lot of tension in the border and he could not get leave. He shed copious tears in memory of his brother and waited for an opportunity to reach home and console his distraught parents. But by the time he could make it, they had already relocated to their village.

When he came to know about the whole matter, Dinesh was very puzzled and upset. His father said that Naresh had been arrested as a suspect in a robbery at the jewelry shop where he worked, and that the boy died of a brain hemorrhage immediately after. Dinesh could not believe this. He could not imagine that his younger brother could in any way be connected to criminals. His sorrow turned into suspicion which grew into a bitter impotent rage. Impotent because the damage had already been done, and besides he did not have the time or the resources to go to the root of the whole problem. After sulking and cussing for a few days, he finally calmed down and went back to his post. Whenever he got spare time, he pondered over the matter. He decided not to rest till he had solved the mystery surrounding Naresh's death.

Dinesh retired at the age of forty five. By then his parents were dead and he was a grandfather himself. His only child, a daughter had married an engineer and was settled in Ahmedabad. Dinesh sold away the property that he inherited, and settled down in Gwalior.

He had a reasonable pension, and he also availed the opportunity to purchase an army truck which he attached to a transport company and began driving it himself. His wife divided her time between Gwalior and Ahmedabad. Now it was time for him to start his investigation.

With his army background it was easy for Dinesh to interact with the police department. He contacted the Inspector who was in charge of the police station where the FIR of the burglary was lodged several years back. The name of the inspector was Puran Singh. He listened to Dinesh's story patiently.

"*If someone had blamed me of such a crime I would have understood.*" Dinesh told the officer in a voice choked with emotion. "*I am a tough guy and could have loved the action. But my brother—*" Dinesh could not speak further.

Puran Singh handed him a glass of water and ordered tea.

"*My brother was the softest person one could come across. Yes, he too wanted to join the forces but that was because he wanted to serve the country. He wanted my parents to be proud of him. And see what happened to him."* Dinesh wiped his eyes.

Puran Singh called for the case file and studied the FIR and the notes. Then he told Dinesh that the case was solved. He also told Dinesh that one Mr. Naresh had been held for questioning but that the man had died of shock in a clinic within hours of being held. Dinesh told Puran that Naresh was his brother.

"Three men were arrested but the loot could not be recovered." Puran Singh told him. *"The accused guys claimed that the loot was with a fourth member, who according to police records was already dead. These three got ten years a piece."*

Dinesh made a quick calculation and found that the convicts would have come out of prison by then. He requested Puran to arrange for a meeting with at least one of them. Puran Singh agreed.

<hr>

A week later Dinesh got a call from Puran Singh. Dinesh rushed to the police station.

"This is Kairy." Puran Singh pointed towards a good looking fashionably dressed man around thirty five years of age. *"And Kairy he is Mr. Dinesh, the brother of Naresh."*

The two men shook hands. Dinesh tried not to show his disappointment. He expected to meet a man with craggy features and flat gangster eyes. But this guy could have blended into any decent social gathering. Kairy and Puran exchanged amused glances at Dinesh's discomfiture.

"Please sit down both of you." Puran Singh said.

Both sat on the long bench in Puran's cabin.

"*I have given him a hint of what you have in mind Mr. Dinesh.*" Puran Singh continued "*So you can ask him whatever you want.*"

"*Thank you Sir.*" Dinesh said. Then he turned towards Kairy. "*I need your help Mr. Kairy. I have been bearing a very heavy cross on my mind for the past several years.*" He paused for a moment. "*How do you know my brother Naresh?*"

"*Mr Dinesh neither I nor my other two colleagues knew him.*"

Dinesh sighed. It could have been relief

"*and what about the other two of your associates? Could they have known him?*" Dinesh asked.

"*One is dead the other has vanished.*" Kairy took a deep breath. "*Then can you tell me how my brother got involved in this matter?*"

"*Mr. Dinesh, the fourth member Kanju, was an old associate. We had done a couple of jobs together. It was he who introduced us to a guy who we knew just as Omi Chikna. Probably his name was Om Prakash, but I am not sure. He was a very handsome man and thus the adage. Omi used to interact more with Kanju than with us three. Only when a job had to be pulled, did we all come together. It wasn't any different in this case too.*"

The snacks and tea that Puran had ordered arrived. Kairy stopped talking. The tea boy served the things and left. Kairy took a sip of the piping hot tea.

"*Omi planned and we four executed. He was also the receiver of stolen property. He knew how to dispose it off.*"

"*You say that one is dead.*" Dinesh said "*Who is the guy?*"

"*Omi.*" Kairy looked at Puran Singh. Dinesh frowned.

"*Actually the Police got a tip that one of those who were involved in the robbery, called Omi Chikna was murdered by his own associates. A badly mangled body was recovered.*" Puran said.

"*We all saw the photograph of the body.*" Kairy continued. "*So the other guy is—*"

"*Kanju.*" Kairy said.

Dinesh turned to Puran Singh "*Sir I think that Mr. Kairy has told me all that I wanted to know.*"

Kairy looked at Puran Singh and then at Dinesh, and then with a swift nod and hand shake, he left.

"*Sir! Please pardon me for bothering you so much.*" Dinesh said "*If it is okay by you, can I see the file?*"

Puran nodded. Then he took the file from his drawer and gave it to Dinesh who shivered instinctively and closed his eyes. For the next one hour, Dinesh studied the file. He saw the photograph of the corpse carefully and took some mental notes. Then he read about how the police had dusted fingerprints from a remote area a few days before the burglary. It was there that they had got Naresh's finger prints which matched when they took the prints of all the employees the day after the burglary.

Dinesh's face clouded. This was leading him nowhere. Kairy was denying knowing Naresh. Then how was it that his innocent brother got stuck in the quagmire?

Dinesh returned the file back to PuranSingh, thanked him for his cooperation and left.

———————◆———————

Unlike Puran Singh or the other cops who investigate a case in a professional manner, Dinesh had a personal interest in this one. So whatever he read or saw he remembered very well and when he reached home, he took a long note book and wrote down everything. Then he began thinking.

The whole problem began with the finger prints. There was a genuine informer. There could also have been more. The first tip that the police received ended with six sets of finger prints landing in the police files. Even if it may be presumed that his brother was somehow involved, then the intention of the informer was to get him arrested. Dinesh could not make out who could have had such an animosity towards his brother. Dinesh closed his eyes and went into a brown study. Suddenly he woke up with a start.

"*Fantastic.*" He ejaculated "*Absolutely fantastic.*")

———————◆———————

Jacob was listening to all this patiently. Puran Singh was also interested now. He was eager to know what Dinesh had deduced that the department had chosen to ignore.

Dinesh could not make out whether it was Kanju or Omi, but he knew that only one person was involved. And this person had some interest in fixing Naresh for good. Dinesh began investigating on my own. Call it luck or Naresh's innocence, but the first lead he got was from the same jewelry shop where Naresh worked.

When Dinesh went there he found that the shop was very big. He went to the owner and introduced myself. He was a young man in his late twenties. His name was Prabhat and he was the son of the gentleman who was Naresh's boss several years ago. Dinesh told him the purpose of his visit. The boy was quite cooperative.

"Mr. Dinesh I was a child when this thing happened. It would be better if you talk to my father."

"I would be grateful if you take me to him."

Prabhat's father Seth Trilokchand was a venerable saintly looking person, who Dinesh met in a temple where Sethji spent most of his waking hours. When Prabhat introduced Dinesh to him, Sethji looked at him with sad yet kind eyes.

"Namaste Dinesh Ji."

"Sethiji I am sorry to bother you."

"Not at all, please sit down."

Sethji pointed at the steps leading to the temple. He then came and sat beside Dinesh. Prabhat excused himself, went in, paid his respects to the deity and left discreetly.

"I was expecting you." Sethji said in a kind voice. *"All these years I have been waiting to talk to someone about the matter that has been weighing down my heart."*

Dinesh nodded numbly.

"Ask me whatever you want to." Sethiji said.

"*Sethiji*" Dinesh began "*Do you believe that my brother was a thief?*"

Sethji sighed. Dinesh looked at his face. His further investigation depended on the answer from this respectable old man. Dinesh was quite tense.

"*No!*" Sethji's voice was firm.

If there was one word, that lifted all the weight off a man's chest. It was this. So relieved was Dinesh that tears streamed down his eyes. Sethji looked at him benignly.

"*Your brother was a very nice boy.*" Sethiji said "*I treated him like my own son. He was intelligent and hard working and we all knew that he dreamt of becoming a soldier.*" Sethihi smiled ruefully "*Soldier in a jewelry shop.*"

"*Then how—?*" Dinesh asked.

Sethji sighed again. "*Yes! That has surprised me too. Police said that they had found his fingerprints matching with that of one of the thieves. We were all stunned. I even told the police to treat the boy with kid gloves, as I was sure there had been some mistake in identity. But before we could take any step towards solving the case, the poor boy hemorrhaged and died.*"

There was a gloomy silence for a few moments.

"*The whole thing affected me a lot.*" Sethji continued. "*As If the loss of property was not enough, the death of your brother shattered me completely. I was never the same again. I hung on for some more years till the business recovered and then gave away everything to my sons and—*" Sethji looked towards the temple.

Despite the gloom that pervaded all around, Dinesh instincts were intact. He sensed that the key for the puzzle lay with Sethiji. He braced himself.

"*Sethiji do you think that Naresh could have been a pawn in a bigger game?*"

"*I don't think. I am sure.*" Sethji said. Startled at the tone Dinesh looked at him. Sethiji had suddenly turned grim. Dinesh waited.

"*I never liked that guy.*" Sethji said in a slow bitter voice. "*If only he hadn't been a good customer, I would have chosen to see the last of him.*"

Now Dinesh was alert.

"*Who?*" He asked

"*One guy came to the shop often, and went straight to Naresh every time.*" Sethji said. "*It is not unusual for customers to choose their own salesmen. Further Naresh was always around, when the guy came.*"

"*What was his name?*"

"*I don't remember. I seldom interacted with him. Ours was one of the biggest shops in town and every day we came across several customers. This guy came only once a month or at the most every fortnight.*"

Then Sethji snorted a chuckle. Dinesh looked at him quizzically.

"*If only that fellow hadn't been a beauty, I would have forgotten him.*"

"*Beauty?*" Dinesh asked.

Sethji nodded.

"*Yes! He was a very handsome boy. Always well groomed, looked like a film star.*"

"*Did he come after Naresh died?*"

"*No*" Sethiji said. "*And in spite of the arrests, the loot was never recovered.*"

"*Omi Chikna!*" Dinesh's thought. He kept a poker face. To make himself doubly sure, he asked Sethiji whether the name '*OMI*' rang a bell. Sethji thought for some time and then shook his head in negative.

"*Thanks Sethiji. I am relieved. It is heartening to know that you believe in my brother's innocence.*" Dinesh said.

Sethji looked at him strangely. Then he got up and took his hand.

"*Naresh was lucky to have a brother like you.*" He said. "*Don't let the boy's unfortunate death go unanswered.*"

Dinesh nodded, saluted Sethiji and left. It was soothing to learn that he was not the only one who was crying for Naresh.

———————◆———————

From Sethji's description of the man, it was evident that Naresh's enemy was Omi and not Kanju. The search had narrowed down a little. From then on, Dinesh stopped thinking like Naresh's brother, and got into the mind of this man who had led everyone by the nose.

Omi had decided to rob the shop even before he began frequenting it. And at that time Naresh would not have appeared in the picture. He was just another salesman. Sethji had said that he did not like him in spite of his good looks. Omi was friendlier with Naresh than he was, with the other guys probably because both were of around the same age.

Omi came, saw, made his purchases as well as his plans, and then hit the shop for good. It was as simple as that. Cut and dried job.

'*But why should he nail Naresh?*' This is what intrigued Dinesh. There is a Hindi proverb—there are three root causes for any enmity or trouble: Land, money and woman. Naresh was not a landlord. He was not rich. And Omi had also succeeded in his own mission. Then what made him commit such a cold yet fool hardy act?

Anyone who had pulled off such a brilliant heist would have made sure that Naresh did not come into the picture at all, lest the innocent guy blurt out something which would be the end of Omi's capers. After spending hours over this puzzle Dinesh came to the conclusion that the answer to the whole puzzle lay with a woman.

As there was a considerable age difference between Dinesh and Naresh, they were not so close to each other. Even nature wise they were very different. Dinesh was the sportive outgoing type, and Naresh was shy and introverted. Yet Dinesh was sure that Naresh was not a frivolous skirt chaser. So the possibility of his and this guy's fighting over a girl was ruled out. Dinesh kept brooding over that matter endlessly.

And then he recalled that kid.

This girl called Sarita was the only child of their neighbor in Maharajpura. Her father Shivlal ran a grocery shop. Naresh and Sarita were in the same school, and were thick as thieves from childhood. Everyone in the locality was amused at the way the two kids behaved like two peas in a pod. Dinesh's friends used to tease him often saying that Naresh had chosen his life partner even before Dinesh. Sarita spent more time in Naresh's home than in her own house.

Dinesh's parents had relocated to their ancestral village after Naresh's death. So Dinesh had lost all touch with Maharajpura. Yet on a hunch he went there and met Sarita's father.

It was an emotional reunion. Shivlal and his wife hugged Dinesh recalled the past and shed copious tears. Dinesh learnt that Shivlal was now a big man. He owned a small departmental store that fetched him a reasonable income. A team of well trained staff took care of the store and Shivlal was enjoying the status of a respectable Seth. Shivlal told Dinesh that Sarita was married to a successful business man based in Chennai, and that his Son-in-law had financed the acquisition of this departmental store. Shivlal was all praise for that man who Shivlal called Mr. Radheyshyam.

"And to think that I met my Son-in-law thanks to the boy who I liked most, your brother Naresh." Shivlal sighed.

This offhand remark put Dinesh totally off balance. He steadied himself.

"Naresh?" He asked most casually.

"Yes. It was a coincidence. My Son-in-law came to my shop and inquired about Naresh's address. They happened to be friends, and so he had come to offer his condolences after the poor boy's

demise. But your parents had left by then. So I invited him to my house for lunch."

Dinesh smiled ruefully. Even now he was not very sure.

"What does you Son-In-Law do?" He asked.

"He is a dealer in gemstones, jewelry etc."

"I see! How is your daughter?"

"She is very happy." Shivlal said proudly. *"My Son-in-law dotes on her. He knows about her affection for Naresh, and so he takes extra care to keep her happy. Now I am a grandfather of a beautiful young girl."*

"I am happy to know that" Dinesh exclaimed. *"And I would be happier if you showed me their wedding album."*

Shivlal, the simple man that he was, obliged readily. As Dinesh opened the beautifully bound volume, his heart skipped a beat. On the very first page he saw the face that he was searching for so long.

———◆———

"Inspector Saab (Dinesh turned towards Jacob) you have seen the dead body. The fellow looked so good even in death. But the photo in the album was several decades older, and despite my bitterness I should admit that Omi Chikna who Shivlal knew as Radheyshyam, was a devastatingly attractive man. He could have been a film star, or a magnate or anything that he wished to be. It was indeed unfortunate that the fellow chose to be a devil."

By the time Dinesh was through with Shivlal, he knew who he was looking for. Tactfully he took Sarita's address in Chennai.

He told Shivlal that he was a transporter and that he may be going to Chennai on business trips. There was a possibility of Omi finding out all about this but Dinesh was ready to take the risk. Dinesh had seen his photograph. Omi did not know how Dinesh looked like.

As a commando Dinesh had learnt that one should never underestimate his rival. And Omi was no ordinary foe. Dinesh planned his next move meticulously.

As a transporter who drove his own truck, it was not difficult for Dinesh to plan a trip to Chennai. The opportunity came a fortnight later. He unloaded his truck at the go down in Chennai, parked the truck, and took an auto to the place where Sarita lived. He got down a furlong away, and strolled towards the house.

As he turned into the street where Sarita's bungalow was, Dinesh stopped abruptly. His heart leapt forward and then began racing. Omi was standing near a gleaming limousine, talking on the phone. Dinesh stepped back to hide himself under a tree, and took a look at the fellow.

Omi looked every inch a prosperous business man. Dinesh was several paces away from him, yet he could see that the man had managed to retain his looks. Dinesh wondered how the devil could have lurked behind such a charming face.

As he stood there unsure of what to do, a young girl came out of the bungalow. She was holding a leather bag of some sort. Even a fool could have made out from her face that she was Omi's daughter. Suddenly Dinesh felt drained. Confronting Omi was one thing. But pointing an accusing finger at him in front of his child was something else. A few minutes later, father and daughter left in the car in the opposite direction. Dinesh kept standing there awkwardly.

But as mentioned before, luck was on Dinesh's side. As a matter of habit he had memorized the registration number of the car that the two left in. That evening, as he was strolling outside his lodge, he saw the same car coming towards him from a distance. It turned into a parking lot near a huge temple. Dinesh walked briskly towards it. He was in time to see Sarita get down from the car and walk towards the temple.

In spite of the time lapse, Dinesh could recognize her. Her sweet plump face had aged a little, but the gentleness and innocence were still intact. He called her by her name, and she turned around. After the momentous shock she came and touched his feet.

It was Sarita who suggested that they should go to the park and have a chat. Dinesh was in two minds now. He regretted having come to Chennai. Life is for the living and Naresh was dead. There was no pointing in digging up old and bad memories. But Sarita seemed to be eager to talk to him.

The conversation began simply though. They exchanged notes about each other's family. Dinesh was relieved that Shivlal had not mentioned about him to her. All the bitterness that Dinesh had for Omi looked insignificant compared to the affection that he had for this girl who he saw as a kid sister. Dinesh wanted to drop everything and leave, after wishing her all the best in life.

And then Sarita threw the vulnerable Dinesh off balance. She asked him casually, how he took Naresh's demise. The question was so sudden and unexpected that Dinesh blurted out what he suspected. And to his horror, Sarita did not contradict him.

When Dinesh told her that he suspected foul play in the Naresh affair, Sarita gave him a sidelong glance and then stared at the ground. And then she began probing Dinesh gently. The tough and taciturn Dinesh was no match to the soft, tactful and sweet Sarita. She drew Dinesh out of his shell by throwing the necessary baits. She said that she was puzzled by the whole matter, and that she regretted her helplessness.

It did not take long for Dinesh to come out with the truth. And when he told her, her reaction was strange. Instead of shouting and cussing at Dinesh, Sarita blushed and began weeping. Now Dinesh was certain that he was on the right track. Teary eyed he explained his position and the mental torture that he had gone through all his life. Sarita got up abruptly, hugged Dinesh tight, touched his feet again and ran away.

Dinesh sat there for an hour or so and then trudged back to his lodge. He had never felt so drained. On one side was justice and on the other was Sarita's life. Omi was her husband, and her child's father. Much as Dinesh hated Omi, he could not bring himself to harm the guy now. It was frustrating but Dinesh had no other alternative except to drop the idea of revenge and leave Chennai for good. And that is what he did.

During his occupation as a transporter, Dinesh had come across people from various walks of life. With some he had a casual acquaintance and with others, he was closer. Rajanand was one from the second circle.

Rajanand belonged to Bhopal. He was a dealer in electronic goods, and was a frequent traveler to major cities. After being a travelling salesman for several years, he had at last set up shop in Pune, with the help of some business associates. Things had become easier for him from then on, and save for frequent drives to Mumbai, he had begun avoiding long trips.

One winter evening, Rajanand was driving back from Mumbai to Pune, when he suddenly had an attack of hay fever. To his frustration, Rajanand found that he had not brought his medicine kit along. With sheer will power, he tried to drive further, but after a few kilometers, he stopped abruptly, parked his jeep on a corner, switched the head lights on, and sat, wheezing and coughing violently. It was in the middle of the night, and Rajanand was stuck somewhere in the western ghats. He had his cell phone but he could not make a call due to breathlessness. He thought that it was the end of the world for him.

AND THEN DINESH CAME . . .

Dinesh was driving his truck from Pune to Mumbai when he spotted the jeep. He stopped, took his cell phone and got down to see what was wrong. Incidents like this were common in that area and Dinesh was a helpful man.

As soon as Rajanand saw Dinesh, he gave up and the attack got more severe. Dinesh picked him up, took him to his truck, gave him a strong shot of brandy, and called the patrolling police. Within half an hour the police came with an ambulance and took Rajanand to the nearest hospital. Dinesh gave his visiting card to the police and left.

A week later Dinesh got a call. It was Rajanand. He was weeping and thanking Dinesh, for the Good Samaritan act. Dinesh was happy that Rajanand was hale and healthy again. Rajanand insisted on Dinesh meeting him on his next trip that side. A month later they met, and Rajanand hugged him, and took him to his family and friends. Dinesh was amused by this show of emotion but he played along. Rajanand took him home and treated him to a splendid dinner. From then on they were close pals, and at Rajanand's insistence, Dinesh made it a point to look him up or call him whenever he was in Mumbai.

Rajanand was a prosperous business man. He also had contacts with other big wigs in different lines of business. Within a year, Dinesh was a regular guest at a club in Mumbai where Rajanand was a member.

On the completion of one year of their friendship, Rajanand invited Dinesh for dinner and drinks. It was on the same day that Dinesh had given a new lease of life to Rajanand a year before. Some of Rajanand's close friends were also invited. The group celebrated the evening, drinking and chatting quietly. Rajanand praised Dinesh sky high, to the embarrassment of the cool headed soldier. As the evening wore on Dinesh learnt that one of Rajanand's guests was a dealer in artificial jewelry and gems. Tactfully Dinesh filed this information away without revealing anything.

This was some months after Dinesh had met Sarita in Chennai.

Six months passed without any communication between Dinesh and Sarita. By now the man had left the problem behind. As far as he was concerned, it was all over. He had scrupulously avoided any trip to Chennai.

One evening, as he was getting ready to take a load of goods to Jaipur, Dinesh got a call. Dinesh looked at the number on his cell phone and frowned. It was from Sarita. He answered the call. Even as they exchanged greetings, Dinesh could make out that Sarita was depressed. He asked her if everything was alright. Sarita began weeping. Dinesh was embarrassed. He tried to console her. But what Sarita said made Dinesh teary eyed. She wondered how Dinesh could swallow such an injustice to the one person who they both loved so much. Sarita told him that from the day she met Dinesh, a part of her was dead. She could not face Omkar anymore. She was disgusted with herself, with Omi and with her affluent but artificial life. She said that she would have been happier as the wife of a nicer though poorer Naresh. The suspicion that Omi had caused Naresh's demise only to wed her, made Sarita hate herself more than she hated Omi.

Finally Sarita told Dinesh that if they left this gross injustice unpaid for, her soul would never rest in peace.

All the way to Jaipur, Dinesh pondered over the situation. The more he recalled his conversation with Sarita, the more upset he got. He could realize that Sarita still loved Naresh, and that her plight was even more pathetic than his own. He had lost a brother. She had not only lost the love of her life, but was forced to live with the very person who was solely responsible for her loss.

At Jaipur, Dinesh got a consignment to be unloaded at Surat. He jumped at it. When he reached Surat, Dinesh called Rajanand. They met at the same club in Mumbai the next evening. Without revealing much, Dinesh told Rajanand that he wanted to confront a man who owed him a huge debt. Dinesh told him that the man was dealing in gems and artificial jewelry and that Dinesh wanted someone who could help him meet this guy. Rajanand agreed to help.

Within weeks, Rajanand and his own gem dealer friend trained a fellow in the rudiments of the business. This guy was a professional conman and he agreed to work for them for a reasonable price. They supplied him with the necessary samples, visiting cards with a fictitious name, and an office address along with a complete list of cell numbers of people from the jewelry line. This guy, who now called himself Lalit Kumar, approached Omkar as a regular dealer in gems, and artificial jewelry.

Over the years, Omkar had become more and more laidback and complacent. Years of rich and peaceful living had eroded whatever suspicion or caution that he had in the beginning. Providentially, Sarita too had chosen to suffer silently, instead of pitch forking the whole family into turmoil by asking Omkar embarrassing questions. When Lalit Kumar's call came, Omkar was the last guy to suspect anything.

Neither Dinesh nor Lalit knew each other. Lalit played his role as a dealer of gems perfectly well. Initially the conversation between him and Omkar was over the phone. Then Omkar looked him up on one of his trips to Mumbai. This foreplay went on for a couple of months, till Dinesh informed that the he was ready for the showdown.

Lalit contacted Omkar and told him that he was coming to Pondicherry on business and that later he would call him so that they could meet. Meanwhile Lalit informed Dinesh about the plan. Dinesh came to Mahabalipuram, and checked into a seedy hotel. The next evening, he got a call from Lalit Kumar that Omkar had arrived. Dinesh gave him the necessary instructions and waited. That morning Lalit had seen Dinesh for the first time. Both had taken the necessary precautions. Lalit had given a wrong forwarding address, and Dinesh had dressed himself up like a well to do landlord who had come to the city for the first time.

Omkar came to the motel where Lalit Kumar was staying and the two went out in Omkar's car. As Omkar had driven all the way from Chennai, Lalit offered to do the driving now. Lalit told Omkar that he had come there to meet an old friend and that the three should have supper together. Omkar nodded. It was already dusk and soon enough it was dark.

Lalit drove the car to the hotel where Dinesh was waiting for the two. On being introduced to Omkar by Lalit, Dinesh played the rustic fool to perfection. He beamed and put Omkar further off guard by making silly statements.

After the two settled down, Dinesh went in and brought a bottle of Whiskey, and suggested that they should have a couple of drinks before going for supper.

The three sat down for the evening. Lalit was the common friend and hence he kept up the conversation for a while. When they were two pegs down, Lalit excused himself to bring cigarettes, and vanished. His work was over.

It was certainly Omkar's Judgment day. His past was catching up with him. A couple of moments after Lalit disappeared, It began drizzling. As it was rainy season, the windows were already closed. This was a seedy dingy rat hole usually occupied by junkies and tourists. No occupant bothered to find out what the other was doing. Everyone had his own problems to take care of.

Dinesh, excused himself, went, closed the door and turned around. Omkar's back was towards him. Dinesh stepped forward and pressed the nerves behind Omkar's ears, suddenly and expertly. Omkar slumped forward. Dinesh, picked him up and took him to the wash room. He then sealed all the doors and windows. Now the two were alone.

Dinesh splashed ice water on Omkar's face. The fellow groaned and tried to open his eyes. Dinesh stared at him.

"*Hello Omkar!*" The silly babble had vanished and the trademark growl had taken over.

Omi winced. He could recall that Lalit had introduced him to this peasant as "*Radheyshyam.*" '*Then how could this fellow call him by the name which even he himself had chosen to forget?*'

"*What?*" Omi hissed.

"*I said hello!*" Dinesh spat "*Omi Chikna.*"

Omi sat bolt upright. He stared at the face which was as stern and hard as it looked stupid and vulnerable just half an hour back.

"*I—I—don't understand!*" He stammered.

Dinesh looked at him and smiled. Then he sat down on a stool. Omkar's mind got clearer. He mistook Dinesh for a police man or a detective who was probably digging up old files.

Omkar was no ordinary criminal. He still retained the same old devilish brain and the confidence of a gangster. In a second he began planning his way out of this situation.

"*What do you want?*" He asked quietly.

"*What do you have?*" Dinesh parried.

"*Ask me.*"

"*I want Naresh back.*"

A mule's kick on the head would not have had a more devastating effect on Omkar than this short line from Dinesh. He jerked backwards, sucked some air and puked on the floor. Then he began coughing wildly. Tears streamed down Omkar's face but this did not fool the soldier. Omkar spat, rinsed his mouth, and then slumped on the closed commode. Dinesh waited patiently.

"*Who are you?*" Omkar gasped.

"*Dinesh! Naresh's elder brother.*"

Omkar stared at the floor for a few moments. Lalit had introduced Dinesh as "*Shri Vilayati Prasad.*"

Omkar felt very exhausted. He tried to say something but words failed him. Now he knew that he can't fool the man who faced him now. Neither his looks, nor his charm, nor all that he had acquired over the years could impress this solid, stolid, specimen of manhood.

"*Tell me what you want me to do!*" Omkar was amazed at his own voice. It wasn't that of a successful, charming, confident business man. Instead he sounded like an aging petty trader who was trying to reason with the authorities who had come to demolish his shop.

"*I want the complete story.*" Dinesh said.

———————◆———————

Dinesh took out a small tape recorder from his pocket. Omkar looked at it disbelievingly. Dinesh placed the tape recorder on a small stool near Omkar.

"*I am going to record every word of what you say. Let it take the whole night. I don't care. But I want the complete testament in your own voice. And listen—*" Here Dinesh leaned forward and peeped into Omkar's eyes

"I know that you know who I am. Don't try to play tough guy with me. I will not blink before snapping your dainty neck." Dinesh displayed his sinewy arms.

Omkar closed his eyes. He indeed knew who Dinesh was. It dawned on him that it was the end of the road for him. This man certainly meant business. Omkar shivered at the thought of spending the rest of his life in a prison cell. He brooded for a few moments. Dinesh was in no hurry. Omkar smiled weakly. He imagined the reaction of his family and those who knew him, once they learnt about the other side of the man who they all knew, loved, revered and respected as Radheshyam.

The name Radheyshyam struck a chord. The gangster shook his head slowly. Dinesh frowned. Omkar looked at Dinesh.

"Okay!" he said finally. *"You want the whole story. You will get it."*

Omkar spoke for hours. What he said made Dinesh wonder whether facts could be so incredible.

Naresh was a salesman in one of the big jewelry shops which Omkar frequented. Besides dealing in such items, Omkar also liked to wear them. Naresh and Omkar were of around the same age group and thus became good friends within a short time. Omkar's house was on the way to Naresh's house and so, Naresh would drop in on weekends for drinks and snacks.

Naresh belonged to a village called Maharajpura in the outskirts of the city. Naresh's elder brother Dinesh was in the armed forces and was posted at the Rajasthan border overlooking Pakistan. It was also Naresh's dream to join the millitary. He had applied once but failed, and now he was preparing again for the written exam.

One evening as they sat in Omkar's house, Naresh told him about his plans. While Naresh was a heavy guzzler, Omkar sipped his whiskey slowly. With a couple of pegs down his throat, Naresh got tipsy and romantic. He slipped into a fond reverie and slurred that he looked forward to becoming a soldier and marrying Sarita.

"*Sarita?*" Omkar smiled. "*Who is she?*"

Naresh screwed his eyes to see Omkar clearly. "*You don't know? Haven't I told you before? She is the love of my life.*"

"*Oh is it!*"

Naresh fumbled into his pocket and took out his purse. He opened it and handed it over to Omkar.

"*See that is her photograph.*"

Omkar threw a casual glance at the mug shot. And then he sat rooted to the chair. It was the face of a very young fresh looking girl, who was pretty in a homely way. If there was something called love at first sight, it was this. Opposites attract. Sarita's delicate features and innocent look hit the cunning Omkar like a thunderbolt. He felt that he and Sarita were made for each other. She was the type who every young man would love to have as a life partner. Omkar was young and he wanted her. He masked his feelings and returned the snap to Naresh.

"*How is she?*" Naresh asked.

"*Excellent choice*" Omkar answered politely.

Omkar's devilish brain began working. That evening, when Naresh left, Omkar put on plastic gloves, took Naresh's glass carefully and placed it inside a cardboard box.

Omkar knew Naresh's address in Maharajpura. Naresh had told him every thing about his family. And now Omkar had learnt that Sarita was Naresh's neighbor.

One evening a fews day later Omkar went to Maharajpura and walked towards Naresh's house.

Omkar was aware that he was unusually good looking and hence his face could get registered easily. It was winter. He wore a huge oversized pullover, and tied a thick blue scarf around his head. He also wore horn rimmed spectacles to be doubly sure that he looked commonplace. In such an attire it wasn't difficult for him to act like a young man suffering from a bad cold. Wheezing and coughing, he entered the street where Naresh lived. To his amazement, Sarita was standing outside her house talking to a small child. Omkar slowed his pace and looked at her without getting noticed himself.

She was wearing a pink color suit, socks, and slippers, and had a shawl draped around her body. Her face was plain, but healthy and glowing. There was not an ounce of guile in her big black eyes. She had a very small mouth and her lips were rosy. Omkar walked towards her wheezing and sweating. As he reached near her, he stopped and began breathing heavily. Sarita and the child looked at him. Omkar gave them a pathetic glance and looked away. In spite of the fact that he had hidden his identity pretty well, Omkar did not want to take any chances. After a few minutes, he slowly walked away without uttering one word.

During a casual conversation with Naresh, Omkar learnt that Sarita's father ran a grocery store near their house in Maharajpura. Omkar filed away the name of the store in his memory.

Now Omkar called the gang for a meeting. It was at the back of an isolated pump set in the midst of a wheat field. It was a very cold night and every one came completely furred up. Besides liquor, snacks, and food for all of them, Omkar had also brought the crockery. He was a good host. As they chatted and discussed about a new job, Omkar deftly slipped Naresh's glass in the midst of other glasses. As the hours passed, Omkar drew out a blue print for the next job.

The Police station at Inderganj, received an anonymous phone call at the wee hours of the same night. The caller gave them specific details of the spot where the gang was planning a burglary, without revealing his identity. He however told them that they could collect several fingerprints from the spot.

The police moved swiftly and took possession of the glasses and the crockery from which they dusted six sets of finger prints.

Exactly one month later, on a foggy night the gang hit the jewelry shop where Naresh worked. It was one of the best jobs the gang had ever done. They came out with a booty that could settle them all for the rest of their lives.

The police came to the jewelry shop and took the fingerprints of all the employees as a routine check. In the evening a police jeep screeched to a halt outside the shop, a couple of hefty cops got down, entered the shop and nabbed Naresh, to the horror of all those inside and outside the shop.

Naresh was too stunned to even mutter something. When the owner asked the cops the reason for their doing so, they told him that Naresh's finger prints matched that of one of the suspects. Naresh swooned there and then. He was carried by the cops to a clinic nearby where he was put on drips. Naresh's parents and relatives were informed and they reached the clinic. His mother threw a fit. Naresh's father and relatives went to the police station and told the inspector that Naresh was a very good boy who wanted to serve his beloved country. A boy with such noble intentions would never do anything so demoniac.

The inspector was sympathetic. He promised that if Naresh cooperated with them, the department would not harm him and may even set him free.

Omkar was a cold blooded scoundrel. He had planned the whole thing very well. The robbery took place on a Thursday night. The police arrested Naresh on Friday evening. Saturday and Sunday were off for courts. So Naresh would have to spend the weekend in the lockup.

Poor Naresh, was a hypersensitive lad. The thought of his being arrested had a shattering effect on him. His imagination went wild. The thought of losing face in the market, the thought of Sarita's reaction to all this and the fear that with a police record, he may be barred from writing the exam for joining the forces, hammered his stunned but subconscious mind repeatedly. He could not imagine why or how all this happened. In the wee hours of Saturday, he suffered a brain hemorrhage and died.

When the news of his death reached Maharajpura, Sarita swooned. Sarita was Naresh's childhood sweetheart. They were waiting for Naresh's selection in the Armed forces before getting married. They studied in the same school, played together and chatted for long hours even when they were kids. There was nothing that the two did not know about each other.

The whole locality was distraught. Every one cried for the young girl. It was with a heavy heart that the people in the area attended Naresh's funeral. As the police could not get any statement from him, The FIR was filed away and the police started investigating without any lead.

When the burglary took place, Omkar was out of town on one of his business trips. A fortnight later, the gang met again, this time at another lonely spot. The loot was handed over to Omkar, who gave them all a hefty advance. The gang celebrated the success with drinks and delicacies and then went back to the routine. Omkar stuffed the loot in the hidden cavity in his car and drove away. He would now focus on disposing it off.

Omkar had been doing this for the past eight years. He was an ace in this field. But now he was getting bored of the grind and was seriously thinking of starting a new life.

Omkar's foresightedness had hoodwinked the cops completely. The gang members lived in separate localities and were seldom seen together. They were five different guys from five different areas. Further, as per Omkar's suggestion, each had carefully cultivated a legitimate image and shunned the company of the bad guys in their own localities. So it was all the more difficult for the police to get any tip about any one of them.

One evening Omkar called Kanju. Kanju and Omkar went back a long way. It was Kanju who had introduced the other three to Omkar. Even now, before taking up any assignment, Omkar and Kanju discussed the plan initially, before disclosing it to the others. Omkar had called Kanju under the pretext that he had a job in mind, that was to be executed at a small township called Dhaulpur. Kanju came to the meeting spot where Omkar picked him up in his car and the two drove away. It was around eleven in the night when they reached an isolated spot. Omkar stopped the car to take a leak. Both stepped out, and Omkar went to a corner. Kanju stretched himself and began lighting a cigarette. With amazing dexterity Omkar reached behind Kanju and shot him dead.

After stripping the body to the under garments, Omkar dragged it to a railway track. He placed the body on the track with the hands on one of the lines. Then he went back to the car and waited patiently. Half an hour later he heard the sound of an approaching train.

At three in the morning the same police station that had been informed about the fingerprints, received an anonymous call. The caller told them that one "*Omi Chikna*" who had participated in the burglary at the jewelry shop, had been killed by the other gang members, and his body thrown on the railway track. He also informed the spot where it was lying.

The police went next day and recovered the body. The hand and the head were completely smashed. So the police could do nothing but to dispose it off after completing the formalities.

Now Omkar was officially dead and had all the loot in his possession. He drove the car to Agra, parked it at an isolated place, removed all the papers, the number plates, the loot from the cavity and his suitcase, and boarded a train to Madras. He knew that the car would be disposed off by professional car thieves even before the train reached Gwalior.

As a travelling business man Omkar had visited several towns and cities. When he decided to start life afresh, he had also thought about where he could lose himself into the crowd easily. After due deliberation, he had chosen this southern metropolis. It was a big city, crowded, yet the population was not so cosmopolitan. With his trade and his skills, he could easily set up a shop dealing in fancy items, artificial jewelry and gemstones. Omkar spoke English well. He had a couple of south Indian friends who were in the same line and who were happy to be of assistance to him. These south Indians knew him as Radhey Shyam which happened to be his official name. Omkar settled down to a peaceful life.

One month later, the police station in Gwalior received the third and final tip. A few hours later Bankey, Gopa and Kairy were arrested. When they were grilled they claimed that the loot was with Omi Chikna. The police laughed. When the three stunned gangsters were shown the photograph of the badly mangled body, they could not make out that it was Kanju's and not Omkar's.

Six months after he settled down in Madras, Omkar decided to make his next move. Talent is what you possess but genius is what possesses you. Omkar was a genius. He had the right combination of talent, luck and pluck, besides a razor sharp brain, and a focus that was truly amazing. When he set his sight on something, he did not rest till he got it. And he had set his eyes on Sarita.

Naresh and Omi Chikna were dead. Radhey Shyam was alive. Now it was time for Omkar to contact Sarita's father Shivlal. And this he did with his typical cunning and tact. He reached Gwalior, and took an auto directly to Maharajpura reaching there just before midnight. He took a room in a small hotel, signing the register as Radheshyam. Next morning he went to Shivlal's shop.

"*Namaste!*" He saluted the elderly man.

Shivlal acknowledged the salute.

"*Mr. Shivlal?*"

"*That is me.*"

"*My name is Radheyshyam. Naresh told me about you.*"

"*Which Naresh?*"

"*Naresh, who was working in the jewelry shop in Gwalior.*"

Shivlal got instantly suspicious. He thought that the man standing in front of him was a police spy who had come to collect information. Omkar was prepared for this. Before Shivlal could say something Omkar dispelled his fears.

"*Sir I know what you are thinking. Actually I was a regular customer in that shop and thus I came to know about him. I am usually on tour and had been in south for the past several months. I learnt about this tragedy through a common acquaintance. I was on my way to Delhi, when I decided to come and pay my condolences to his family. I don't know his address, but I remembered his telling me that his neighbor ran a grocery shop. So I came to you.*"

Shivlal relaxed a bit. He offered him tea. Then Shivlal told him that Naresh's family had left the town and gone back to their village which was in a remote area. They chatted for some time.

"*Oh I see.*" Omkar sighed. Then he sipped his tea quietly. Shivlal asked him about his business. Omkar gave him his business card. Shivlal looked at the handsome, affluent looking young man, and thought about his own unfortunate daughter.

"*Actually Naresh was more than a neighbor to me.*" Shivlal said sadly.

'*Here it comes*' Omkar thought "*Oh! Really?*"

Shivlal nodded. "*He was to become my son in law.*"

"*Oh! I see.*" Omkar said sympathetically. "*I am sorry.*"

"*Are you married?*" Shivlal asked suddenly.

"*Me? No Sir. Actually I have settled down just now. Further, my parents are both dead, and so—*" Omkar let it hang.

"*There is none to look for a suitable match for you.*" Shivlal completed the sentence.

"*That is right.*" Omkar smiled feebly. "*How long would you be in Gwalior?*"

"*I was thinking of leaving tonight. Is there anything you want me to do?*"

"*No, I just thought that as you are Naresh's friend and his family is not here, you may drop in for lunch at my house.*"

Omkar smiled "*With pleasure Sir if it does not bother you and your family.*"

"*Not at all, It's a pleasure.*"

Shivlal would never know how deliriously happy Omkar was. This was the chance he was waiting for. And it had fallen in his lap in a most unexpected manner. On the way to Shivlal's house that afternoon, Omkar insisted on purchasing sweets, and fruits. He gifted the parcel to Shivlal's wife, and floored her with his charm, sweet talk, and manners. Sarita was nowhere in sight.

Omkar left after lunch with a promise that he would return a week later, on his way back to Madras. That evening Sarita's mother and Shivlal had a long chat about Sarita's future. Both had seen Omkar, and liked what they saw.

When Omkar came the next time, Shivlal told him that he had a daughter who was well educated, young, pretty, and was supposed to marry Naresh but due to his unfortunate and unexpected demise, he was searching for a suitable match for her.

"*Sir if you consider me for the alliance, I would feel obliged.*" Omkar said softly.

"*That is the reason why I requested you to drop in on your way back.*" Shivlal smiled. "*Wait I shall call my daughter.*"

Sarita came with her mother into the hall, and stood shyly. Omkar's throat went dry. As he got up to greet her, his legs were shaking.

"*Namaste.*" He said softly.

Sarita folded her hands in return. Both stood there awkwardly for a few moments.

"*Sit down Mr. Radheyshyam.*" Shivlal said affectionately.

Omkar sat down and stared at the floor. Shivlal smiled at Sarita and she went back discreetly.

From her room, Sarita saw Omkar. He was certainly a very handsome man. Far better looking than any one she had met till now. Naresh and she used to exchange notes often and she knew a lot about him, his employer, his colleagues etc. But she could not recall Radheyshyam's name. Probably he was just an acquaintance. Yes, her father mentioned that he was a regular customer in that shop.

Being a worried father Shivlal wanted things to happen fast. Omkar and Sarita got married a month later. Sarita came to Chennai with her mother and set up her household. Omkar was on cloud nine. He had achieved what he wanted. When Rashmi was born a year later, Omkar cup was full.

By the time Omkar came to the climax of his strange life story, it was already midnight. Dinesh had to change the tapes a couple of times to record the complete monologue. Now he had the poison to nail Omkar for good.

"*Yes, I wanted Sarita badly*" Omkar concluded "*but I never intended to kill Naresh. I knew that he was a soft guy but—*" He looked at the floor

"*Believe me I was shocked on learning about his death.*"

All through this period something was nagging at the back of Dinesh's mind. He knew that Omkar was telling the truth. He also realized that this testament would be Omkar's ticket to hell. And that wondered him. How could Omkar be so docile?

"*Is that all?*" Dinesh asked.

"*What else? You wanted the complete story. I gave you more than you asked for.*"

Dinesh took the tapes, put them in his pocket along with the recorder and opened the door to go out. With lightening speed, Omkar lunged forward.

With the dexterity and cold bloodedness of a professional criminal, Omkar attacked Dinesh with the long thick wooden brush that he had spotted at a corner of the wash room. Omkar was shorter and softer than Dinesh, but he was desperate. His future depended on the tapes that were now in Dinesh's pocket. He needed them so badly that he stopped thinking of the consequences of such a foolhardy act.

Dinesh smiled instinctively. He was ready for this. He turned around grinned, stopped the reckless blow with his left hand and in one swift move punched Omkar on the face.

As Omkar spotted the fist coming towards him, he tried to ward off the blow. In the process, he slipped on the wet washroom floor. His head jerked back, and the punch that should have landed on his jaw, hit his chest.

Omkar gasped, fell backwards and lay still. Dinesh stared at the prostrate figure. He knew that Omkar was not built for a punch like this. He kneeled down and placed his palm under Omkar's nose. A moment later he got up and went out.

Dinesh kept the cassettes and the tape recorder on the table, made himself a stiff shot of whiskey, and gulped it down.

———————

Omkar's sudden death shook Dinesh. If only he had not been the tough guy that he was, Dinesh would have panicked. The whiskey had the desired effect. Dinesh relaxed and tried to think.

Naresh's death had been vindicated. This relieved Dinesh. He felt light after several years. Omkar had paid his debt. He did not deserve anything better. But now Sarita was a widow, and the child Rashmi, who Dinesh hardly knew, had lost her father. This pained him.

Dinesh went and stared out of the window. It was pouring cats and dogs. Dinesh went and peeped into the wash room. Omkar was still motionless. Dinesh came back and stared at the table where the cassettes lay. And then he spotted the bunch of keys.

They were lying at the other end of the table. Dinesh picked them up and frowned. Then he realized that they were Omkar's car keys. Dinesh went back, stripped Omkar to his under garments, and carried the body to the bed. Then he checked his clothes.

Dinesh had taken his bath early in the morning and then he had been using only the wash basin. The washroom had not been used for some time. Yet as he had fallen in the wash room, Omkar's clothes were slightly wet.

Other than the usual wallet, handkerchief, a packet of cigarettes which was now almost empty, and an expensive lighter, Omkar was not carrying anything with him. Now Dinesh realized, what had bothered him for so long. Omkar was not carrying a gun or any weapon. It spoke volumes about the dead man's complacence. Without wasting much time, Dinesh dressed Omkar up again. The whiff of perfume still emanated from the man's handkerchief and clothes. Omkar was some dandy.

A few hours before dawn, Dinesh opened the door and strolled out. The rains had stopped. He looked around to assure himself that all was quiet. He went and opened the front doors of Omkar's car. Then he returned, picked up the body, which now weighed a ton, and took it to the car.

Placing the body in a sitting position on the front seat, Dinesh drove away. He had to move fast before rigor mortis set in. Driving steadily, he crossed the toll gate and sped towards Chennai. After a couple of kilometers, Dinesh began looking for a suitable place to dump the body. His nerves were taut and he was observing everything astutely. Dinesh could not afford to make any mistake now. As there was not much traffic, he could drive at the centre of the road, so that he could see both sides easily.

After driving for around forty five minutes, Dinesh spotted a ditch on the right side. He drove towards it and stopped on the road a few paces away. Then he studied the ditch.

In spite of the heavy down pour the ditch was somehow only half filled with rain water. Dinesh switched the head lights off and waited for some time. During the drive he had thought of all the precautionary steps. He got out of the car, and stepped on the tarred road. Carefully, he caught hold of Omkar's right arm, and began dragging him slowly towards the driver's seat. For a strong man like Dinesh it was not very difficult. Once the body was in the right position, Dinesh lifted Omkar's stiff hands and placed them on the steering wheel. Then he closed the door and windows tiptoed to the back of the car. Dinesh had already taken the cell phone, the cigarette pack, the lighter and the car keys in his possession.

Slowly, with all his strength Dinesh pushed the car into the ditch. It went in with a splash. Carefully tiptoeing a few steps towards the ditch, Dinesh leaned forward and made sure that the car had landed well. He then began walking towards Chennai. A couple of kilometers later he saw buildings on both sides.

Dinesh was one lucky man. The police patrol car had not spotted him till now. He entered one of the buildings on the left side. Standing in a dark corner, he lit one of Omkar's remaining few cigarettes and began thinking.

Now he planned his next move. He called the police using Omkar's cell phone, informed them about an accident at East Coast Road, removed the SIM card, and threw it into a gutter. Then he walked into a small lane that passed through a sleepy locality and reached a broad road that led to the main bus stop in a place called Thiruvanmiyur. There he boarded the first bus that took him to the other end of the city. By the time he reached there, it was already early morning. For the next couple of hours Dinesh whiled away his time, filling his belly with snacks and numerous cups of tea.

After lunch Dinesh took a circuitous route back to his hotel, and checked out at 6 PM. Then he went to one of the transport companies where he used to unload his consignments as a trucker, and managed a trip to Bangalore in one of the trucks. And thus he hitch hiked his way back to Gwalior.

"I still have the tapes which I used to record Omkar's monologue." Dinesh told Jacob, Puran Singh and Chellappa. *"If only I had known the purpose of my being called here I would have brought them along. As I had mentioned before, Omkar's death was an accident. If my intention had been to kill him, I would have done that long back and that too with ease. I have told you everything that I know. Now it is for you to decide my fate."*

Dinesh stopped talking. The room was quiet again. Puran Singh looked at Jacob. Jacob sat playing with the paper weight on Puran Singh's table. Chellappa kept staring at the floor.

"*What time is my train?*" Jacob asked Puran.

"*Eleven Thirty.*" Puran Singh deadpanned.

Jacob looked at the clock on the wall. It showed 9. 45 PM.

"*How did you come?*" Jacob turned towards Dinesh. Dinesh frowned for a second.

"*Oh I came by Auto.*" He replied still puzzled at the question.

Jacob smiled at him.

"*Sorry Mr. Dinesh. I don't have a ticket for you to Chennai.*"

Jacob waited for a moment. Dinesh tried to make out what Jacob said.

"*But if you want I shall drop you home on my way back.*"

Dinesh closed his eyes. The gesture was so disarming that he dropped his guard. Tears streamed down his cheeks. Chellappa smiled at Jacob. Jacob placed his hand on Dinesh's back. The tough soldier began sobbing.

A visibly relaxed Puran Singh rang the bell. A constable came in.

"*Get some snacks and tea for four.*" Puran said. "*And ask the driver to be ready to drop Jacob Saab and Chellappa Saab at the station.*"

The constable nodded, looked at the weeping Dinesh, shook his head disbelievingly and went out.

RAKSHA

In that class of tenth standard students, it was the history period. It was around 4 PM, and the students sat in rapt attention, as Krishnamurthi took them to the medieval period.

With his well known mastery over dates and names of various historical figures Krishnamurthi analyzed the first battle of Panipat threadbare, and discussed the plus and minus points of both armies. Such was his description, that the students could see the action in the battle field themselves. When Krishnamurthi taught, students did not take notes. They learnt far more by listening to his monologues, than they would by reading books.

Krishnamurthi was an intellectual and his favorite subject was history. After doing his B.Ed, Krishnamurthi had been appointed in this school as a teacher. That was 25 years ago. During this period Krishnamurthi had completed his post graduation, and his M. Phil. He had written several articles on various topics in history, and his book on Emperor Ashoka had been published by a reputed publishing house. In that school in Gokulpet, Krishnamurthi was a respected and loved man. His colleagues admired him and the students adored him.

Gokulpet is a small town some 150 kilometers south of Chennai. Half a century back it was just a village. But due to its proximity to the capital, Gokulpet got its share of material progress. An industrial township was built in the northern outskirts of the town a decade back. Small hillocks dot the western side of the town and there is more vegetation per acre in Gokulpet than in Chennai. The weather is not so hot, and during winter time Gokulpet enjoys a cool balmy weather so sought after by the city dwellers.

Krishnamurthi lived in a small but independent house, with his petite and pretty daughter Swarnalatha alias Swarna. He had constructed it in the outskirts of Gokulpet. It was a beautiful house with a small garden in the front, a sit out and a shaded parking space at the right side.

Krishnamurthi had two children. Bhadrachalam alias Bhadra, his elder child and only son was a tall well built, boor with a sadistic, criminal mind. Like all prodigal sons, Bhadra was pampered and spoilt by his simple but highly emotional mother Sharada. A problem child right from the beginning, he was tolerated in the school thanks to Krishnamurthi's goodwill.

Bhadra was a consummate trouble monger and was regularly hauled up by the administration for disciplining. Many a time Krishnamurthi had been warned by the Principal, that the management was eager to kick this incurable brat out. But every time Krishnamurthi tried to hammer some sense into the boor, his wife Sharada would rush at him like a protective hen, and accuse the Krishnamurthy and his school of harassing her pet son. Sharada believed that Bhadra was a very good boy and that every one including her husband was prejudiced against him.

Bhadra and his gang seldom attended the classes. Thanks to his father's genes he was Intelligent enough to scrape through in the final exams, without failing regularly in each class. Despite that, he had plucked a couple of times, and was one of the oldest in his class.

Bhadra, had a rival in the school, a ruffian called Girish who was as much a pain as Bhadra. The two along with their respective gangs were at logger heads with each other all the time. The students of Bhadra's and Girish's classes knew that their animosity would culminate in something serious sooner or later.

On a Saturday, which was a half day, when the students and the staff had gone home for the weekend, the two gangs confronted each other in the school playground. It was supposed to be a meeting for temporary truce between them, but neither was ready to take any chances. Armed with hockey sticks, chains, cricket stumps and bats and other such weapons, the hot blooded youngsters glared at each other. There was too much bad blood between them, and the fellow who was selected to mediate was at his wits' end.

What began as a mild trading of accusations, soon turned into a heated slanging match. The issues mainly concerned bruised egos and childish squabbles over cricket, hockey and football matches. Before the mediator could realize what was on, some one from one of the gangs threw the first punch. The battle of Panipat had begun. And Krishnamurthi was not there to record it.

It was no ordinary slugging out between kids. It was a full fledged Street fight in which weapons were freely used. Bones got broken, heads got split and every one including the mediator received his share of decorations on his body. Krishnamurthi was at home, reading a book on modern history when a police van pulled up outside the gate. It was 7 PM. The officer walked up the lane and reached the sit out. By that time Krishnamurthi had come out of the drawing room to see what the commotion was all about.

"*Mr. Krishnamurthi?*" The inspector asked politely.

"*That is me.*"

"*You have to come to the police station.*"

A stunned Krishnamurthi stared blankly at the police man who waited patiently.

By that time Sharada and Swarna were also near the door.

"*What is it?*" Sharada asked.

Before Krishnamurthi could react, the inspector said

"*Your son has been arrested.*"

When Krishnamurthi and a raving Sharada reached the police station, they were attacked by a mob of angry parents of other boys. The police formed a protective ring around the two and took them to a safe place. It was there that Krishnamurthi learnt that In a fit of demoniac rage, Bhadra had caught hold of Girish, dragged him to a nearby pole and strangled him to death with a bicycle chain.

Including the mediator, there were nine participants in the fight. Every one was injured and Girish was dead. Bhadra's face was swollen, and his body was badly bruised. All the boys were already in the hospital. Sharada indulged in a showdown with the other parents, and Krishnamurthi shed copious tears. He was a soft man, and this was not the place for him especially on a weekend. When after the essential paper work, the police drove them to the hospital, Krishnamurthi was totally drained.

On Monday when the school reopened the seven boys including Bhadra were terminated. Girish was already dead. The mediator was pardoned with a stern warning that if he did not cooperate with the administration and the police department, he would be thrown out too.

As soon as Bhadra was discharged from the hospital, he was arrested and presented at the court. After spending a fortnight in police custody, he was released on bail.

One month later the case came up for hearing. Based on the arguments of the prosecution, the Judge, disapproved the smirk on Bhadra's face, sent him to a juvenile school.

Sharada fainted in the court and had to be admitted to the hospital. The once shrewish Sharada finally realized that it was her love that had spoilt her son. She became distraught, and her guilt took its toll on her health. Within weeks, she was a shadow of her old self. Refusing to eat anything, Sharada lost her senses. Weeping and murmuring to herself she died a month after Bhadra's sentencing.

Ironically, life for both Krishnamurthi and Swarna improved after the two fold tragedy in their family. Bhadra was several years older than Swarna. Right from her childhood, she had been a witness to the regular sight of Sharada trying to shout her father down while Bhadra the hulk sulked in a corner. A scared Swarna would spend her nights weeping and clinging to her father.

Swarna had grown up pitying her father and hating her brother. Due to that fellow, her mother had always ignored her. So, when Sharada died, Swarna did not feel the sorrow that a child would feel on losing a parent. Krishnamurthi doted on his pretty and well behaved daughter. As long as Bhadra and Sharada were alive, he did not get an opportunity to show his affection to the child. But now things were different.

A few months after Sharada's death, Krishnamurthi got a promotion and an increment. The publishing house requested him to keep writing and gave him a token advance. Krishnamurthi threw himself on his work and within months, came up with a book on Ancient history. It was published, and was recommended by the council for education. Krishnamurthi was congratulated by his colleagues, and the Principal announced that the school was proud to have him as a teacher.

Swarna was a delicate and pretty girl. She was an average student, but she never failed in any class. She was also well behaved and quiet. Krishnamurthi liked to indulge the child and he got her various colorful dresses, toys etc and took her on outings during week ends. Swarna and her father grew closer and closer with each day.

Swarna was nine years old when her mother died and Bhadra landed up in the juvenile school. Now she was in her teens.

———————◆———————

Arumugam looked at his watch. It was 6.45 PM. Nandini had asked him to meet her there at 7 and she was never late. This spot was selected by Nandini as the pickup point and Arumugam marveled at her choice. This corner near the Besant Nagar crossing had the crowded look and the privacy that went with busy thorough fares. No one bothered to notice who was seeing who.

At exactly 6.59 PM Nandini's bike screeched to a halt near Arumugam. With a slight nod of greeting, he got on the pillion and the bike rolled away. It crossed the signal and sped towards Adyar. After a couple of furlongs, Nandini turned to her right abruptly and went through a dark lane with houses and trees on both sides. Despite being a Sunday evening, the place was quiet. Probably everyone was glued to the television. Threading her way through a couple of smaller lanes, Nandini came to the road that ran alongside the beach. She again turned to her right and drove to an old dilapidated structure and stopped. Both got down and walked towards it.

There could not have been a better pair of opposites. Nandini was a woman. Horatio Arumugam was a man. Tall, dark, and slim Nandini was a police officer. Short, fair, very athletic Horatio Arumugam was a thief. Nandini belonged to a respectable and educated family and had joined the police force as an IPS officer. Horatio's parents had died when he was in his teens and he had been brought up in juvenile homes.

Beginning as a vagabond, he had joined a gang of boys of his age and background who created a lot of nuisance and were hauled up regularly by the police. In these tough schools, Arumugam had learnt to read, write and fight for survival. Perpetual existence on the razor's edge had made Arumugam's senses taut and ever ready for trouble. He had got an opportunity to learn martial arts and he proved to be a natural student. It was his hobby, and his addiction. Whenever he found time, Arumugam worked out religiously and considered this as his only source of entertainment and enlightenment.

From playing harmless pranks, Arumugam and his gang slowly graduated to committing burglaries in shops, houses and godowns. Because of his build and agility, Arumugam could wriggle through a small space, climb up great heights and do all sorts of acrobatics that were needed in his profession. After a spate of such crimes, there was a public uproar and the department decided to take action. The crackdown resulted in complete annihilation of the gang. Many were jailed, and some were killed in the raids. As fate could have it, Arumugam was not in Chennai when this took place. Loaded with cash that he had earned as his share of the loot, he had gone on a sightseeing trip.

And this innocent excursion backfired.

When his gang members found that this fellow was nowhere in sight, they got viciously angry and suspected that had tipped the police off about them. When Arumugam, returned, he found himself squarely between a rock and a hard place. Both, the underworld and the law were gunning for him.

Not that Arumugam was scared of death. He had witnessed it at very close quarters several times before. But he did not want to land in a grave without telling his side of the story. He contacted the only person who could save him.

Her name was Pavitra and she was a social worker who interacted with the poor people in his locality. Arumugam had heard her speak about the importance of being good human beings. At that time he did not give a second thought to her noble advice. But now he realized his mistake and wanted her to emancipate him.

Pavitra was a fifty year old plump and kind lady with a sympathetic ear for people in distress. After listening to Arumugam, she arranged for a meeting with Nandini.

The meeting was held at Pavitra's office. Based on Pavitra's dope on Arumugam, Nandini thought that he would be the typical dark, brutal looking tough slum hood she routinely encountered in her police station. She came prepared for the meeting accordingly. But Arumugam's over grown school boy looks came as a big jolt to her. So much so, that the first question she asked the scared guy was

"*How old are you?*"

"*Twenty four, I think.*" Arumugam whispered hoarsely.

Nandini looked at Pavitra, '*Are you sure, this is the guy you were speaking about?*'

Pavitra nodded.

"*Okay tell me.*" Nandini said.

Arumugam bared his heart to the pretty looking police officer. Even he was not prepared to meet such an amiable person. He told her everything about himself. He said that, he did not want to be tortured to death by either the police or his own colleagues, without someone knowing the truth. Nandini heard him patiently.

"*What do you want to do now?*" She asked finally.

"*I don't know.*"

Nandini thought for a minute.

"*Okay stay with Pavitra Amma till I get back to you.*"

Arumugam nodded. Before going back, Nandini turned around and said "*Incidentally you did the right thing by contacting Pavitra. Don't worry I will help you.*"

Arumugam's eyes went moist.

After studying the file on the gang, Nandini realized that Arumugam was not as high up the underworld ladder as he claimed to be. He was just a hyperactive kid who had been used by the bigger guys in the gang.

Being an IPS officer, Nandini had good contacts with other powerful people in the department. After a round of discussion with her seniors, she decided to use Arumugam as her tool in the fight against crime.

The first thing she did was to arrange for "*a gangland slaying*" of Arumugam in Sivagangai, a place in the south of Tamilnadu.

A fortnight later the news papers reported that the Sivagangai police had discovered a body of a young male in the jungles. And that the finger prints matched with that of one of the missing members of the gang, which had terrorized Chennai and its suburbs, and which was smashed by the police a few months back. The dead man was identified as Arumugam of Korrukkupet.

With Arumugam officially dead, Nandini took him under her wings. She kept him hidden in a remote village near Tindivanam for some months and then reintroduced him to the Chennai circles as Horatio which indeed was his first name and which was rarely used by his cronies, while addressing him.

Arumugam got a job as a clerk in a clearing agents' office, run by Nandini's friend. This was his official source of income. His real job was to help her as an underworld informer. Having been brought up in gangland, it was easy for Arumugam to blend in, as Horatio. Though he was too small a fry to get noticed there, Nandini asked him not to take any chances. From his previous North Chennai region of Korukkupet, Horatio relocated to the southern suburb of Injambakkam with a new name and appearance.

Horatio Arumugam had all the talents which go with people who have small, compact, and athletic bodies. As an extension of his martial arts, he had also learnt gymnastics. He could climb up buildings with amazing dexterity and speed, and it was this which had earned him a place in the previous gang. Now Nandini decided to use his talents for the department. Within weeks of landing in his new surroundings, Arumugam fed in a remarkable amount of information to Nandini. Though most of it was trash, it was retained nevertheless to find a needle in the hay stack.

Nandini selected the place for their rendezvous. Whenever she called him, Horatio would go and give her the latest update on the underworld. That day she had called him for an urgent meeting. And now they entered the dilapidated building near the beach.

For the past few years, the Chennai police department had been following a hunch that some of the most sensational crimes in the city and around were planned and masterminded by an enigmatic person.

Be it a bank robbery, a jewelry heist, a murder, or any other felony, the jobs were executed with such clockwork precision that the law men were baffled. Every time a case came up they marveled at the sheer genius of the perpetrator and doubted that this could have been the brain child of some ordinary hood. Many guys were arrested and questioned but none could give any clue about the brain behind all the commotion. The jobs were planned in such a way that nothing could be traced back to him.

After months of slogging, running around and following threads that lead nowhere, one of Nandini's subordinate inspectors hit pay dirt.

During a routine check of vehicles, cops stopped a car which was speeding towards Pondicherry. When they checked the papers of the car and that of its sole occupant the two did not jell. The fellow was nabbed and brought to the police station along with the car which was evidently stolen.

The man was fingerprinted and it was found that they matched with the prints in some of the scenes of unsolved crimes. On interrogation it was found that the man was high up the rung of a well oiled criminal outfit. But the cops suspected that he was not the chief.

After a methodical grilling the fellow got more pliable and disclosed that that the man who headed the organization was addressed by the initials—GS. The cops went ballistic.

GS i.e. Girija Shankar was not only a filthy rich business man but also a highly respectable socialite known for his philanthropy and high profile. He moved in the highest circles, and was on back slapping terms with the elite in the city. Penetrating through his veil of respectability, was impossible. So well had GS carved a niche for himself, that it was difficult for the ordinary cops to even approach him let alone arrest the man.

But every criminal makes a mistake and GS was no exception.

GS was a bachelor and he resided in the fifth floor of a building in a posh area of Chennai. He was alone and did not have servants. The only maid who did the cleaning work did so under his eagle eye. People were seldom invited there and no one had a key to his house except GS himself. Despite taking so many precautions, GS slipped in two matters.

First of all he had no alarm system in his house. Secondly, except for the automatic Chinese lock on the only door of his house, GS did not use any other lock when he went out.

After a lot of brain storming and meetings, the top brass of the force decided to bug his house. And for this work Nandini needed Arumugam.

"How are things?" She asked as they sat on the small wall of the building.

"Fine! No further development on that end. I think the guys are waiting for the right moment to strike."

Nandini smiled inwardly. Arumugam was talking about some small robbery that was supposed to take place. He thought that he was giving a vital tip to his boss. Nandini had more important things in mind. Nevertheless she humored him by making the right noises.

"*Aru, can you climb up a building*" She asked suddenly. A puzzled Arumugam nodded slowly "Sure."

"*Can you do that for me and for my department?*"

"*Sure.*"

Nandini smiled at him. "*If you do this I would say that you have helped me.*"

"*I shall certainly do it if it benefits you.*" Arumugam declared.

Exactly a month after this conversation, at 3 AM on a Friday, Arumugam went up the drain pipe of GS' building, priced open the window, jumped in, and opened the front door. By the time a bunch of IT professionals from the department entered the flat to do their job Arumugam was already half way down the same pipe. After landing on the floor, Arumugam trotted to the underground parking where Nandini waited for him in the darkness.

Without exchanging a word, the two rode away on her bike and left the building by a side gate. At the railway station, Nandini handed him a thick wad of notes and a ticket to Gokulpet As she waved him goodbye, Nandini said "T*ake care boy. If you need something let me know.*"

The experts worked on GK's house all night. They bugged the whole place, and placed cameras at all strategic angles. And then they went for his laptop, gleaned every bit of information and made a perfect copy.

For the next three months, Nandini and her team worked day and night on the assignment. They extracted data, and information from the hard disc, the cameras and the bugs.

One weekend evening, GS stepped out of a fashionable massage parlor after his regular manicure, and smiled broadly at the security guy, who had opened the door for him. The fellow bowed respectfully and closed the door. GS looked around to see if anyone was waiting to catch his eye. There were the usual pan wallahs and small shopkeepers. The driver brought his car and stopped it right near him. Then the fellow got out and opened the back door. It was already dark and GS was getting late for the beauty pageant where he was one of the respected judges. As he trotted down the steps and tried to get into the car, he saw someone already on the other side of the seat. It was a woman.

GS frowned at her.

"*Good evening GS.*"

"*Who are you?*" He demanded.

Nandini waved her card on his face.

With a sudden jerk, GS stepped out and turned away. The driver was nowhere in sight. But the huge fellow who had opened the door for him moments ago, was blocking his path and grinning at him.

All the veneer and suave façade that GS had so carefully cultivated over the years vanished instantly. Cursing like a low level slum hood, GS made a desperate attempt to run through the motley crowd of horrified onlookers. Hefty police men closed in on him from all sides. They knew that he was not armed. GS would remember later, that the car and the driver were on hire, as his own limousine had been sent for servicing in the morning.

GS' arrest made the most sensational news of that month.

NANDINI GOT A PROMOTION, CASH REWARDS AND A MEDAL.

Arumugam read and reread the news till he had it by heart. He was the happiest man in the state.

When the brawl that sealed Bhadra's fate took place, R. Adityan was one of his class mates. Not that they were friends. Bhadra wasn't probably aware of Adityan's existence. They were exact opposites. Bhadra was a back bencher. Adityan was always in the first two rows. Bhadra seldom attended classes. Adityan was one of the best students in the school. Bhadra never scored more than the minimum pass marks. Adityan was regularly in the merit list.

Adityan did his schooling with science and Mathematics, came second in the school, and got a seat in a reputed engineering college in a nearby town. He opted for mechanical engineering and stood in merit in his first three years of his college.

Now he was in the final year and had come home as usual, for his Diwali holidays.

The day after he landed, Adityan took his breakfast and left home for a walk. The weather was nice and breezy and he strolled along watching the passersby, looking at the posters on the walls and brooding over some mathematical problem. As he turned back after a few furlongs to return home, he realized that he was very near his own school. Adityan did an about turn and began walking towards it.

As he reached the gate, Adityan realized that it would be Diwali holidays for the school too. However he strolled on, hoping to find someone to chat. Adityan Identified himself to the security man, who asked him the purpose of his visit. "*Just to say hello to the teachers*" Adityan smiled. "*I am an ex-student.*"

The security man found him decent enough and asked him to sign on the register. Then he let him in. Though the holidays were on, Adityan knew that the teachers and the staff would be working. This was the time when some teachers brushed up their knowledge about their subjects, checked answer sheets and took notes. Adityan strolled towards the staff room looking here and there trying to spot someone, but the long galleries were empty. Adityan peeped into the staff room. There was none inside. It was slightly before 1PM, and probably they had all gone for lunch. Adityan sighed and turned around to walk back.

And then he stopped. Swarna had just turned into the far end of the gallery. Dressed in an orange color suit, and holding a basket, Swarna walked slowly towards him, her anklets making a pleasant tinkling sound with every step. As She passed him, Swarna smiled. Adityan stood watching her walk to the other end, turned right and disappear. To Adityan she seemed like the most beautiful girl he had ever come across.

Adityan was a brilliant student. Till now his life revolved around his books and a small group of equally studious male friends. He had had his usual share of sports activities in the school but he was no great shakes in any extracurricular activity. He had no sisters, a younger brother Kannan who was a bigger book worm than him, if that was possible, and till now he had no interaction with the opposite sex. The only woman he was close to was his own mother.

Swarna on the other hand, was precocious enough to realize the impression she had made on this guy who she hadn't seen before. This was not the first time that her looks had attracted people. Wherever she went everyone gave her a second look.

She knew that she was attractive, but this did not swell her beautiful head.

She knew that the guy's eyes were following her and that he would possibly try to find out who she was. Swarna kept walking. Her intuition was right. As she went across the lawn to the library at the other wing, Adityan slowly walked and stood behind a pillar to watch her. A few minutes later Swarna came out of the library with Krishnamurthi. Both went to the lawn and sat on a bench. Swarna opened the basket and began laying out the lunch for her father. It was in a steel tiffin carrier. Krishnamurthi began eating with a spoon. She kept the water bottle by his side.

Krishnamurthi ate slowly, and took a sip of water. Then Swarna poured coffee for him from a flask. At his insistence, she poured some in a tumbler for herself. Adityan watched this, all the time looking around furtively to see if anyone had spotted him. The only one who knew about his existence was Swarna.

Krishnamurthi was working on a new book on Bhakti movement. It was only an excuse for him to spend his time in the library. Everyone in the school knew that he would have lived there if he were allowed. Like a dedicated student, he would ride to the school every morning and bury himself beneath huge dusty volumes. He would read and take notes religiously. Swarna in turn mothered him by bringing his lunch and coffee. When he returned home, she would be ready with coffee and snacks. Father and daughter lived for each other.

Even before they had finished, Adityan trudged back to the school gate thoughtfully. By now he knew that the girl was Krishnamurthi's daughter. That was good. But that also made her Bhadra's sister. And that was a problem. Adityan waited patiently under a tree. Presently she walked out and turned to her left. Adityan watched her but could not move for a moment. He was very scared and nervous. Somehow he steeled himself and went to her.

"*Excuse me.*" Adityan was surprised at his own confidence.

Swarna turned around "*Yes.*"

"*Adityan.*"

Swarna frowned.

"*My name is R. Adityan. I am an ex-student of this school.*"

Swarna's eyes widened. R. Adityan and R. Kannan, the two brothers were supposed to be among the best students in her school. Their names appeared on the display board of meritorious students, and she had heard a couple of times from her teachers and senior students about them. Moreover, Kannan was her senior in the commerce batch. He had passed out with flying colors and was doing his chartered accountancy course.

"*Oh!*" Swarna smiled.

Both stood awkwardly waiting for the other to speak. Then suddenly Swarna spoke,

"*I am Swarnalatha. Mr. Krishnamurthi's daughter I am in the eleventh standard, commerce batch.*"

"*Commerce?*" Swarna nodded.

"*Do you know Kannan?*"

"*Heard about him*"

"*He is my younger brother.*" Adityan's voice had a tinge of pride. Kannan was a merit holder in the twelfth board.

Swarna nodded and smiled. They both began walking towards the bus stop. Adityan's brain was in turmoil. This was new to him. He did not know why he was behaving so odd, but he could not help it. He was a decent guy and was keeping a respectable distance from her. Yet his heart was thumping wildly and he was sweating. As long as they were walking, it was okay. Adityan thought of something to continue the conversation, but his brain was blocked. Thankfully her bus arrived even as they reached the stop. Swarna got in, nodded at him and the bus moved away.

Adityan reached home in a trance. His worried mother gave him a good tongue lashing.

"*Where were you for so long? Couldn't you phone?*" She shouted at him.

Adityan looked at her and mumbled some explanation which neither could understand. Then he went to his room. Kannan was in the corner surrounded by a huge pile of reading material ranging from spiritualism to organized crime. Unlike Adityan who read only about his course subjects, Kannan lived to read. Despite being good in mathematics and science, he had opted for commerce in his school. Even as a school boy, he would go to his uncle's C.A. firm during his vacations and write cash books and work on the computer.

Now Kannan was in his C.A final.

Adityan looked at him for a few moments. Then he had an idea. "*Do you know Mr. Krishnamurthi?*"

Kannan looked up from the latest issue of a business periodical, with a blank expression on his face.

"*Yes?*" It was a question.

Adityan repeated patiently.

"*Which Krishnamurthi*"

"*Our history teacher*" Adityan snapped.

"*Yes. What about him?*"

"*Nothing, I saw him today.*"

Kannan could not make out where this conversation was heading. Both he and Krishnamurthi were permanent fixtures in the school library and though, after taking up commerce, he did not come in direct contact with the history teacher, yet because of their similar addictions, they were on nodding terms. Kannan read anything that was readable, and this had got him an approving smile from the intellectual Krishnamurhi a couple of times.

"*Where?*" Kannan asked.

Adityan told him the whole story.

Adityan believed that Kannan was too much of a fool to understand the nuances of romance. But he was in for a shock.

"*Do you love her?*" Kannan asked in such a flat tone that Adityan just stared at him open mouthed.

"*What do you mean by that*" He demanded trying to do the big brother stuff. It did not impress Kannan one bit.

"Man it's a simple question Yes or No."

"Yes! I think I like her." Adityan's replied demurely. *"Okay. Tomorrow we both go to the school."*

"For what?" Adityan was shocked. He did not want to do anything which would embarrass any one.

"Nothing man." Kannan had read his mind. *"I know Mr. Krishnamurthi personally and I can introduce you to him."*

Adityan looked at Kannan disbelievingly. His brother had certainly learnt a lot from his books.

Despite her sobriety Swarna was tickled by the morning incident. Being an average student herself, she wasn't a part of the elite in her own batch. The studious guys were a class apart and they seldom mixed with the mortals. She could not believe that Adityan her senior by several years and a member of the royalty in her school, would come and strike up a conversation with her. Her humility brushed off the passing thought, that he was attracted to her by her looks. She chose to believe that either he saw her as a teacher's daughter, or that he was plain bored and wanted to talk to someone. She tried to convince herself but could not.

And that delighted her.

When Krishnamurthi returned in the evening, he found Swarna more cute and happy than usual. As they sipped their evening coffee, he smiled at her affectionately and she blushed. He was puzzled.

"Look quite vibrant today!" He observed *"Any favorite film on the TV?"*

"*No:*" Swarna tittered and blushed deeper.

"*Well! Well! Someone is in a festive mood*" He quipped. Swarna hid her face in her palms and giggled till it hurt.

'*Something out of my range*' Krishnamurthi thought '*Women have always been an enigma.*'

Next day the two brothers went to the school library at around 11am. Krishnamurthi was already there. He looked up and saw Kannan and Adityan. The brothers smiled and bowed. Krishnamurthi nodded and smiled back. They both went to the racks at the back end of the library. Krishnamurthi kept reading and taking notes. Kannan took up an encyclopedia and buried himself in it. Adityan began fooling around with some old magazines. Half an hour before the lunch break, Kannan peeped out of the shelf into the front room. Krishnamurthi was yawning and polishing his glasses.

"*How are you Sir?*" Kannan went and asked.

"*Fine Kannan long time no see.*" Krishnamurthi smiled and extended his hand for a shake.

"*Yes Sir. Busy with my CA final. This is Adityan My brother, you might be remembering him*"

"*Of course I do! I think you are from the science group.*" Krishnamurthi shook his hand too.

"*Yes Sir. I am in my engineering final.*" Adityan said politely. "*How are you here today?*"

"*We were just strolling around and thought that we could look in to say hello to our teachers*"

"*Very good! Very good!*" Krishnamurthi laughed.

Adityan could hear the sound of anklets. Swarna was coming towards the library.

"*Lunch break*" Krishnamurthi smiled as she entered. In spite of seeing Adityan there she kept a poker face.

"*She is my daughter Swarna.*" Karishnamurthi said. Smiles and greetings were exchanged.

Politely declining the invitation to join him for lunch, the two boys took leave.

Krishnamurthi was in a good mood that day. He had put in some hours of solid work, and had taken several pages of notes. The meeting with the two boys had lifted his spirits still higher. Krishnamurthi had his lunch and then father and daughter sipped their coffee. Swarna knew that he would be saying something about the boys, and she waited patiently.

"*It is nice to talk to good boys*" He said finally. Swarna nodded indifferently. "*This fellow Kannan*" He chuckled "*Is worse than me. I pity the guy.*" Swarna looked at him.

"*I wonder how he can read his boring subjects and still remain a bookworm*" He said with a twinkle in his eyes.

Swarna hadn't seen her father so mischievous before.

Back home as Kannan disappeared into his heap of volumes and Adityan indulged in day dreaming.

On the Diwali day, Adityan got up early, took his bath and wore his new set of clothes. After bursting a few crackers, and gobbling some sweets, he left home under the pretext of taking a walk around the town. Kannan was aware of his plans, and he gave him the Krishnamurthi's address. Adityan took a bus and got down at the stop near that house. Then he began walking towards it.

When two persons love, there is an inexplicable telepathy between them. Swarna had a hunch that Adityan would be thinking about her. As usual she was dressed in her best that morning, and could be seen running up and down the house. Every year she would be going to the temples, or to her friends' houses to wish them on Diwali day, but this time she was more interested in knowing whether her guess about Adityan was right. As she peeped out of the gate, she saw him.

There was an exchange of smiles, and Adityan jogged towards her. Luckily everyone in the neighborhood was watching the colorful programs on television.

"*Happy Diwali.*" Adityan beamed.

Swarna reciprocated.

There was an awkward silence for a few moments. Adityan did not want to lie that he had just been strolling around and had seen her by chance. He knew that she was too smart to believe it.

"*How is Sir?*" He asked politely.

"*Come. He is inside.*" Swarna invited him.

By the time Adityan stepped into the bus back home, Swarna was sure that he was in love with her. Before taking leave, Adityan gave his phone number to Krishnamurthi and informed just casually that he would be returning to the college the next day by a bus that left at 9.PM.

The call came next morning. It was from Krishnamurthi for Kannan. But Adityan was delighted.

"Hello Kannan Krishnamurthi here."

"Yes Sir." Kannan replied.

"Adityan gave me your phone number and I wondered if I could ask you for a Favor."

"Sure Sir. Please."

"My daughter is a commerce student in her eleventh standard. Can you give her some tips about scoring better in the exams?"

"My pleasure Sir"

"Very good! Just a minute."

There was a pause and Swarna came on the line.

Kannan told a giggling Swarna that all his notes would be delivered to her by the weekend. He also told her that he can give her a list of important questions on all subjects, and help her get fantastic grades. Swarna blushing and thanked him.

"Anything else?" He asked her.

Swarna looked around. Krishnamurthi had gone to the kitchen.

"Nothing, your brother came here yesterday."

"And he is here now. He would like to talk to you."

Once back to the college, Adityan became the conscientious student that he was. Kannan assured him that he would keep him posted about the developments. Adityan threw himself on his books with a vengeance, and worked hard. Whenever he thought about Swarna, he would take a long notebook and write his feelings. This was Kannan's suggestion.

In school and at home, Bhadra was the big bully who the good guys avoided, and the not so good guys treated with awe and reverence. But in the Juvenile school, things were so drastically different, that in the initial stages he was himself scared. It was a mini prison, meant to straighten up guys like him. The students were all his mould and the teachers too were tailor made for the job. They were not like his father or others in the ordinary school. Punishments were more frequent than tuitions. Inmates getting whipped or tortured for small faults was a common sight.

However Bhadra, got used to the new atmosphere fast enough. He was game to his share of torture sessions and when he showed that he could take it all like a man, he earned the respect of his colleagues.

Among the inmates, Bhadra got particularly close to one Elango. Elango belonged to a family of unsavory elements and both his elder brothers were an alumni of this great institution. Elango was already there when Bhadra checked in. After observing him for a couple of months, the shrewd and experienced Elango felt that this fellow could be his associate in crime. They became close and with the help of other sidekicks, Elango took over the place. They offered protection from themselves to the others for a price, and to drive their point home, the gang broke a few bones of inmates who refused to toe the line. Because there was no love lost between the inmates and the management, the latter looked the other way when Elango and his men terrorized the others. Kick backs from Elango to the staff, served a dual purpose. The management was getting extra payment for not doing there own duty, and there was a discipline of sorts in the institution.

Because Bhadra had killed Girish in a gang fight, his case was treated as culpable homicide by a minor. There were too many technical loopholes and the parents of the deceased were not interested in pursuing the case. There son was dead any way and even alive, he was as big a headache as Bhadra was to his own parents. Besides, they preferred to spend their time and energy in bringing up their remaining kids who were better behaved.

This went in Bhadra's favor. At the time when Adityan was getting to know Swarna, Bhadra was released from the juvenile home. Not that it made any difference on either side. Even at the funeral of his mother, Bhadra had made it quite clear to his father Krishnamurthi that all relationships between them were over and that he would be going his own way. The only person he loved was his mother and she was dead. To Swarna he was a stranger and to Krishnamurthi a burden.

Elango, who had been released a couple of weeks earlier, was waiting for him when Bhadra came out. Elango introduced him to his eldest brother as his best friend. Bhadra was impressed by the warm reception that he got from the family. He decided that this is where he belonged.

As a legitimate front, Elango's family owned an automobile workshop in the seedy quarters of the town. Every policeman in the town knew who they were and what they did. There was no illegal activity that the family did not indulge in. Elango's second brother Gajji was one of the best contract killers in the underworld, and his eldest brother specialized as a receiver of stolen property.

Elango arranged for Bhadra's accommodation in the locality and got him an initial job of collecting payment from shopkeepers who came under their jurisdiction. Bhadra loved the job, and the fear [*which he misunderstood as respect*], that he saw on the face of his debtors. Bhadra got a remuneration for his "*services*" and he was elated by the sudden improvement in his "*social status.*"

One day Bhadra went to a near by town, where there was a shop which sold knives of different varieties. While inspecting several kinds, Bhadra came across one that caught his fancy. It was a beautiful piece, with a steel blade some six inches long, a carved black colored handle and a velvet sheath that fitted the blade to the T. When he asked the price, the shopkeeper told him that it was an expensive item which had been brought from some where in the north and that they had only two of such pieces of which one was sold a few days back. This item had a strange yet perverted specialty. There was a hidden cavity at the tail end of the handle which could be braced open with a tiny knife that came along with this piece. This cavity was big enough to hold some thing like a stamp size photograph or a small slip of paper.

The shop even arranged for embossing any name inside the cavity, that the owner wished to engrave, to show that it belonged to him. The perversion came from the fact that, any one who had used it for some crime would be giving away his own identity to the law men, in the event of its being found at the scene of the crime. Bhadra purchased it without bargaining.

Through a campus interview, Adityan got a job in a reputed company with its unit in the industrial estate at the outskirts of Gokulpet. Adityan and Kannan completed their respective courses at the same time. Kannan got a gold medal in taxation which was his favorite subject. He joined his uncle's firm as an associate.

Swarna was generous enough to share her notes with her friends and they all scored far better than they had done before. In the twelfth standard she was looked at with more reverence by the studious group. After seeing his daughter's results, Krishnamurthi was delighted and he personally thanked Kannan for the help. Kannan gave her his other notes too and offered to guide her in her board exams right from the beginning. Now both Kannan and Adityan were closer to Krishnamurthi. Krishnamurthi congratulated both on their achievements and was glad to know that the two boys had settled down.

In the twelfth standard the students are not very particular to attend the classes after six months and the teachers also tend to be more lenient towards them. Swarna too stopped going to the school regularly after some time. She began studying at home and practicing the important questions that Kannan had given her for the board exams. With Krishnamurthi in the school, she had more freedom, and with prior arrangements, she would chat with Adityan on the phone whenever he was free. They kept this quite discreet, and seldom met in person.

Swarna was very particular that she should get the best marks possible in her board exams. And being the studious guy that Adityan was, he agreed to this wholeheartedly.

Adityan found the new job to his liking. He was a mechanical engineer and this company was into automobile business. He was posted at the workshop as an apprentice and he worked hard and learnt a lot. Now he could make out the difference between theory and practice. Within six months he had gained a lot of experience and was now more confident about his caliber than he was as a student.

Adityan used to work shifts. The factory ran round the clock and as an apprentice, Adityan was assigned a new shift after every two months. The factory bus would pick him up from a bus stop and drop him there. Six months after he joined the company, one evening at around 7 PM, Adityan got down from the bus. And he ran into Arumugam.

Arumugam had arrived in the town sometime back and had taken up lodgings in a bachelors' mansion where every one minded his business and no one asked any questions, as long as you did not come in their way. Years of experience had taught Arumugam how to keep a low profile. In the entry register he had given his profession as documentation clerk. It was the designation he had been asked to mention by his clearing agency while handling consignments at the yards. Arumugam dressed well, looked decent and his soft voice and gentle manners prevented any one from getting suspicious.

That evening he had gone to a movie and was standing in the stop waiting for a bus. When Adityan got down, Arunmugam stared at the bus and made a move to board it.

"*Company bus:*" Adityan smiled at him.

It was a routine thing in that stop, and Adityan had said this many times before to other people. Arumugam stopped, looked at Adityan and then chuckled as the bus roared away.

You meet several strangers daily and nothing clicks in your mind. But suddenly out of the blue, you come across someone who you do not know from Adam, but you feel a sense of dejavu'. In Adityan's case this happened when he saw Arumugam. Adityan was born and brought up in the same locality where he resided now. Except for the years spent in the college, in a different town, he had always hung around this locality. Though he did not have many friends, he could make out who was new and who was old in the area. Arumugam's face, seemed decidedly new. But then he recalled that the fellow was waiting to board a bus. *'Probably he was from some other locality.'* Adityan thought, at the same time wondering, why he was thinking about him.

A week later, Adityan was having his lunch in the factory canteen, when a fellow came and sat beside him. Casually Adityan turned around and saw that it was Arumugam. Both exchanged glances, and Adityan smiled. Arumugam frowned. He was trying to recall the face

"*Bus stop. Company bus.*" Adityan said.

Arumugam chuckled again. And Adityan liked the smile instantly.

As both ate, Adityan introduced himself. Arumugam introduced himself as Horatio, told him that he was a clearing agent, posted in Gokulpet to supervise loading and unloading of goods. Adityan was surprised at his own friendliness towards this stranger.

That evening, when Arumugam rode back in the same bus, as a guest, Adityan had him sit beside him. It was an hour's ride, and by the time they got down, Adityan was chatting away as if they were childhood chums. A fortnight later, on his day off, Adityan took his father's bike and went to Arumugam's lodge. They both rode through the streets of Gokulpet, with Adityan doing the guide act. They had tea and snacks at various shops, and Arumugam started liking this fellow who he did not know at all a month back.

After being the talk of the town for a fortnight, and fresh with the new found success, Nandini was a happy woman. The promotion and the rewards were immediate. Now she was an important officer and she was entrusted with the GS case.

After all she had arrested him herself. Womens' organizations congratulated her and Pavitra was especially happy for her.

There was a valid reason for Nandini's sending Arumugam out of the city. She genuinely cared for the boy, and he had done her a valuable service. He was indirectly responsible for her prize catch. She knew that as soon as the case became public, tongues in the underworld would begin wagging and speculations of all types would be rife. Underworld too had informers within the department and very soon they would be able to get an idea of how the whole operation was carried out. In spite of the precautions, she had taken to keep Arumugam's slate clean, she did not want to take any chances of the guy being spotted by some old acquaintance.

Elango's brother Gajji, the contract killer, belonged to a fast widening network of like minded members of the underworld, who took such assignments for a price. The network was spread all over the state and had contacts with such gangs operating in other states too. Gaji was an important member who had proved his mettle more than once in such jobs. It was an extremely secretive society and had its own set of rules which were laid out carefully and were meant to be followed unquestioningly. One of the founders of the network, a person who had used this system most effectively was, a very powerful Don called GirijaShankar alias GS.

When Bhadra joined the group, Gajji was away. Even in his own family, no one asked Gajji any questions. He came when ever he wanted and went away as suddenly. He seldom talked and never ever interfered in any one's affairs. The plus point with him was that when ever he came he would bring a thick wad of currency and give it to the eldest brother. He had been doing this for the past ten years and had not once asked for any account of the money spent. Love it or leave it, his family had prospered from Gajji's activities and his resourcefulness.

Till now Gajii had been working with one or two accomplices who were chosen from the regular underworld, and who had been co operating with him more for the money than because of any personal liking for him. Gajji was itching to have someone who could be the perfect foil for his set of talents, and who could treat him as his mentor and boss. When Elango told himabout Bhadra, Gajji became thoughtful. Unlike his own brother Elango who was just a thief, Bhadra had started his crime career with a killing. The fact that he was a minor then and that it was booked as culpable homicide, did not change the fact that Bhadra had taken a life. Sensing that Bhadra could well be the guy he had been looking for, Gajji agreed to see him in his hideout in Chennai.

From what Bhadra had learnt about Gajji from Elango, he had formed an image of Gajji as a scary predator. Hence the shocked look on his face, on seeing the man for the first time amused, both Elango and Gajji.

Gajji, with his tea brown complexion, a long very sharp featured face, waif like body and a beautiful set of white teeth, was like a mannequin in a garment showroom. Bhadra would learn later that Gajji always looked like that. No one had ever seen him dirty or uncouth in appearance. It was ironical that this cute guy was a deadly killer. Gajji always wore dark glasses.

"*Hello*" He extended his hand for a shake. Bhadra took it and felt the cool soothing soft flesh of Gajji's palm. The voice was husky and as attractive as the man. '*No wonder the police department can not suspect him.*' He thought. And Gajji read his mind.

Over cups of hot tea and snacks, Gajji listened patiently to what Bhadra said. In between he would ask questions and clarifications. By the time Bhadra had concluded, Gajji could make out that he had in his hands a very rough stone which when polished, could turn out to be a gem. After two hours, Elango returned and Bhadra remained with Gajji.

A fortnight later, Gajji, accompanied by a man of around forty, came to a godown situated in a lonely spot. It was in an area called Pulianthoppe in North Chennai, and this place was the headquarters of the city's underworld. Deftly opening the lock with a wire, they opened the door and went in. It was totally dark, yet they could make out that the room contained merchandise which could fetch them a good price. The man with Gajji was a criminal himself and had recently started the business of receiving stolen property. Gajji switched on his pen torch, for the man to have a better look at the material. As the fellow screwed his eyes and peeped at the bundles, Bhadra crept up from a corner noiselessly, and delivered a sharp tap at the back of the man's head. The fellow fell face down with a sigh.

That night Bhadra learnt how deceptive appearances could be. In front of his horrified eyes, Gajji the fairy, coolly dismembered the body. The victim had betrayed some powerful people and Gajji had received the contract to dispose him off. The body was packed in polythene bags and put in a wooden box. Gajji took out a three wheeler which was parked behind the godown. The carton was placed in it, and as Bhadra spent the rest of the night washing the blood stains and finger prints, Gajji drove fast through by lanes, to the sea shore. He stopped near a lamppost and got out. After a few minutes, shadows from nowhere closed in on him. They were three in number. They looked at Gajji and then inside the vehicle. There was an exchange of nods, and one of the guys drove the vehicle away. By seven the next morning the body of the unfortunate man would be consigned to the sea. Bhadra was surprised at the amount he got for this work. Gajji had always been honest in money matters.

After the job was over, as per the advice of Gajji, Bhadra went back to Gokulpet, and contacted Elango. He learnt driving and purchased a second hand three wheeler delivery van with the money that he had earned. Now he was self employed, and he began carting loads within and around the city. It was his legitimate front. After a few months, he got in touch with other people in the business, and began frequenting the industrial estate where Adityan worked. There were a lot of small and medium sized units which regularly needed the services of such transport, and soon enough, Bhadra was earning a decent income. This job got him the necessary freedom and facilities to indulge his main career.

Swarna's board exams were over on March 25th. Most of the questions that Kannan had listed, had appeared in the exam. Being a merit student himself, Kannan had also taught her how to prepare and write the answers. Swarna and her friends performed very well. She thanked him profusely for his fantastic guidance. That evening, Swarna met Adityan after several months. It was at a huge temple, surrounded by an open area full of trees and plants. This temple was the meeting ground for people of all ages and sexes. Children played, old people gossiped and devotees worshipped their favorite deities. Shops selling pooja items, tea stalls, and fancy stores lined upon two sides of the temple. Evenings were quite busy and every one was occupied with his or her work.

"*How were the exams?*" Adityan asked her. Draped in a printed Sari, Swarna looked like an angel to him. It was impossible for him to keep his eyes off her.

"*Fine. I thanked your brother in the afternoon.*" Swarna replied.

"*Very good. Very Good.*" After a pause and before Swarna could say something

Adityan said abruptly "*I want to talk to your father.*"

Swarna blushed a deep red when he said this.

In spite of being a good father, Krishnamurthi did not miss his only son Bhadra one bit. He felt guilty about this in the initial stages, but as time passed, he got used to it. According to him there were several reasons for this indifferent attitude. First of all, the boy had never given the father anything other than endless pain and humility. Secondly, he was the main reason for Sharada's untimely demise. Not that Krishnamurthi missed her either. But Swarna had lost her mother, and this hurt him. A girl needs a mother while growing up, and the poor child had missed the love, care and affection that only a mother could give to a daughter. And finally, though Krishnamurthi avoided thinking about it, the fact remained that he had seen true happiness and success only after the mother and son had gone out of his life.

Krishnamurthi was a nice man, but he was as human as any one else, and no human being would choose hell over heaven. Krishnamurthi had stopped visiting Bhadra three months after the boy landed in the juvenile home. Even the few meetings that the father and son had, began with mono syllables and ended with stoic silence from both sides. They had begun to realize that they had always been strangers to each other. So when Bhadra was released, Krishnamurthi was relieved that he did not return home. Yes, Krishnamurthi did shed silent tears when he was alone, but he did not allow his pet daughter to know that he cared for her brutish brother. What ever love he had in him, Krishnamurthi showered lavishly on Swarna. And he thanked god for giving him such a sweet child.

On Tamil new year day, Adityan told his parents about Swarna. The parents were aware of the girl, after Kannan had introduced her to them in a temple, as Krishnamurthi's daughter. Kannan's mother had invited her for a pooja during October and she had attended it. When Adityan disclosed his feelings for her, and Kannan vouched for his choice, Adityan's parents decided to take up the matter. His father rang up Krishnamurthi the same evening.

A numb Krishnamurthi put the receiver down and sat on the chair. He could not believe what he had heard from Adityan's father Mr. Raman. Mr. Raman, had first introduced himself and then requested an appointment from him. When he had politely asked for the matter to be discussed, Raman had told him about Adityan's wish.

After draining a glass of water, Krishnamurthi began to rack his brains. Being a history man, he had a way of recalling incidents. The first meeting with the brothers, Adityan's dropping in on Diwali day, & Kannan's generous gesture in helping Swarna with her studies, flashed through his mind. As the exams were over, Swarna was a free bird, and she and some of the neighborhood women had gone to a festival in some temple where supper was provided to devotees.

Krishnamurthi was reading a book when Swarna returned. She gave him some prasadam and went into the pooja room. Krishnamurthi smiled inwardly but said nothing.

"What did they serve for supper?" He asked pleasantly as Swarna switched on the TV.

"Very different this time." Swarna smiled *"Three different varieties of sevai."*

"Lots of crowd?"

"Yeah!"

"*Festival time! Festival time!*" Krishnamurthi said grandly.

Swarna frowned at him. Krishnamurthi pressed her cheeks gently and said

"*Adityan's parents want to meet you.*"

Swarna's mouth popped open. She tried to smile but could not. Krishnamurthi hugged her. She grasped him tight. Krishnamurthi kissed her forehead.

On the day of the engagement a fortnight later, the women in the neighborhood took over, and shooed Krishnamurthi out of the house. He did not know whether he was the host or the guest in the ceremony. He and Raman chatted at the lawn as the women prepared the food and drinks. The crowning glory was that Adityan's mother was given the responsibility to doll up the bride. It was Adityan's day off, but Kannan had gone for an outstation audit. Though it was basically a family function, he decided, with the permission of his parents, to invite Arumugam.

Adityan had already introduced Arumugam as Horatio to his father. Mr. Raman had shook hands with him and found him to be a polite and decent young man. On that day when Arumugam, dressed in a light blue full shirt and slacks, came to the function, Raman recognized him, and introduced him to Krishnamurthi. Arumugam had his lunch with Adityan, and left for work.

The engagement ceremony went off well. The women who had seen Swarna grow up were all praise for the girl, and some of them got emotional when the ceremony was concluded. The priest fixed the date of marriage. In the evening father and daughter went to Adityan's house for supper. Kannan called and congratulated them.

It was around 10 PM in the night, and Bhadra sat on his three wheeler, parked on the road outside Krishnamurthi's house, staring at the closed door. His heart was bleeding. There had been a ceremony in that house, which many had attended, and he Bhadra, the only son of the host was not even informed, let alone invited. Bhadra did not know what the event was all about. He did not care. Due to their age difference, Bhadra still believed that Swarna was a pig tailed tot full of sobs and giggles. He had always ignored her. She did not exist for him. As far as he was concerned, there were only three in that family, he, Krishnamurthi and Sharada.

Bhadra had always been the eye of the storm in the family. The fact that his father detested it, was immaterial. Bhadra believed that life in that house, revolved around him. He thought that Krishnamurthi would fade away after the death of Sharada, his mother. Even in the juvenile home, he missed his mother more than his father. That is why when he was released, he had used this new found freedom to keep away from his family. With the mother gone, there was no point in going back to his house. And Krishnamurthi's indifference had helped.

Gokulpet is a small town, and in spite of the time gap between his going to the juvenile home and now, Bhadra was wary of being recognized by some one who had know him as a child. So he mostly hung around the industrial area, and was ever ready to go to neighboring towns and villages instead of frequenting the streets of this town. However on that day, he had to bring a load to a godown, which was a couple of kilometers from his house. On his way back after the work, Unwittingly, he had turned the vehicle towards the colony. Realizing his mistake fast, Bhadra turned the vehicle around but came across a street, where a huge lorry had blocked the path. Cursing no one in particular, he wrapped a towel around his face and hit the street where his house was situated. He wanted to cross it as fast as possible. But as he passed the house, Bhadra saw a lot of activity. People were moving around, chatting and laughing and colorfully dressed women were standing in the verandah. Bhadra went to the end of the street stopped the vehicle and looked back.

Krishnamurthi was standing and talking to a priest. His thick mop of hair had gone a shade greyer, but he looked healthier and was in a better mood than Bhadra expected him to be in. For a second, Bhadra wanted to get down and barge into the house. But he controlled himself. He tried to imagine the reason for this celebration, but his mind was numb. Bile rushed up to his throat. '*How can this man throw a party when neither the son nor the mother were present?*'. Then he remembered Swarna. She was no where in sight. Bhadra accepted albeit regretfully that even if she were around, he could not have recognized her. He could not even recall her face. Before the whole sight could get unbearable, he started the vehicle and drove away.

After buying a bottle of country brew from a local liquor shop, Bhadra went to his room, locked the door and the windows and gulped down the stuff. The more he drank, the more savage he got. Like all guys of his nature, he blamed every one except himself for his sorry plight. He cursed Krishnamurthi from the bottom of his heart and shed copious angry tears. Then he went to the loo and puked out all the brew. After lying in a stupor for a couple of hours, he fell asleep and got up at 8 PM. He took a bath, and went to a nearby hotel where he filled his empty belly with junk food. Then he took his three wheeler and went back to Krishnamurthi's house to confront him, but found it locked. And now he was sitting opposite it glaring at the door.

A little before eleven he heard the noise of a vehicle approaching him. It was a scooter and it stopped near the house. The pillion rider got down. It was Krishnamurthi. He went and opened the gate and the rider, drove the scooter in. From the spot where Bhadra sat watching, he could see every thing clearly. With the verandah light shining brightly, he observed the rider remove the helmet. And then he realized that it was a young woman. She was wearing a churidar suit and she parked the vehicle on one side. By that time Krishnamurthi had opened the door. As the woman too followed Krishnamurthi into the house, Bhadra could see her profile clearly.

'Swarna' He thought. 'Could the snot nosed kid have grown so big?' He wondered. And then an evil suspicion gripped him 'Or the old man had got married again.'

Any ordinary man would have brushed off this stupid thought immediately and felt proud that his sister had grown up and that she and his father were happy now. But Bhadra was no ordinary man. He wasn't even a human being. Seeing them so relaxed and happy, filled him with a blind rage. His first thought was to barge in right away and make life miserable for them. But the hangover from the afternoon, had drained his energy. And what he saw now had made him still tired. After staring at the dashboard and murmuring to himself for some minutes, he drove away.

After a very long time, Swrana had enjoyed motherly love from Adityan's mother Ratna. Her own mother Sharada had been aloof, because of her preoccupation with Bhadra and Swarna had always felt ignored. If it hadn't been for Krishnamurthi, she wouldn't have had any love. But Krishnamurthi, was after all a father. He could not have given her the soft feminine care that any child needs from a mother. And Ratna gave it to her in plenty.

Ratna had only two sons and for her, having a teenaged girl child around was a a beautiful experience. She was reminded of her own younger days. Ratna knew about Sharada and Bhadra and what the family had gone through. When Ratna hugged Swarna for the first time, Swarna got breathless, and tearful. The two hit off wonderfully. When Krishnamurthi and Swarna came for supper, on the day of the engagement, Ratna took her straight to the kitchen and they chatted and cooked the food together. *"Consider me your mother."* Ratna said and Swarna nodded vigorously. To an amazed Adityan, Ratna looked like a woman who he had never seen before.

Life resumed as usual and Swarna started going to college. After years of wearing the school uniform, now she could wear her best clothes. Ratna had taken her to a shop, and got her some suits, as a gift. Both the women were enjoying each other's company. Ratna too learnt a lot about the new trends from the sweet looking teenager.

Krishnamurthi's new book was complete, and was sent to the publishers. It was a well researched work, and they sent a few copies of the first edition to the council of education. As his work on Ancient History was already a popular one, it was easy to get the recommendation certificate for this one on Bhakti movement too. Many of the college students who had grown up on his books as school kids, purchased this new arrival, and it was a hit in the market.

Kannan applied for, and landed a job in a multinational company. As per his uncle's advice, he accepted it and was sent to Mumbai for training and first posting. Adityan's apprenticeship was over and he was confirmed with an increment. He became a supervisor in the shop floor.

Krishnamurthi's school became popular because it was mentioned in the copies of his every book, that he was the head of History department of that school. But he politely refused any offer for a better job in other schools, in Chennai or other big cities. He was an asset to this institution and preferred to remain that way.

The publishing house was situated in a busy commercial complex in the heart of the city. There were lots of offices, shops, establishments and go downs in that building which had three wings with four stories each. The publishing house had its go downs in the basement, and offices at the first and second floors of one wing.

It was 6 PM in the evening on a week day when Swarna and Krishnamurthi rode the bike to the parking space at the back side of the building. Krishnamurthi had been called by the publishers for a meeting to discuss about some new subject on which the man could work. As they parked and turned around, they were greeted by a pleasant faced man

"*Good evening Sir!*"

Krishnamurthi turned around and frowned "*Hello!*"

"*Horatio! Adityan's friend! Came to the engagement!*" The man said. "*Ah! Ah!*" Krishnamurthi recalled now. "*How are you?*"

"*Fine Sir. I came hear to load a consignment to Chennai.*"

"*Very Good! Very Good!*" Krishnamurthi smiled. By then Swarna had joined them. The man smiled at her and she nodded. Both father and daughter went inside the building. Unknown to the three, Bhadra was watching them from a dark corner.

Having lived in danger all his life, Arumugam had a well developed sixth sense for trouble. As he met Krishnamurthi that evening, he could suspect that he was being observed. But the gut fear that usually came along with such a feeling was missing. This intrigued him. '*Was it just an imagination?*' He thought, but he knew better. There was no doubt that he was being watched. He looked around, but could see no one. He spotted a three wheeler parked under a tree. He could guess that the person, who ever he or she was, was in that direction. Arumugam went inside the building, crossed the galleries and came out from another door. Nimbly he trotted to one lonely spot and looked at the vehicle parked a few meters away. By habit, Arumugam read the registration number and memorized it. Then he looked at the big bearded man sitting on the driver's seat. He was still staring at the direction where Swarna's scooter was parked. Arumugam could bet on his cute head that this fellow belonged to his world.

Raving and ranting for a couple of days after that night, Bhadra had at last come to his senses. He still hated Krishnamurthi, but did not know how to confront him. Meanwhile Gajji had called him to Chennai. There had been a couple of meetings in various seedy hotels and bars, and every where Gajji had introduced Bhadra to his associates as a rising star in there profession. This had boosted Bhadra's ego and made him forget his family. Two days back, he had returned and resumed his work. That evening he had brought a load to be kept in one of the go downs. After the work was over, he had gone to a tea shop. As he was about to leave after smoking a cigarette, he had spotted Krishnamurthi and Swarna entering the building. He had come back got in to his vehicle and looked at them. And then he saw the fellow with whom Krishnamurthi was talking and smiling. The guy looked decent enough, in a light colored full shirt and dark slacks. But even from that distance, Bhadra could make out that something was amiss. He had not seen this guy before, but was certain that he was out of place in the company of people like Krishnamurthi.

The meeting was over at 7 PM. Krishnamurthi and Swarna came out and Swarna went to bring the scooter. As she wheeled it back, turned it around and pushed it towards where Krishnamurthi was standing, she stopped abruptly. A big shabby looking guy was standing a few feet from Krishnamurthi. Both were staring at each other. Swarna stopped.

"*Remember me?*" The fellow asked. His voice was a growl.

"*Sure.*" Krishnamurthi said in a flat voice.

"*Thought that I was dead! eh?*

Krishnamurthi ignored the question. "*What do you want?*"

"*What do you have?*"

The man turned towards Swarna. '*Oh my god! Bhadra!'*

She stood rooted to the ground. There was an awkward silence.

"*I came there the other day.*" Bhadra growled again. "*You were celebrating.*"

Krishnamurthi looked at Swarna. Neither could understand what this fellow was talking.

"*What was the occasion? My mother's death anniversary?*"

"*Bhadra, this is no way to talk.*" Krishnamurthi said in a soft tone. "*We are seeing each other after ages.*"

Then he said sweetly "*And your sister can't even recognize you. She was a kid when you left.*"

Instead of softening him these words irritated Bhadra. He stared at Swarna again and gave an imperceptible nod.

"*How are you?*" Krishnamurthi asked.

"*Do you care?*" Bhadra snapped back. "*If you had done, you would have come to that hell hole to see how I was.*"

Krishnamurthi gulped down his emotions. Yes it was a mistake. After all Bhadra was his son. But the father could not recall when the son had given him a moment of pride or peace.

"*Okay! What happened, happened son. Let us make up for the loss now.*" Krishnamurthi said soothingly.

And then it happened. With a roar of rage Bhadra was on his throat. Swarna let out a shrill cry. Bhadra was trying to strangle Krishnamurthi. A stunned Krishnamurthi tried to let himself free but the fellow was too strong. Krishnamurthi Could feel his breath cut off. He reeled, and shook, but Bhadra did not loosen the grip.

From the shadows, a figure emerged and was on Bhadra in a second. Horatio Arumugam, let go a solid punch on Bhadra's broad face. The shot sounded like a dull thud. Bhadra's hand jerked back and he fell flat on the floor. Arumugam immediately hugged Krisnamurthi and supported him. Krishnamurthi was now coughing loudly. Swarna came running and took him from Arumugam's arms.

Bhadra glared at Arumugam. Then he began cussing savagely. Arumugam said nothing. By now he knew that Bhadra was Krishnamurthi's son. Bhadra tried to get up, but his nose was bleeding. Gallantly Arumugam lifted him up and sat him on a raised platform.

Though to the father and daughter it had looked like ages, the whole thing had happened within a matter of three or four minutes. Krishnamurthi was shivering uncontrollably.

Arumugam helped him sit on the scooter. Swarna gave him some water from a bottle, to drink. She and Arumugam then looked at the hulking Bhadra. Arumugam took the bottle from her and went to him.

"*Go to hell!*" Bhadra roared at him.

"*I am sorry, I can not recall your name.*" Krishnamurthi said and smiled at Arumugam.

"Horatio Sir." Arumugam replied.

"Yeah! Yeah!" krishnamurthi chuckled. "I am a history teacher and I could not remember such a beautiful name."

After the incident, seeing that both father and daughter were badly shaken, Arumugam had suggested that they should go by Auto, and that he would follow them on their scooter. They had reached home safely, and Krishnamurthi had invited him in. Swarna brought coffee and biscuits.

"Thank you very much young man." Krishnamurthi patted him on the back. "Glad to know that Adityan has got such a good friend."

Arumugam looked at the floor shyly and Swarna beamed. As they sipped their coffee, Arumgam ventured a question

"Sir! Is he your son?"

"Was!" Krishnamurthi replied. "Till today." Arumugam looked at Swarna, and said nothing.

"I am seeing—"

"Appa—" Swarna tried to stop him.

"Let me speak." Krishnamurthi said "I am seeing him after several years. I thought he would have changed. But he has gone even worse."

The other two sipped their coffee silently. It was embarrassing for both.

"Look at my daughter. That fellow is her own blood. The rascal did not have the decency to say even a hello to her."

Both Swarna and Arumugam began blushing. Arumugam wanted to kick himself for asking the question.

After some time Arumugam took leave.

"Drop in some time Horatio." Krishnamurthi said.

"Sure Sir. Please let me know when ever you need me. Good night."

Arumugam came out into the open air. He was so elated that he pinched himself hard to confirm that what had happened was indeed true. Such decent people had treated him so well. And he had not done anything special. He wondered how a saint like Krishnamurthi got a Satan like Bhadra for a son.

Krishnamurthi was in a daze after his tiff with Bhadra. When a shivering Swarna and a calm Arumugam, helped him out of the building into a waiting Auto, He was not thinking correctly. He had not bothered to check, how Bhadra was. Shock, fear, anger and sorrow had clouded his intelligence, and he was more worried about his daughter's safety. As the whole incident had happened at dusk, at the backyard of the building, there were no witnesses, more so because it over in moments.

Bhadra sat there sulking, for sometime. He had been caught unawares by the short cutie. The punch was a marvel, and his nose was now a crimson bulb. Slowly he got up, and went to the tea chop. He took a glass of water and washed his face, in a corner. There weren't many there and thankfully, none noticed him. Mopping his face, he asked for a tea. After draining two cups in one go, he lit a cigarette. Now he was thinking clearly. He grimaced at his own stupidity. The first meeting had ended in a fiasco. He should have been more tactful. Now Krishnamurthi would avoid him still more.

Pea brained Bhadra wondered who this punk was. At the first glance itself, he had guessed correctly that the fellow did not belong to Krishnamurthi's circle.

' Was he that snotty Swarna's boy friend?' He wondered. Did not seem so. Swarna was still a kid. There was a big age difference between Bhadra and her. And this fellow looked even older than him. Bhadra accepted albeit reluctantly that the guy was as tough as himself, if not more. As soon as he thought this, something flashed in his mind. ' This guy was more up his own street. A genuine under world character. '

As per their agreement, none of the three, mentioned this incident to Adityan. He was a soft guy, and it would throw him off balance at this juncture. Adityan was genuinely scared of Bhadra and he did not want that fellow to come in his life. Every thing was normal, and Swarna even went to his house on week end. Ratna had invited some of her friends and they had all gone to a festival in some temple. Adityan called Arumugam and the two watched a new movie in the best theatre in town. Later they went to Arumugam's mansion and chatted for a while.

Arumugam had memorized the registration number of Bhadra's vehicle. He knew that the fellow was in the transport business. Arumugam had to take the services of transporters for his own work. He had made some contacts with people in that line. Now he decided to put his talents to work. Without any one getting suspicious, he found out that Bhadra was a new comer in the trade and that he had a curious habit of taking those assignments which took him away from the town. It was on one of the rare occasions, that he had come to that commercial complex that evening. When Arumugam was told that Bhadra worked the industrial estate, he smiled inwardly.

Within a few trips to the estate, Arumugam had gathered an astonishing amount of information about Bhadra. Now he was certain that the fellow was a regular gangster. This worried Arumugam. He suspected rightly, that Bhadra too would be inquiring about him. The cat and mouse game between the two ex-alumni of juvenile homes had begun.

Nandini had strictly warned Arumugam against getting in touch with any one from the Gokulpet underworld. Arumugam had realized that it was for his good and had obeyed accordingly. But this incident had put him on guard once again.

Sitting alone Girija Shanker alias GS, had all the time in the world to look back in anger. He was a prize catch and had been allotted an independent cell by the authorities. Nandini's jeering smile, came between him and his sleep almost every night. He hated her. He could not accept that this chit of a girl, had stripped him to his birthday suit in front of the whole world.

GS believed that he was too smart, for all the police men in the country put together. He had planned it all so perfectly. He was so well insulated. Yet somehow the lawmen had come sniffing and grabbed his goat. When the initial cussing sessions, aimed at putting the fear of devil into his tormenters failed,

GS reconciled to his fate as a state guest. Now he was thinking clearly.

His house had been bugged. The evidence produced in the court was too damaging to have been fed by some accomplice. None of those close to him, knew so much. But how did they manage it? He was in the fifth floor and there was security outside. The lock on the door had not been tampered with. GS lived alone. And no one had the keys to his flat. Then how could the egg heads get in and play all night? After a lot of brain storming, GS concluded that some ape had trotted up the drain pipe. That needed skills which only some one from his planet could possess. GS regretted that such a genius was not in his payroll.

As per prison rules, GS was allowed to meet the other inmates every day for two hours, in an open area closely watched by guards. Many of the small fry waited for this opportunity to say hello to the great man. They waited for a nod, a smile or any other sign of recognition from GS to make their day. And being asked to run some errand for him, was an honor that every one dreamt of.

In prisons there is an unsaid code of conduct. The authorities do not interfere in personal conversation between inmates unless and until it affects the law and order directly. They know that there is a two way flow of messages between the guys in the slammer, and those waiting outside. They do not eves drop into such communication. Even then, to be on the safe side the inmates use code words.

On that day when GS walked in, there was a hushed silence. GS smiled broadly at no one in particular, but every hood thought that it was meant for him.

"Kathir!" GS called in his soft modulated voice.

Several heads turned towards the lucky man, a dried up convict who was to be released that week. As every one stepped back to make way, Kathir shuffled towards GS and stood with folded hands.

"When?" GS asked.

"Day after tomorrow Sar!" Kathir told him his release date. "Tell Roja that I want to see him."

"Yes Sar!"

Roja was the nickname, that GS had given to Gajji for his deceptive looks. Kathir knew him. He would be suitably rewarded for giving this message.

On Friday, at around midnight, one guard came to GS' cell. GS was awake. The fellow opened the door and nodded. GS got up and came out. Passing through various grilled gates and steel doors, which the guard unlocked and locked meticulously, they reached a long dark gallery. Passing through it they came out into an open verandah. GS peered into the darkness. The guard threw a beam of light with his powerful torch. There was a shuffle of feet, and someone draped in a shawl appeared from the shadows. A moment later, GS slowly turned and looked at the guard. He nodded and stood there. GS walked slowly towards the shawl man.

"Hello Boss.!" Gajji said. "Hm."

"Called for me?" "Hm!"

"Tell me."

"Some clown from our brotherhood, is servicing the sweetheart who nailed me. Knows how to climb up drain pipes."

GS stopped and looked at Gajji. "Oh! I see!"

Find him and send him to his ancestors."

Gajji understood every word of the message. Sweetheart was Nandini. Clown was the fellow who climbed up the drain pipe and opened the door of that inaccessible fifth floor flat. Gajji had to find him and kill him.

"Sure!"

"How much?"

Gajji told him the price of the contract. There was no haggling. They had done business several times before.

"Done!" GS said. "Now it is your baby. I want to just read the news in the papers."

"Perfect." Gajji replied.

"Good! And tell Senthil to send the amount this fellow asked for this favor." GS said nodding towards the guard. "Sure."

"That is all!"

Gajji nodded a salute, stepped back a few paces and dissolved into the shadows. GS picked up the packet, that Gajji had dropped on the dewy ground. It was a polythene bag containing ten packets of GS' favorite cigarettes. GS walked back And was in his cell ten minutes later.

Gajji had got an assignment of a life time from GS. If he completed it successfully, his position in the underworld would increase manifolds. The news of his getting this job, had spread like wild fire in the underworld. Unknown faces had sent messages to him, offering their services in nailing the guy.

GS had said that some clown from their brotherhood, had been servicing the sweet heart, who had grinned at GS's smooth polished face that fateful evening. Gajji imagined the scene and chuckled. GS had always considered him self a ladies' man.

Her name was Nandini. Gajji began his search from there. It as a very difficult job. She was a senior officer, and the department as such did not have any affection for Girija shankar alias G.S. It would be all the more difficult to glean information from the regular contacts in the force.

Gajji dug out all the stuff about Nandini, he could lay his hands on. She was an IPS and had joined the police force, on a senior level. Her career graph had been quite routine, and regular, till she had hit the jackpot in the form of G.S.

Gajji now shifted his gaze towards the clown. G. S. had said that he was some one who could climb drain pipes. Typical cat burglar. Gajji began tapping his sources in the underworld for information on such guys. Here he met with some success. One of the informers told him that there was a burglar gang in the city which was smashed a couple of years back. Many of the guys had been killed but some of them had been jailed. Gajji got the names of a few who were still alive and in prison. One of them was a fellow called Sethu. He was serving his sentence in Palayankottai prison. Gajji immediately made a trip to the city.

Gajji had contacts in that prison. Through them he got in touch with Sethu. Luck was on Gajji's side. Sethu had been given a two day permission to go to his village which was nearby, to attend his mother's funeral. Gajji immediately rushed to the village, and was waiting for Sethu there when the convict arrived. Sethu had already been told about Gajji, and when Gajji came with the funeral procession as part of the family, Sethu hinted that he should stay in his home that night.

The villagers, entertained the police men who had come with Sethu. He was not a VIP catch any way. Only a thief whose term would be over in a year. More over Sethu had been an ideal prisoner. So the police men did not bother much. They did there routine vigil, had their supper, and sat at the verandah waiting for the dawn when they could take the guy back and hand him over to the prison officials.

Inside the house, in the small attic Gajji and Sethu sat talking. "What was the name of the guy you said, had vanished?"

"Arumugam."

"Arumugam" Gajji repeated the name slowly. Sethu chuckled and Gajji looked at him sharply. "What makes you laugh?"

"Nothing." Sethu replied. "I don't know why we are discussing this but this kid was too small a fry in our outfit."

"What do you mean was?"

"He is dead."

"Dead?"

"That is what I said."

Beads of sweat appeared on Gajji's face. "Are you sure?"

"Can't be otherwise. I learnt from the sources inside the slammer." "How did he die?"

"No idea." Sethu shrugged. "The Sivagangai police found his body." Gajji sighed deep. His tone changed. He was quite soft now.

"Tell me Sethu, could this guy really slither up pipes?"

Sethu nodded. Gajji hugged him." Brother you don't know what you have done for me. If I suspect right, you have quite a sum waiting for you when you come out."

"Thanks." Sethu grinned.

Next morning, as soon as Sethu left, Gajji took leave from the family, after giving them some money for the hospitality. He went to the bus stop and boarded the first bus to Sivagangai.

Gajji went to work like a true professional. Due to his member ship in the network, he had contacts all over Tamilnadu. Moreover guys had offered him help, after he had got the assignment. On landing in Sivagangai, Gajji called his contacts and explained the situation.

"Please get me all the dope on this fellow, Arumugam's 'unfortunate demise.'

The feed back began within hours. No one had seen the body. Police claimed that it was in a bad shape, and they had disposed it off after the necessary formalities. The man in charge of the case was one Inspector Natrajan. And then Gajji got a needle in the hay stack. One of the eager to please wise guys observed casually, that Natrajan was a disciple of the awesome detective Jacob Janardhanan.

Gajji's face was taut with excitement and tension. He had a strong suspicion that Arumugam was alive, and in a new avatar.

Sethu had described the boy in detail. Now Gajji had to find him.

"Please do me one favor, brother." Gajji requested the wise guy after pressing a wad of notes, into his palm. "Find out where Jacob is posted now."

The Northeast monsoon had begun. Chennai and the surrounding areas had started receiving their share of rainfall for the year and Gokulpet was no exception. Being nearer the mountains, and thanks to the vegetation, Gokulpet experienced heavy downpours this season.

S.S.P Jacob Janardhanan sipped his umpteenth cup of tea. The sky was cloudy and there had been heavy rains the previous night. Even now it was drizzling, It was dawn in Gokulpet.

The phone started ringing and he picked it up. It was from the patrol team. Jacob listened to the message carefully and said:

"Okay don't do any thing. Wait. I am on my way." He drained the cup, took his helmet and walked out of his cabin.

"The patrol team has found a body. Let us go. "He told the assistant.

The young man stopped writing his report, and joined Jacob. They got on Jacob's bike and rode away. Jacob always preferred the bike to the jeep, during an emergency because it took him to the spot faster. And the fact that it was drizzling did not change this preference. He was more comfortable riding a two wheeler.

Six foot two inches tall and extremely thin Jacob, looked more like a college professor which he wasn't, than the policeman that he was. He was forty five and had joined the department twenty years ago. Considered to be one of the best sleuths in the state, the intelligent police officer, always believed in solving a crime with brains rather than brawns.

Having showed his mettle in various towns and villages, and having solved several complex cases, Jacob had won medals, rewards and promotions. Now he was posted in Gokulpet, as in charge of a police station.

The drizzle turned into a shower, and Jacob had to peer through the plastic shade of the helmet to see clearly. Normally it would have been a thirty minute ride at that early hour, from his office to the spot which was a kilometer from the industrial estate. But due to the rains, Jacob rode slowly and reached there in forty minutes.

The previous night, the Patrol car had been cruising through the highway connecting the city to the industrial estate, when they had spotted a three wheeler parked on one side around hundred meters from the road. It was three in the morning, and the police men thought, that the occupants had parked it to wait for the rains to slow down. It was indeed a heavy down pour and they themselves were finding it difficult to drive.

After making the rounds of the estate, the team had driven further into the villages, to see if any one was stranded or needed help otherwise. While coming back, when they passed the spot, they saw the vehicle still there. On a hunch they stopped to see what was wrong. One of the police men went near it and peeped in. Five minutes later, Jacob got the call.

The sole occupant of the three wheeler was a young man. He was found in a sitting position on the driver's seat, with his hands gripping the handle. The side doors were both closed, and the body of the vehicle was locked. As per Jacob's instructions, the police men had not touched any thing because it was evident at first sight that the victim was dead for some hours.

Within seconds of Jacob's arrival, the ambulance came. Two men wearing gloves, got down and walked towards the vehicle with a stretcher. As there had been quite a down pour, and the thick growth of shrubs in that area was ankle high, foot prints could not be depended upon for any clue. Yet every one was treading warily.

Dexterously, the fellows opened the door, extracted the body and placed it on the stretcher. Rigor mortis was beginning to set. Jacob peered at the dead man closely.

The man was in his mid twenties, around five foot ten, and very sturdily built. His hair was long, and he had a thick black beard. He was wearing a dark pant and a shirt which was of a light shade but was now soaked with his own blood. There was a grey colored leather box on the dash board. Jacob opened it and looked at the contents inside it.

The finger prints on them matched that of the dead man, identified as Bhadra, a man with a criminal record. It looked like a gang land job. The grey box which evidently belonged to Bhadra, had an empty velvet sheath, and a tiny knife. Jacob smiled to himself. The knife which was supposed to be in the sheath, was missing.

The victim had been involved in some kind of scuffle, in which the killer had got the better of him. The victim had been hit on the head with a blunt object, and stabbed several times. The medical report said that he had died due to excessive loss of blood leading to a fatal cardiac arrest. The killing had taken place somewhere else, at a time when it was raining. The killer, had put the body in the vehicle's container, driven to the spot where it was found, extracted from the container, and placed on the driver's seat in that sitting position. It looked like a professional job, but still Jacob's instincts pointed at some loose ends. The body was sent to the morgue after the post mortem.

Jacob wrote down the F.I.R. and started a new file for the case. The finger print people gave their report. They had extracted a lot of prints but almost all of them matched that of the dead man. Those which were different, were carefully code numbered and filed.

Jacob was an expert detective. The case looked like a simple open and shut one, and he allowed the other officials to believe it that way. After looking at the box, he had decided to investigate this case on his own. It was a job which needed careful study, and extraordinary tact.

Jacob marveled at the killer's luck. Not even the brainiest of criminals, could have planned a crime to be executed on a rainy day, even if it was the monsoon season. Nature is too unpredictable for that. The killer, who so ever he was had the devil on his side.

Krishnamurthi read the news item in the paper, and went numb with shock. He felt that someone had kicked him on the chest. He stared at the clip.

GANGSTER KILLED

The Gokulpet police found a body, in the outskirts of the town, which supposedly belongs to a gangster named Bhadrachalam alias Bhadra. His body was found in his own three wheeler, with several stab wounds. It may be recalled that Bhadra was the main accused in the killing of a schoolboy called Girish, some years back. Bhadra had spent his time in a juvenile home, and had been released an year ago. Reliable sources confirmed that Bhadra had resumed his illegal activities after the release and was connected to the Gokulpet and Chennai underworld. The police is investigating the case.

Krishnamurthi tried to get up from the chair, but couldn't. All the energy in him was drained. He was feeling breathless and his mouth popped open. He sucked in some air and tears started flowing from his eyes. He wanted to say something but had lost his voice. Swarna had gone to the college. Her classes started early and ended at noon. He turned around and saw the coffee pot. He poured a tumbler and gulped it down. Now he felt slightly better. The phone rang. It was Adityan's father Raman,

"Good morning Sir.' "Morning."

"How are you Sir?"

"I am fine!" Krishnamurthi's voice was choked. There was a pause.

"Sir! I read the news."

Krishnamurthi did not reply.

"I am very sorry Sir." Raman seemed genuinely distraught. His voice was a sob. Krishnamurthi was still silent.

"Sir, can I come to see you in person?" Raman pleaded. "Please please."

"Thanks. I am on my way." Raman kept the phone and rushed out.

When Raman reached Krishnamurthi's bungalow, some of the neighbors were already there. There was a pall of gloom. Krishnamurthi was sitting on the sofa. Raman went and hugged him. Krishnamurthi began crying and that made others tearful too. No one was speaking. One lady went to the kitchen and made coffee for all.

Swarna was in her last class, when the peon arrived and told her that some one had come to see her. Swarna frowned and excused herself from the class. When she came to the corridor, she raw Ratna there. Ratna smiled at her and tookher hands. Swarna looked at her quizzically.

"Sorry for disturbance."

"Its okay." Swarna still looked at her askance.

"I could have called but I did not know the college phone number." Swarna nodded.

"Your father, and Adityan's father have gone for some work. So I came myself to take you to my house till they returned."

Swarna nodded slowly but could not make out any thing. Ratna looked away. "Finish your class. I shall wait." Ratna said finally.

Adityan was doing night shift, and had returned home at seven am. Straight away he had gone to bed. When he got up in the afternoon, he was happy to see, Swarna in the kitchen. Ratna and Swarna were having lunch.

"Hi!"

"Hello!"

Adityan looked at Ratna.

"Wait I shall bring your coffee.' Ratna said.

Adityan nodded, beamed at Swarna and went to the drawing room thoughtfully.

Swarna wanted to ask a lot of questions but was tongue tied. More over Ratna fussed around her so much, that she could only stare and the woman. Ratna was a good actress. She had cried her heart out even before going to the college. Raman had told her to keep Swarna comfortable, till he and Krishnamurthi returned.

Sitting in his den, Gajji pondered over the news that he had just received from Elango. Gajji was back from one of his mysterious trips, and had called him for a meeting in Chennai. When Elango told him that Bhadra had been done to death, he was stunned. Elango had assured him that it had nothing to do with their own family business, or any rivalry pertaining to that. According to him, it could have been the result of some brawl that Bhadra was always notorious for.

Gajji liked Bhadra. He believed that the fellow would be the best associate in crime, once he was perfectly polished. Gajji had great plans in mind. He wanted to have his own outfit, which would cater to the cream of the underworld all over the country. The sudden whacking of Bhadra had come as a great hindrance. Actually he would have been the best guy to keep a tab on Jacob. Gajji knew that Jacob was in Gokulpet.

"I am really sorry that Bhadra is no more." Gajji told Elango. "But he is dead and of no use to us any more." I am on a very big job, the details of which are immaterial to you. What I would have liked Bhadra to do, I want you to do now. Use what ever contacts you have to find out every thing about Jacob. Where he goes, who he meets, and especially if he contacts some one who is around twenty eight years old, short, light skinned, and of compact built. If he does, find out the name of that guy and what he does."

The brown colored car came to where Jacob stood and stopped. At that hour the highway was empty except for a lonely lorry, roaring down towards the city evry now and then. The driver opened the front door and peeped out.

"Morning Mr. Jacob?" "Hello."

The driver slid back to the steering wheel. Jacob got in beside him. The car drove away. It took a U turn after a furlong and sped back in the direction that it had come. Driving at a steady speed, the driver went through a couple of roads, till he turned right into a broad road flanked by shady trees. There were rows of independent houses on both sides. The car went to the end of the avenue, and stopped near a huge gate to the right. The driver honked and someone opened the door. The car slipped in and stopped at a garage. Both of them got out. The driver walked into the house followed by Jacob. They stepped into a huge well furnished and decorated hall. The driver climbed up the stairs, on the right side and went into a room. It was equally well furnished. By that time, one of the servants and come running to wait at the driver, who was actually the owner of the house.

"Please sit down Mr. Jacob. What will you have, hot, cold—"
"No thanks."

"Please, no formalities." "Coffee."

The servant heard this bowed and left.

Jacob sat on a leather chair. The other man sat behind the huge brown table. "So, Vaitheeswaran what news?" Jacob began the conversation.

"Every thing fine." The man whose name was Vaitheeswaran replied.

Vaitheeswaran belonged to a family of wealthy business men whose main activity was trading. Vaitheeswaran managed an antique and fancy item shop in a township near Gokulpet. This shop sold expensive items mainly brought from North India.

Jacob took out the grey colored box from his bag and placed it on the table. Vaitheeswaran looked at it and smiled.

"Recognize this?" Jacob asked. "Sure."

"Can you tell me whether you sold it?"

"I must have. Actually I don't have any more of this variety with me now. But I had two some time back. Both sold." "Only Two?"

"That is right."

Jacob nodded thoughtfully.

"Can you recognize the guy who you sold them to."

Vaitheeswaran chuckled "I don't know whether it is a miracle, but actually I do remember one of them."

"Fantastic." Jacob said. Then he took out Bhadra's driving license.

"See" He said pointing at the small photograph on it" Whether it is this man?" Vaitheeswaran stared hard at the photograph. Then he tapped at his forehead "Ha."

"What happened?" Jacob asked. "This is the other guy?"

"What do you mean?"

"I told you that I remember one of them. But this guy is the other fellow. He bought the second piece."

"Oh I see."

"Mr Jacob" Vaitheeswaran continued, "This guy looks like the normal customers, who come to my shop every day especially to buy items like this. "He pointed at the box. "I can recognize the other fellow, because he looked different. When he came, I thought he wanted to buy some gift for his girl friend. I was a trifle surprised when he went for the knife. It would have looked out of place on his person."

"What makes you think so?"

"He was a toy boy. Short, very fair, and bright looking."

Jacob smiled at the description. Vaitheeswaran was a fancy stores' man. He should know who would buy what.

"So now we have the description of both the buyers of this item."

Jacob opened the box. "The knife in this is missing, Vaitheeswaran. I wish I could know how it looked like." "Just a minute."

Vaitheeswaran took a plain paper, and drew a rough sketch of the knife.

"Is the other piece in the box?" He asked.

"You mean this?" Jacob pointed at the tiny knife. "Yes." He chuckled. Jacob frowned at him.

Vaitheeswaran slid the sketch towards Jacob. "The knife looks like this. The tiny piece is meant to open the cavity here." He pointed at the handle.

"For what ? Loading bullets?" Jacob quipped.

"No! No! "Vaitheeswaran grinned. "You will not believe if I tell you." "Try me."

"The owner of the knife can keep something there to identify that it belongs to him."

"What is it ? A bad joke?" Jacob snorted. "I am serious."

"No wonder it is missing now." Jacob said a moment later.

Jacob stepped into the station and looked around. He saw a pair of middle aged men sitting on the bench. They looked distraught. It was not new. No one in a holiday mood came to his office. As soon as they saw him one of them got up. Jacob looked at him. The other police men saluted Jacob. Jacob looked at the couple and went to his cabin. A moment later he rang the bell. The assistant went in.

"Any news?"

"Sir they are waiting to see you." "Who are they?"

"One of them is Bhadra's father."

"Hm! Send for some tea and ask them to come in."

Jacob received Krishnamurthi and Raman, kindly. Krishnamurthi looked shattered.

"I am sorry for what happened Mr. Krishnamurthi." Jacob held his hand. "I was. expecting you. I had gone through your son's file and found out that he was your son. I wanted to come myself, but thought that it could embarrass a decent person like you.

"Thanks for your concern Sir." Krishnamurthi said in a hoarse whisper.

"With your permission, I would like to take possession of my son's body." As he said this his shoulder slumped, Raman hugged him gently.

As soon as the permission was granted, Raman made a few calls. The first one was to Ratna. He told her to break the news gently to Adityan and Swarna. Then he called some of Krishnamurthi's neighbors. After the formalities, the body was taken straight away to the electric crematorium.

With tears streaming down his face, Adityan looked at the body of the guy who he hardly knew, but who was his classmate a few years back. In death, Bhadra covered from head to toe looked at peace with himself. No one could have said that this guy had led a violent and trouble some life.

Swarna wept bitterly and clung to Ratna. Krishnamurthi completed the religious rites and then the few who attended the funeral, paid their respects to the departed soul. When the body was consigned to the flames, Krishnamurthi let out a wail that left every one sobbing. All the time Adityan and Raman were as supportive as possible to the bereaved man. For once Krishnamurthi thanked god for sending such nice people.

Next morning, Jacob picked up Krishnamurthi from a prearranged spot. Jacob was driving a car, that he had borrowed from some one. Dressed in a white colored Safari, Jacob did not look one bit like the police man that he was. The two drove away and began cruising towards the industrial estate. After some time, Jacob pulled over, opposite the spot where Bhadra's body was found.

"When did you last see Bhadra?" krishnamurthi told him in detail about that evening. Jacob listened to it patiently. When Krishnamurthi stopped speaking Jacob asked

"You said, Horatio?"

"Yes Sir. That is his name."

Jacob nodded. "You say that he is a clearing agent."

"Yes Sir."

"Can you tell me how he looks like?"

Thankfuly, while describing Arumugam's appearance, Krishnamurthi was looking through the wind shield. If only he had turned to his right and glanced at Jacob, he would have been shocked. Jacob's face was a granite mask. Horatio Arumugam was Vaitheeswaran's 'Toy boy' customer.

But that was not the reason for Jacob's face turning to stone.

He suddenly relaxed, smiled at Krishnamurthi, thanked him for the valuable information, and took him to a hotel where they had coffee and snacks. Then he dropped Krishnamurthi at the same stop from where he had picked him up.

Jacob wasn't called an ace sleuth for nothing. Time and again he had surprised his colleagues and superiors, with his dedication, brilliance and an uncanny ability to see the unseen. He never ignored any bit of information. He had learnt and memorized many things from his past cases, and they had come handy while solving complex problems.

Next morning, sitting in his cabin Jacob ordered some tea, and sat thinking. He took a paper and began doodling as he thought. He was trying to remember dates, occasions, people. As he thought and scribbled away, he suddenly got a flash. Jacob immediately tore the paper into bits, popped it in his mouth, chewed it for some time and spat it into the flush. Then he placed a call to Chennai.

While in Chennai, When ever he found time, Jacob would visit the Besant Nagar church, to light a candle for the umpteen people, whose murders and accidental deaths he had investigated. On one such occasion, as he was striding towards the church gate, Jacob suddenly stopped. Blending easily with the surging crowd, he stood in a corner and observed a couple on the opposite side a hundred meters from him.

A woman dressed in a tight full shirt, and jeans, was sitting on a bike, wearing a polo cap. She looked like the many young girls one would find on weekends, in that area, heading for the beach. A small very attractive man was getting on the pillion. The bike moved towards Jacob's direction. Hidden behind the people, Jacob could see the two clearly. The young man was light skinned, had curly hair, and wore a bright T shirt and dark pants.

The woman was Nandini. Jacob had no doubt about it. 'The fellow on the pillion could be some relative or friend' Jacob thought. But his intuition hinted otherwise. Bowing to his sixth sense, Jacob had filed all this away in his remarkable memory.

A couple of years back, when Jacob was posted to a station in Kanchipuram, he had received a call from a young IPS officer, called Nandini. She told him that he had been recommended by her seniors for a job which needed utmost secrecy, efficiency and tact.

Nandini wanted a favor from him. Jacob was to arrange the fake killing of a person whose name she mentioned as Arumugam. Jacob did not know who he was. However from her words, he could guess that the young lady was cultivating an informer. In the police department every one respects the right of the other to protect the identity of his or her informer. Jacob did not ask any questions.

Jacob masterminded the whole operation of erasing the identity of Arumugam, through a 'gangland slaying' of the man in Sivagangai, where he had very good contacts. The whole thing had worked like a charm under his supervision, and Nandini had personally thanked him for his service.

Now as he drove towards Nandini's office, for an appointment with her, he recalled all this. The man he had seen with Nandini's that evening, had an uncanny resemblance to the man mentioned as Horatio by Krishnamurthi and as the buyer of the knife, by Vaitheeswaran. He had placed a call in the afternoon, and asked Nandini whether she knew any one by the name of Horatio. She had listened to him for a minute and asked him to come straight away.

"Good evening madame." Jacob saluted her.

"Good evening Mr Jacob. Please sit down." Nandini waved at a chair. They were in her well furnished office, and Nandini had specifically instructed the staff not to disturb them.

"Please tell me."

Jacob told her every thing in detail. The killing of Bhadra, the knife matter, and Krishnamurthi's incident. Nandini listened without commenting. Once Jacob had concluded, she asked him:

"What made you ask me whether I knew this Horatio?" "A hunch! "Jacob replied politely.

"Come again."

"Madame I go to Besant Nagar Church often." Jacob said and looked at her. Nandini stifled a smile and played with the paper weight.

"Hm."

"The description of Horatio that I got from the knife seller, was similar to the one that Mr. Krishnamurthi gave of a guy called Horatio. Both times, I felt that I had seen some one like that before, but could not place him. And then when I did a methodical thinking back, the sight of a similar guy with you flashed in my memory. Before making any move I decided to contact you."

"Good! I appreciate your wisdom Mr. Jacob. Yes I know that fellow." Jacob sighed and smiled.

"Do you suspect him of killing the man?" Nandini asked.

"No madame." Jacob said in a low measured tone giving weight to each word

"On the contrary I suspect him of hiding the identity of the killer."

Nandini looked at Jacob with visible surprise. She knew Jacob. He would not say any thing without meaning every word of what he said.

"I shall explain the logic behind this theory." Jacob said. Nandini nodded. Jacob placed the grey box on the table. Nandini saw it and Jacob gave her a description of the missing knife and its properties.

"I would repeat that it is only a suspicion. I may be wrong but with my experience, I feel that I am on the right track. It is just a coincidence, that both Horatio and Bhadra purchased the same type of knife, independently from the same seller. If Horatio had such a knife, one may presume that he also knew, how to use it. I still don't know whether this fellow is something other than the clearing agent that Krishnamurthi said he was.

Krishnamurthi confirmed that Horatio saved him from Bhadra once. So the two fellows knew each other. From the facts that we have collected on this case, it would appear that the killing took place else where, and the body was dumped at the spot where the police found it. Bhadra was a criminal, and this looks typical gangland. To be honest, I would choose to believe that the whole operation was executed by a professional." Jacob took as sip of water.

Nandini was all ears. She was amazed at the way Jacob was going about the story with perfect clarity.

"However I am forced to think otherwise. Bhadra died of concussion and cardiac arrest resulting from excessive loss of blood, and not due to a fatal stab wound. The injuries in the body suggest that the killer had madly and repeatedly swung the knife at the victim without actually bothering to know about the consequences. It is a case of culpable homicide and not of cold blooded murder. As a professional detective, I would say that the killer was probably a first time offender."

A man came and placed a pot of tea, two cups and a plate of snacks on the table. Jacob waited till the man poured the tea in the cups, and left. Both took a sip.

"Now I look at it from the eyes of the novice killer. After realizing what he has done, the killer would have run away from the spot in panic and may have reported the matter to the police. No such message was received by any police station or check post. So there was some one at the spot other than the killer. This someone had a more cool head, and he not only transported the victim to a different spot, but also disposed off the weapon of crime which could probably be the knife from this box. Ie. Bhadra tried to use this knife, but it slipped from his hand when he was hit at the back of his head. And the killer used it to kill the owner himself.

Why I suspect Horatio of being the other man? Two reasons. First, he could be the owner of a similar knife, and hence knew about its strange property. And that is why he either destroyed it or threw it some where. Secondly, Horatio knew Bhadra, and was probably there at the time when the incident took place. And I can safely guess that a fellow who could buy a knife, who could floor a fellow like Bhadra, even if it was to save another man, could also be smart enough to put the law off the track by transporting the body." Jacob concluded.

Nandini kept quiet for some time. Then she suddenly asked

"What is your future course of action?" "That is why I came to you."

"Me? For what?"

"To ask whether I can close this case." "What? Don't you want to question Horatio?" Jacob shook his head vigorously.

"Why not?"

"Madame! You may find it strange, but for once I genuinely regret my skills."

Nandini smiled at him "And why?"

"I am afraid that I will solve the case, arrest the killer, and hate myself for doing that. When I was young and hot blooded, I had done that a couple of times. I thought that I had done my duty and was happy with the rewards. But as I grew older, I could not erase the memories of genuinely nice people being convicted of crimes that they had indeed committed, out of circumstances beyond their control."

Nandini looked at him. "Tell me how many people know the whole story?"

"None other than you and me."

"Okay! Thanks for confiding in me. I shall help you."

"Thank you madame. It's a weight off my chest." Jacob said and took leave.

"Horatio!" Elango said.

"Wow. Great job Elango. Are you sure?"

"As sure as, you being my brother." Elango chuckled." I saw Jacob coming out of the fellow's office just now."

"Fantastic Elango. I am proud of you."

"I never saw the two meet. "Elango accepted. "But I saw this fellow at a distance. Actually he was easy to find. The guy is working in a private company here. One guy from our stable showed him to me. Same description that you gave, Short guy, light tint, well dressed. To make sure that he was indeed the guy, I tapped my sources, near the office, and just now it was confirmed that I was right. When Jacob went in, this guy of ours followed him and heard Jacob inquire about Horatio. The fellow was not there."

"Superb Elango. Now drop Jacob, and tail this kid. Don't repeat Don't do any thing else."

"Done."

Once he was gone, Nandini sat on her desk thinking about the whole matter. Jacob was brilliant, but Nandini was no fool either. She knew that Jacob would not have dared to come and ask her about Horatio without doing his homework properly. Jacob had rung her up at 3 PM. He had reached her office at 7.30 PM.

Jacob had mentioned that he met Krishnamurthi the day before, in the morning. Nandini was sure that with more than twenty four hours at his disposal, Jacob had made a lot of discreet inquiries about Horatio.

And then it struck her.

Jacob had put two and two together. From the mansion, he had found out when Horatio arrived in Gokulpet. Some of Jacob's colleagues were part of the operation which nailed GS. Through the grape vine he had learnt about the whole thing. 'On a hunch', as he had politely said, he had compared the dates, and found out that he was indeed on the right track.

Horatio had arrived at Gokulpet, the day after the bugging operation. Jacob's intentions were noble. He did not want to do something which would put Nandini in an embarrassing position.

Her thoughts now shifted to Horatio Arumugam. They had been keeping in touch over the phone, but she hadn't met him for sometime. Nandini had specifically told him to keep away from trouble.

' Then what made him get into this, supposing that Jacob was right?' She wondered.

Nandini knew Horatio like the back of her hand. He was too nice and intelligent to disobey such a sane advice, especially when it was for his good. A small brawl was one thing. But this was serious matter. And Arumugam was no fool to believe that the police would not see through the façade. She had assured Jacob that she would help him. Now she decided to take over the case.

Gajji was an extraordinarily cautious and patient man. He never took a step without confirming that he was in the right direction. When Elango gave him the registration number of the bus, which Horatio Arumugam had boarded that after noon, Gajji had finished all his routine work, and come to the Chennai main bus stop where the Gokulpet bus would arrive. Even here he hadn't taken any chance. Before terminating at the main bus stop, the bus dropped commuters at two other halts. Gajji, had placed two of his best men in the two halts. They had confirmed to him that no one answering to

Arumugam's description, had got down from that particular bus.

Gaji finished his third cup of tea and went near the bay where this bus would arrive. He stood inconspicuously near a magazine shop, pretending to browse. The bus arrived a few minutes late, and the commuters began disembarking. As soon as Arumugam got down, Gajji tensed up.

The pickup point and time were the same. The only difference was that Jacob was not hiding behind the crowd, but as per Nandini's advice, he was standing a couple of yards away from Horatio Arumugam and studying him. Nandini came exactly at 7 PM and Jacob scratched his left arm with his right as a signal that his intuition was right. As Nandini stopped the bike and Arumugam got on the pillion, Jacob crossed the road and vanished.

From the bus stop, Arumugam had taken an auto. Immediately Gajji, who had planned it all perfectly, got into another auto, which he had brought with him, and followed him. Arimugam got down near a restaurant, a stones throw away from the church. He went in, had a cup of tea and then walked towards the spot where Nandini would pick him up. On a hunch, Gajji drove slowly behind him, like a guy searching for a customer, and then he spotted Jacob.

Gajji parked his auto discreetly in a corner and waited. Presently Nandini arrived, and picked up Arumugam. As soon as the bike hit the main road, Gajji began tailing it from a safe distance. When the bike turned towards the road leading to the dilapidated building, Gajji stopped at a place and waited.

"So Aru! How are you?" "I am fine madame."

"Don't seem so."

"No madame, I am fine." Horatio smiled feebly. "Hm! How is the work?"

"Okay."

The usually bright and enthusiastic Arumugam, looked dull. The glow on his face was missing. He looked tired.

Nandini wanted to ask him point blank about the Bhadra case. She was after all a police officer, and this would have been the best moment to make the guy spill the beans. But she did not. There was a reason. She had called him to just make some gentle inquiry about his welfare. But Horatio had expressed the desire to meet her in person. This had intrigued her. No one who has been party to a capital crime, would in his right senses, request an audience with a police woman, unless and until there was more than it met the eye. She had agreed, tipped off Jacob, and now she found a totally dejected Horatio in front of her.

"Madame." Horatio said in a voice which looked like a sob. "Yes!"

"Can I come back to you?"

"You are with me." Nandini smiled.

"No! No! The way it was before." His tone was pleading. "Why, anything wrong?" Nandini probed gently.

Horatio sighed. "I feel very lonely and—"

This was not the answer Nandini expected from him. She thought that Horatio Arumugam would ask her to save him from a situation that he had found himself in. But the fellow's attitude was of total surrender. Nandini recalled Jacob's statement "I suspect him of trying to save the killer."

Horatio had taken a great risk, against her advice by doing what Jacob suspected him of. That too against Nandini's advice. He should have been avoiding her now. But he had come to her onhis own. Her experience said that, this attitude did not jell.

"I was very happy when I was with you, running your errands. It was the happiest period of my life. I felt that I was doing some thing really good." Arumugam said. "You saved my life, and I wanted to be at your beck and call all my life."

Nandini nodded.

"And when you sent me to Gokulpet, I took it as a command from you. But now I want you to take me back, or give me some work, where I can be with you all the time."

It was impossible for Nandini to keep a straight face. Without even knowing it, Horatio Arumugam was falling into her lap. What he would not do for her?Jacob wanted to bury the Bhadra case. In return if Nandini gave Horatio as an informer, Jacob would be grateful to her. She would be hitting two birds with one stone.

"Sure Aru. Why not? I too want you to help me just like before." Nandini smiled.

"When can I return?" Arumugam asked. For once he was the same old guy again. The enthusiasm that she had always seen in him, was back.

"Very soon! In fact we can start as soon as you return to Gokulpet." Arumgam smiled broadly for the first time that evening.

Gajji wanted to hug himself. He never knew that he was so brilliant. To tie up Jacob with Arumugam's disappearance was indeed a stroke of genius. Now he had seen Jacob at the spot where Arumugam stood waiting. No wonder GS had chosen him for this assignment.

The girl had to be Nandini. There was no doubt about it. But there was a small suspicion in the back of his mind. 'Why didn't Arumuam and Jacob recognize each other? Or they did so but Gajji could not notice as it was through some gestures. Yes Jacob had scratched his left arm with his right.'

From where he sat in his auto, Gajji could see Nandini's bike. What they were doing in the building, did not bother Gajji one bit. Presently the two returned.

Nandini started the bike and Arumugam got on. She rode back and suddenly stopped on the opposite side of where Gajji had stopped his auto. Arumugam gestured towards him. Gajji's heart began racing.' Had they seen him following them?' He started the auto and drove near them.

"Koyambedu." Arumugam said. His voice was husky. "Sure." Gajji was proud of his steel nerves.

Arumugam got down from the bike, nodded at Nandini and got into the auto. Nandini nodded back and rode away.

Gajji pinched himself hard to believe that he was indeed so lucky that evening. His prey was sitting in his auto so close to him. Gajji drove the vehicle at a normal speed, and hit the main road. After a furlong, he turned to his left and drove fast for some time till he came to a very dark, very shaded and small alley which connected the main road to the one leading to Adyar. It was a road which was seldom used by people during nights. Gajji slipped his hand into his pocket and braked suddenly. The auto stopped with a sudden jerk. Arumugam's head bumped against the roof of the three wheeler.

"Ha! What happened" He said sharply.

Gajj turned around, and pointed a small revolver at his face "Hello Arumugam." That was the biggest Faux pas Gajji would ever make. If only he had said Horatio, things would have been in his favor. But the name Arumugam got a reaction which even Gajji was not ready for.

The next second Horatio Arumugam hit Gajji very hard on his face. It was the same punch that had floored Bhadra some time back. But even here Gajji was fast. He saw it coming and tried to block it with his left hand. The punch landed above his elbow and he winced. And then it hit the right arm. A shot rang out and the gun slipped from his hand. The two fellows were at each others throats and they too spilled out of the vehicle. They fought furiously punching,. kicking, grunting and rolling over each other.

Suddenly, Gajji pulled out a flick knife and buried it into Arumugam. Arumugam made a sound like a deep sigh, and in a knee jerk action, kicked Gajji very hard on the groin. Gajji puked and fell on the ground. Arumugam broke himself free and ran to the auto to take his bag. His feet hit some thing.

It was the pistol. Gajji heard the sound and pounced to pick it up. He was late by a fraction of a second. Horatio Arumugam took it and blew Gajji's head off.

Nandini entered the hall in her spacious flat, and headed straight to the fridge. She lived there with her mother, who was watching the TV. Nandini took a bottle of cold water and drank half of it.

"Coffee?" Her mother asked.

"Sure." Nandini closed the fridge and plonked on the sofa.

Her mother was watching some serial. As soon as a scene was over, there was a commercial break. Her mother got up to go to the kitchen. The phone rang.

Her mother picked it up. It was a male voice on the other end. The man confirmed that he had dialed the right number, identified himself, and asked for Nandini.

"Its for you."

Nandini got up and took the receiver.

"Mam. Good evening. I am Inspector Pulendran from the Adyar police station." "Yes! Tell me!"

After listening to what Pulendran had to say, Nandini mumbled some thing and rushed out to her bike.

"Coffee." Her mother reminded her. "No thanks."

Nandini rode fast from her house to the big hospital and screeched to a halt near the patrol van outside the gate. The two police men leaning against its fender, stood to their attention.

"Pulendran." Nandini asked.

He is in the reception madame.

Nandini strode towards the reception with one of the police men running after her.

Pulendran was a middle aged well built man, who greeted her. "Where is he?" Nandini asked.

"CCU madame." Pulendran said politely.

As soon as the first shot rang from Gajji's gun, Pulendran, who was patrolling the area a furlong away, turned his jeep towards the direction and drove fast. As soon as he reached the mouth of the blind alley where Gajji and Horatio were fighting, the other shot rang. Pulendran immediately rushed in, to see two guys and an auto. One was lying prostrate on the ground and the other was swaying like a drunk. On seeing the headlights, this guy began walking towards the jeep. Puendran ran and held the fellow.

"Madame," Pulendran said "The man said his name was Horatio. 'Please inform ACP Nandini'. The fellow had shouted. He was delirious. He kept saying

'Madame, Madame'. I rushed him to the hospital and then I called you."

"You said he was in the CCU. What happened to him?" Nandini asked.

"He had a knife buried to the hilt through his heart Madame." Pulendran's voice was pathetic. "The doctors are trying to remove the thing."

Nandini went numb. CCU meant critical stage. Just half an hour back, she had promised the pleading Horatio, that she would take him back.

Suddenly she asked "How is the other guy."

"Dead . . . He is in the morgue. The finger print guys have been informed."

Nandini looked at the closed door of the CCU unit. "Can we go to the morgue first?"

Nandini stared at the body of Gajji. There was a hole on his left temple, which had given his chiseled face an ugly twist. Otherwise he was of medium height and build and there was nothing macabre about him. One thing was certain. Nandini had never seen him before.

"Where is the auto driver?" Nandini asked.

"There were only these two madame." Pulendran replied. I have already called for the information about the auto.

The body went back to its slot and the two returned to the main building. Pulendran went and talked to a young doctor outside the CCU. The doctor nodded and looked at Nandini.

"ACP Nandini" The doctor asked politely. "That is right."

"Madame his condition is critical." The doctor said in the tone which they use while breaking a bad news to relatives of patients. Nandini felt a hollow sensation within her. She nodded.

"Can I see him?"

"Sure. But before that you may inform his relatives." The doctor suggested softly. "I am his only relation doctor."

Horatio lay on the bed totally unconscious. A couple of doctors and nurses were standing and watching him. Tubes were attached to his body and there was a monitor which showed his condition through graphic lines. When Nandini entered the crowd of medicos looked at her. Nandini went as near him as possible. The doctor had said that it was a hopeless case any way. They were just waiting for the inevitable to happen. Nandini knelt down and took Horatio Arumugam's hand.

On feeling the soft touch of her flesh, the body shivered a little. A moment later, tears started flowing down Arumugam's eyes. The doctor looked at the monitor. Arumugam's hand gripped Nandini's and pressed it gently. He began fidgeting. After some incoherent murmers. He started slurring.

"Madame, Nandini madame, my—" He gripped her palm tight. Nandini blushed." Baby give the knife. Baby run. Baby run away."

Every one there heard these words clearly, Nandini frowned and looked at Arumugam's face. He began moaning and got breathless. The doctors pushed Nandini away and began pumping his chest. They tried all their methods to revive the guy. Arumugam's body shook violently and gave up.

Nandini took complete charge of Arumugam. She informed Jacob, Pavitra and Arumugam's employers. The police had found out that the auto had a fake number and was most probably stolen one. However from the finger prints they could identify the dead man as Gajji, a criminal from Gokulpet. Jacob sent his condolences and Pavitra attended the wake at Besant Nagar Church. Nandini paid all his bills and got him a decent burial. Gajji's body was disposed off by the police.

In spite of such a tragedy in the family, Krishnamurthi insisted that Swarna's wedding should take place as planned. His logic was that the wedding celebrations would bring a new wave of peace and happiness to the family. Raman agreed.

The wedding was a gala affair, in a hall in the center of the city. Kannan came from Mumbai. Swarna's friends and Adityan's colleagues too attended. Adityan tried to contact Horatio but was told that he had gone for some work to Chennai and that he had not left any forwarding address. Adityan returned dejected. He would have been happy to have him at such a beautiful moment. Every thing went off like a charm. There was a reception on the evening before the wedding, and Krishnamurthi gave away the bride the next morning at the auspicious hour. In the afternoon, the newly wed couple went with select friends and relatives to the marriage registration office and completed the legal formalities. Raman and Ratna were witnesses from Adityan's side, and Krishnamurthi and Kannan for Swarna. In the evening, Krishnamurthi went with Adityan's family to their house for dinner. Swarna and Adityan went to a hotel in the city.

After Horatio's funeral, Nandini began working on the case. She did a lot of brain storming. ' Baby give the knife, baby run, run fast' These last words from Horatio kept haunting her. To be doubly sure, she had confirmed from the hospital staff who were in that room that evening, that she had indeed heard right.

The finger prints on the knife that killed Horatio, matched with that of Gajji. So he was the killer. Then which knife was Horatio referring to? She presumed that it was the one that snuffed Bhadra's life out. 'Baby! Baby run fast!' Who was this baby ? Horatio was new to Gokulpet, and except for his company staff, it was doubtful that he had any acquaintances. ' Baby give the knife!' Jacob had said that Horatio had tried to save the killer.

Jacob had also said that the killer was most probably a novice. ' Baby!' Did he mean that literally ? Certainly not. How can a baby or even a small child do such a job? Krishnamurthi? Ha! No man in his right senses would address a middle aged man as baby.

Jacob said he would be happy to close the case. Why? Jacob was a very experienced detective? What did he suspect?

It came as a sudden flash. Nandini could not help chuckling.

A fortnight later, the couple went for a honey moon to a hill station near Vellore.

It was winter time and the weather was quite chilly. They had booked a room in a decent hotel which also arranged for their sight seeing trip. It was afternoon and they had landed in the hotel only a few hours back. The hotel was situated at a small hill and one had to go to the city for even small purchases.

Adityan and Swarna dressed up and came to the lobby. They ordered a pot of coffee and sat on the lounge, glancing at the papers and sipping the coffee. There was another couple standing near the counter. They looked like newly arrived guys waiting for their keys. The male came to Adityan.

"Excuse me." He said. Adityan looked up.

"I needed some one to come with me to the city. I have my bike."

Adityan looked at Swarna and smiled. They were just then discussing how to get some medicines from the city.

"Can I?" Adityan asked.

"Sure. Actually my wife{ He pointed at the woman near the counter} does not want me to go alone in this new place."

"No problem I shall come."

Adityan and the man went out to the bike. Swarna kept sipping the coffee. The bike started and after a roar, the two rode away. There was none in the lobby except Swarna, the woman and a male receptionist sitting on his desk.

The young woman came to Swarna and smiled. "Hello!"

"Hi!"

"I am Nandini ACP." She Said and sat beside Swarna. She flashed her card at Swarna.

Swarna paled. Her lips quivered. But she contained herself.

"Oh" She smiled and nodded.

"I know that you are Swarna and that was your husband Adityan." Nandini spoke in a voice slightly above a whisper "The man he has gone with is my colleague." Swarna's throat went dry. She gulped down some saliva.

"I want to talk to you. I could have done that in front of Adityan but—" She looked at Swarna. Her face was a white sheet.

"I am more human than one could think police men are."
"Where?" Swarna licked her dry lips.

Nandini admired the kid's composure. "Your room?" Nandini smiled.

Swarna sat on the double bed and Nandini on the chair. There was a jug of water and two glasses. Nandini poured the water into one and gave it to Swarna. Swarna emptied it. She was shivering slightly.

"Are you okay?" Nandini asked politely. Swarna nodded.

"Can we talk?"

Swarna looked at Nandini "Are you the madame Horatio speaks about?"

In spite of detecting a slight tone of accusation in the question, Nandini smiled

"I think so."

Swarna fidgeted with her dupatta. "What do you want me to tell you?" She was tense and angry.

"Every thing." Swarna gulped.

"I would like to know what Horatio told you. I don't want—" Swarna stopped suddenly and looked at Nandini.

Nandini took Swarna's hand and pressed it gently "Baby, Horatio is dead."

Swarna shook as if she had been goosed with a hot iron rod. Startled, she stared at Nandini's calm face. Swarna's mouth popped open and she began breathing heavily. Nandini got beside her and hugged her. Swarna shook uncontrollably and started crying. It was the wail of a kid who had lost her favorite toy. Nandini rubbed Swarna's back gently.

"I loved him." Swarna said in between her sobs. Nandini kept rubbing her back.

"He was the strongest man I had ever seen. Adityan is sweet, very sweet, but soft. Just like my father. But Horatio was brave and tough. He saved my father from the beast, my brother Bhadra."

"Hm!" Nandini nodded. She gave Swarna another glass of water. Swarna looked at Nandini "I killed Bhadra."

"Hm."

"Horatio was Adityan's friend. I did not know that he had attended my engagement. One evening when Bhadra attacked my father, Horatio appeared from nowhere and saved my father.

That evening he came to my house and my father thanked him for the timely help. I brought coffee for all, and saw my father so happy. I looked at Horatio. To me he looked like a super man. When he left, I realized that I had fallen in love with him." Swarna took a sip of water.

"Did I feel guilty? I don't know. It was not my fault. It just happened. Seeing my father praise this young man so much, gave me a lot of confidence. I worship my father. He is every thing to me. Adityan is a dear boy. He really loves me, but do I deserve him?" Swarna began weeping again.

"Adityan came one day to my house. I, my father and Horatio had agreed among ourselves that Adityan should not know about the incident. Poor kid, he brought Horatio along with him and reintroduced him to me."

"I don't know whether it was my body language or my behavior, but Horatio immediately realized my feelings for him. He got scared. He did not want his best friend Adityan to suffer. Suddenly out of the blue, he mentioned that he had a friend in Chennai who was a police officer. He said that he called her Madame. I don't know what Adityan made of it, but I knew that he was hinting to me to forget him. I think I blushed deep. Adityan took it in a different way. He joked that Horatio should introduce her to him."

Swarna looked at Nandini. "But the heart has its reasons madame. Horatio began avoiding me after that. My father met him a few times and called him home, but he made some excuse or the other. My father openly quipped a couple of times that he wished, Horatio was his son instead of Bhadra. This made me love him even more."

"One evening I had gone to the temple nearby. My father was working on some book and was spending his evenings in the school library. It was very cloudy and I hadn't taken the scooter. The temple was not far from my house. I wanted to rush back and heat the supper."

"It began as a drizzle but before I could realize, a heavy downpour started. In a moment I was completely drenched. There is an open area, a furlong away from my house. I ran to cross it fast. I was not able to see properly. It was already dark and the thick clouds made it darker still."

"Suddenly I saw some thing. Two guys were fighting like wild cats on the right side of the ground. I got very scared and started running. There was no soul other than the two in sight. And then I heard Bhadra's voice. He was one of the two and he was cursing and punching the fellow. To my horror I saw that the other guy was Horatio. I rushed towards them."

"Both of them saw me simultaneously. Before Horatio could say something, Bhadra let out a growl and gave me such a hard push that I was flung across.

Horatio pounced on him and they began kicking and punching again. I fell hard on the ground and squealed. Bhadra came charging towards me. And then I saw that he had some thing which was gleaming. Horatio immediately hit Bhadra with a stone. It caught him at the back of his head. Bhadra winced, lost his balance dropped the thing, and kicked Horatio very hard on the stomach.

"Horatio began rolling on the ground. This animal Bhadra, who was supposed to be my own brother, looked like a monster to me then. Every girl loves her brother and wants to mother him. But this demon did not deserve any affection. He was always a pain. He had always been against those who I loved and who were good. My mother died because of him, he had tried to strangle my father who meant the world to me, and now he was trying to kill the man who I loved. Who knows he would have harmed the sweet Adityan who I was engaged to then?"

"A blind rage gripped me. I took the thing that was lying on the ground and began swinging it like a mad woman. It was a knife. I don't know how, but every time I did so, it caught the wretched fellow some where or the other. It was raining cats and dogs, and the ground was slippery, and full of mud. Bhadra tried to shout but his voice was muffled and he fell to the ground with me on him cursing and hitting with the knife."

"I promise on my husband that I don't know what I was doing. I don't know how many times I did that. Suddenly Horatio came from behind and picked me up like a rag doll. He pulled me away from Bhadra. Bhadra was making a gurgling sound. I was still very angry. I tried to break away from Horatio but he was too strong."

"Both of us stared at Bhadra who was lying motionless. The rains just did not seem to stop."

"'Baby give me the knife' Horatio said. I did not understand. He repeated. I looked at the knife in my hand. Then I pulled my hand to my back in defiance.

' Baby please. Give me the knife. ' Horatio pleaded. I looked at him stubbornly.

' Baby for Adityan's and your father's sake give me the knife.' I began crying.

' Baby, if you have any love for me, if you are the good kid that I know you are, give me the knife.' He said."

Swarna began weeping. Nandini looked away to hide her tears.

"I had gone numb. He took the knife from me. ' Run baby run. Forget what happened. Don't open your mouth. Run fast.' He said. I walked away slowly, and then I ran like I had never done in my life. I went home, removed all the clothes, squeezed away the water, put them in a polythene bag and put it in my shoulder bag. When my father came, we had our supper and I did not mention anything to him. I told him that I had a special class the next morning and that I had to leave early. He said something about the rains and I nodded without knowing what he was saying. Next morning the rains slowed down. I took my bag, and put on my rain coat. I walked fast to a very big canal that was behind my house, and which was now over flowing with muddy water. I looked around, saw no one and threw the polythene bag into it. The thing was out of my sight in a moment."

"That day I attended the classes as usual but my mind was else where. It was only the next afternoon that Adityan's mother came to my college to pick me up. It was impossible to keep an innocent face but I some how managed. And when the news of Bhadra's death was broken to me I played the part of the bereaved sister to perfection."

"All the time I was worried about Horatio. I had decided that if ever he was caught for what he had not done, I would go and tell the truth to the police. But nothing happened." Swarna stopped and began playing with her dupatta again. There was silence for a few moments.

"Perfect baby perfect." Nandini said. Swarna looked at her askance. "You are going to arrest me?" Swarna asked in a small voice.

Nandini shook her head. She got up and began strolling up and down for a few minutes. Swarna kept staring at her. Then Nandini dialed a number on her cell

"Okay you can return." She said to her colleague.

Nandini came near Swarrna, pressed Swarna's cheeks gently. "Horatio was right. You are a nice kid."

Back in her room in Gokulpet, Nandini took out the bag which she had picked up from Horatio Arumugam's room. She had the key, and the lodge keeper had no objection when Jacob had come with her and identified her as Horatio's sole relative.

Nandini put on her gloves, opened the bag and emptied the contents on the bed. There were the usual clothes, shaving creams, lotions, etc. She ignored them all and picked up the item which was tightly bound with strips of polythene and fastened with sticker tape. She took a pen knife and slit it open gently. The grey colored box that came out, was the same that Jacob had shown her once, and which was still with the

Gokulpet police department. She placed it on the table and opened it. The velvet sheath inside had a knife in it. She took out the knife. From her experience she could make out that it had never been used. She was looking at the piece for the first time. Jacob could not recover the knife that had killed Bhadra so he had not seen it either. Nandini looked into the box and found the tiny knife within. She remembered Jacob telling her that there was a small cavity in the handle, where the buyers could place something to identify that the piece belonged to them. And the tiny knife was meant toopen the cavity. She took it, felt under the handle of the big knife and gave a slight push. There was a click and the upper part of the knife moved side ways to show the cavity within. She peeped in.

Embossed clearly, in golden letters was the word" NANDINI". At last, Horatio Arumugam had bared his heart.

THE
FINAL ORBIT

It was 8 PM on a December evening in Gwalior. Thanks to an unexpected rain the night before, it had been foggy all day. But now the visibility was slightly better and all the street lamps were in working order. Yellow beams of light filtered through the mist to illuminate the broad road that connected one end of the city to the other. Well furred up commuters rode on their bikes, eager to reach home to the comforts of warm beds, hot tea and hotter suppers. Even compulsive shoppers, were desperate to rush back.

Inspector Puran Singh sat in his jeep and watched the gradually thinning crowd. The driver had parked the vehicle at a strategic spot from where they could keep an eye on the traffic, besides getting an endless supply of tea and cigarettes from a nearby kiosk. The Walkie talkie kept blaring routine messages from the control room.

Puran Singh yawned. Despite four cups of piping hot tea he could not shrug the fatigue off his bones. It was VIP duty the night before and he hadn't slept a wink for several hours now. Love it or leave it a cop had to be on duty all the time. Not for him the luxuries of the average family man.

"Let us go back." Puran drawled.

The Jeep took a U turn and began sliding slowly into the main road between the railway station and the city. The Walkie talkie crackled again.

"An abandoned car has been spotted in a mango grove at Govardhan Pura." Puran Singh sat bolt upright. The spot was under his jurisdiction. Instinctively the driver looked at him, and the jeep picked up speed.

Govardhan Pura with its share of markets, middle class residential complexes, roads and by lanes, schools, dispensaries etc. was at the southern side of the town. Puran Singh had been posted to the station a year back and he hoped to be there for a couple of years more. The mango grove that the walkie talkie mentioned stood at the tip of Govardhan Pura. Around 500 meters away was the highway that connected the city to the rest of the country.

Puran Singh was at the spot within ten minutes. Two constables were already there. They saluted him and he acknowledged it. Then he walked briskly towards the car which was parked under a huge old mango tree, with its left side a yard away from the tree trunk.

It was a light colored Maruti esteem. All the doors were locked. Puran Singh peered in. There was none inside. He checked the registration number.

The two constables belonged to his check post. One of them had received a message from an anonymous caller that the car had been standing there for the past two days.

"When did you receive the call?" Puran asked the constable.

"Just fifteen minutes back Sir." The constable replied. "We sent a message to the control room immediately."

"I know."

Puran made a few more phone calls to various check posts and inquired whether anyone had heard anything about a car with that registration number. He left a message that he should be contacted immediately in case of any development. Leaving the constables there, Puran Singh returned to his office.

Thirty five year old Inspector Puran Singh belonged to a family of police men who had settled down in and around Gwalior centuries ago. The family owned several thousand acres of land and was one of the wealthiest in the district. There was no need to work for a living. Beginning from his grandfather's generation, the family had joined the police force and now almost three fourth of Puran Singh's kith and kin held various posts in the department. Not surprising that Puran Singh too nurtured a childhood ambition to wear the uniform.

Puran Singh graduated in Commerce and joined as a sub inspector in the city. He continued his studies, and completed his post graduation in the same subject. Then he did a Law course. A voracious reader with a healthy appetite for knowledge, Puran Singh was well known in the department for his sincerity, dedication and hard work. Thanks to an inborn interest in his job, Puran had a wide knowledge of several cases that came within his jurisdiction besides information that he gleaned from police records and gazettes. Puran Singh believed that as a lawman he should be aware of happenings in in other towns and cities too. His superiors recommended him for various conferences and meetings that took place regularly. Puran Singh used this opportunity to meet some of the best brains in the business.

The cell phone rang and Puran Singh picked it up. "Hello! Yes that is me! That's right."

Puran listened to the voice on the other end and frowned

"Indore? I see, just a minute."

Puran Singh grabbed the pad on the table.

"Yes please tell me. The owner of the car is Mr. Bhupathi. I see! Did he lodge the complaint for the missing car? No? Oh the owner himself is missing. I see. His wife lodged the complaint. When was it? Two days back?"

Puran Singh looked at the calendar.

"But the car has been here for the past two days. Yes! No, there is none inside it. Sure! I was there myself. Okay. Sure. I shall do that. Thank you. That was fast. Bye."

The phone went dead and Puran stared quizzically at the wall.

Indore is a small commercial town south west of Gwalior near the Maharashtra border. According to the caller, the car belonged to a man called Bhupathi who lived in Indore. Two days back his wife had lodged a complaint with the police station near her locality that her husband was missing with his car.

And the car, minus the owner had turned up several hundred kilometers away in Gwalior.

The fingerprints on the car were carefully dusted. Strangely there were no papers or documents that are usually found in the glove compartment of any vehicle. There were no clues either except for the usual foot prints on the ground, which obviously belonged to the occupant of the car. Probably Bhupathi had driven it all the way from Indore to Gwalior for some reason best known to him, parked it at the spot where it was found and vanished. There were no traces of struggle of any kind inside or around the vehicle.

The car was towed away to the garage that the department used for vehicles that were exhibits in criminal cases. Puran Singh thanked his stars that Indore and Gwalior belonged to the state of Madhya Pradesh. Thus, the legal and bureaucratic hassles one would have faced in an interstate crime (if it was a crime), could be avoided.

Bhupathi lived in an independent house in a respectable locality in the north east of Indore city, with his wife Sonia and a teenage son Vimal. It was his own house and he had built it a few years ago. Bhupathi was a Tamilian who had settled down in the city some twenty years back. He was a successful dealer in grocery and dry fruits. But instead of having his own shop or go-down, Bhupathi had chosen to work as a commission agent. He had several business contacts in the neighboring countries, South East Asia, and Middle East. Besides his main occupation, Bhupathi was a consummate speculator in commodities and futures and had over the years, made a neat pile for himself and his family.

Once the official formalities were over the car was delivered to a distraught Sonia.

The city was stunned at the sudden disappearance of the respectable, middle aged businessman. Bhupathi's photo appeared on the newspapers and the television, with an offer of a handsome cash reward to anyone who gave any clue about the missing person.

Puran Singh was entrusted with the case and the Indore police department welcomed him gladly. They were aware of his reputation.

Puran Singh went about the case with the meticulous planning that he was known for. The first person he questioned was Sonia.

Sonia told him that Bhupathi operated from their house with his laptop and his cell phone as his sole assistants. He even carried them whenever he went out. Both the things were missing now. Sonia had tried to contact him but his cell was dead and the e-mails remained unanswered. A devoted family man, Bhupathi never failed to keep in touch with her. Hence his unexplained silence was all the more intriguing and scary.

The business community in the city offered all assistance to the department. Bhupathi was a likeable man, loyal and trustworthy. By his brilliance and hard work he had made many shopkeepers and business men prosperous. It was vehemently denied by one and all that Bhupathi's disappearance could have had anything to do with his business or profession.

When another fortnight passed and still there was no sign of Bhupathi, Puran Singh suspected something fishy. His instincts pointed at Sonia. Unknown to her, the department had tapped the phones of the house hold and she had been tailed by professional female detectives. But nothing interesting happened. Sonia turned out to be a genuinely suffering house wife who was waiting for her husband to return.

Yet, Puran Singh felt that only she could lead him out of the dead end.

It was afternoon and the kid had gone to school. Puran Singh had informed Sonia in advance that he would like to talk to her. The meeting took place at her house in the presence of Sonia's parents. To make things more discreet, Puran Singh took a lady inspector along.

Despite the seriousness of the situation, the meeting looked like a gathering of close friends chatting the long hours away over cups of hot tea and biscuits. After realizing that the department was genuinely concerned about the welfare of her family, Sonia opened up. Where ever she fumbled her parents intervened gently.

According to what Puran Singh gathered from the chat, Sonia was a north Indian girl who Bhupathi had fallen in love with and married a couple of years after he landed in Indore. Bhupathi was at that time a tenant in the flat opposite the one where Sonia lived with her parents.

The flat which Bhupathi rented belonged to a local wholesale trader who Sonia's father Trilok Chand knew well. Trilok Chand was a clerk in a bank.

Bhupathi was around five foot ten inches tall, dark and slender, with a thick mop of curly black hair, a long saturnine face and a sober demeanor. He did not talk much but his tone was gentle and polite. As a bachelor he lived alone, handling his own cooking, washing and cleaning. The owner of the house had arranged for a landline connection immediately after Bhupathi had moved in and as Sonia had already mentioned, he did most of his work through phone and written correspondence right from the beginning. He would also go on business trips every month.

Beginning with a formal greeting during the initial stages, Bhupathi had gradually got closer to the Trilok Chand family. He even attended functions at Trilok Chand's house. Once the ice was broken, Bhupathi began running small errands for them, like bringing provisions, fixing a bulb, calling the plumber and the like. Later on he would leave the keys of his house with them during his business trips.

Sonia's father was impressed by the young man's resourcefulness, hard work and business acumen. Trilok Chand nurtured an unfulfilled desire to own a shop. Due to lack of finances and other family obligations in his youth, he had to take up a job. Whatever dynamism and enterprise he still had, got sapped once he got married and fathered two kids both daughters.

Sonia was the younger of the two. She was delicate and pretty, and had just started going to college when twenty six year old Bhupathi entered her life. For the first one year neither acknowledged the presence of the other. Sonia was busy with her studies and her friends and Bhupathi with his business. It was a new place for the young man and he did not know much Hindi either. By sheer perseverance, he developed his contacts and soon enough proved his worth as a valuable business associate.

One evening around nine, Trilok Chand was sitting in his drawing room watching TV, when the call bell rang. Trilok Chand went and opened the door to find Bhupathi there. He had just returned from one of his regular business trips and looked tired and weak. Bhupathi greeted him, apologized for the intrusion and asked for the key of his own flat. Trilok Chand invited him in.

As he drained a glass of water that Trilok Chand offered him, Bhupathi heard the sound of anklets. He looked up and saw Sonia standing shyly at the corner of the room. She was dressed in a light colored suit and looked incredibly fresh and lovely. Bhupathi got up to greet her, but his throat went dry. Sonia smiled at him came near the table and handed the keys to her father.

Bhupathi smiled weakly and turned towards Trilok Chand. "You look quite tired." Trilok Chand said.

"Yeah! It was a hectic trip." Bhupathi gave a hollow chuckle. "Have you eaten something?"

"I had lunch in the morning."

"Just that? Sit have a cup of tea."

"Oh no, thanks I shall manage." Bhupathi blurted out but his tone wasn't convincing.

"Come On! No formalities." Trilok Chand said. Bhupathi sat down.

That evening Bhupathi not only had a tea but also a steaming hot meal cooked by Sonia. Her mother had gone to her sister's house for a couple of days and she was in charge of the house hold. The food was simple but tasty and Bhupathi relished every morsel.

As he left after thanking the father and daughter for the hospitality, Bhupathi did not realize that he had fallen in love.

Bhupathi dealt in spices and cashew nuts. He had been referred to the dealers in these commodities by a business man in Chennai. Bhupathi became a middleman cum commission agent between the north Indian dealers and the south Indian Cashew and pepper growers. Once he had closed a few successful deals, benefitting both the parties, he earned the trust and respect of both.

Later on, Bhupathi branched out into other products. He became a two way agent. Now he also handled distribution of grains, fruits, vegetables, pulses etc. produced in North, in various parts of Tamilnadu. In all the deals he was content with a reasonable commission. He worked alone and his expenses were minimal.

Two years after he landed this new profession, Bhupathi had a stroke of unexpected luck. During one of his trips to Coimbatore, Bhupathi came across a prosperous business man from Malaysia. This guy got an immediate liking for Bhupathi and offered him a new line of business. On his return to Indore, Bhupathi chatted up the dealers there and began importing goods from Malaysia, Singapore and other south east Asian countries. Slowly the business grew and soon enough Bhupathi was dealing with customers in Srilanka, and middle east. It was a two way street with goods being both exported and imported through him.

Bhupathi's method was simple. He not only negotiated a deal but also supervised the transport of goods from one place to another, without having his own establishment. Amazingly efficient and meticulous, he was also good in public relations. By his thirtieth year, Bhupathi had made a name for himself as a much sought after middleman.

Bhupthi was now like a family member in the Trilokchand household. On coming to know about Trilokchand's unfulfilled desire, Bhupathi offered help. When a new guy tried to set up a small shop, Bhupathi put in some money of his own on behalf of Trilokchand and purchased a partnership. Trilokchand was delighted. Being a bank employee, he could not own a business in his name, so at Bhupathi's suggestion, Sonia's mother signed the partnership deed. Trilokchand was now a busy man.

When one gets the job he craves for, he puts in an extra effort. The man who used to laze on the sofa after office hours and on holidays, now began working late. Every evening Trilokchand would leave his office and land at the shop. The other partner would have a cup of tea with him and then leave the shop in Trilokchand's care. Trilokchand would work there till nine PM, close the shop, give the key to the servant to be delivered to the other partner and go home. On Sundays he would spend the whole day there. The servant would bring the lunch cooked by Sonia's mother, to the shop. Trilokchand was on cloud nine.

The love between Bhupathi and Sonia grew with utmost discretion. Bhupathi was a sober guy. Like a true business man he thought about every matter from all angles.

After some time Bhupathi went to the owner of the house and bared his heart to him. The bemused old man pondered over the situation and agreed to talk to Trilokchand on his behalf. This was a year after Trilokchand became a business man. Bhupathi's landlord told Trilokchand that Bhupathi would like to marry Sonia.

Trilokchand was stunned. Not because he did not expect this from Bhupathi but because he was stumped by the young man's honesty, and level headedness. The landlord told Trilokchand that Bhupathi was a man of character and that Trilokchand may not find a more suitable match for his child in his own community. Trilokchand had a word with his wife who was even more surprised by the sudden offer.

Unlike Trilokchand she was a house wife and had had more opportunities to meet Bhupathi than Trilokchand did. Not only that, Bhupathi had come to their house often. But even she had never noticed anything in Bhupathi's behavior that even remotely hinted at his feelings for her daughter. After discussing the matter over, the parents asked the girl. Sonia nodded her acceptance.

Trilokchand had learnt that Bhupathi belonged to a town called Gokulpet a few hundred kilometers from Chennai. His father was a petty shopkeeper and had died when Bhupathi was two years old. His mother had tried to run the shop but was forced to sell it after a few months of her husband's death. Finding it difficult to make both ends meet, she had at last given up and married another young man from the same town. That guy had taken care of Bhupathi for a few years till he got a job in the Andamans. After pondering over the situation, the couple decided not to take Bhupathi along with them. Instead they had him admitted to an orphanage. Bhupathi was four when he saw his mother for the last time.

After several rounds of discussions with his relatives, Trilokchand nodded his acceptance to the alliance. Bhupathi and Sonia got married.

Bhupathi turned out to be a loving and caring husband. He took Sonia on a honey moon to Srilanka, and purchased a flat in their joint name in the same locality where her parents lived. Their first and only child Vimal came a year later.

Vimal was studying in one of the best schools in the city. The kid was a good student and had a normal healthy and carefree childhood. Meanwhile Bhupathi got into speculation and came out in leaps and bounds. The family was financially secure.

Then all of a sudden Bhupathi vanished without a trace.

Neither Sonia nor Vimal knew the password for Bhupathi's email id. Getting any clue from that end was ruled out. Puran Singh tried the various bank accounts which the family operated through online. No withdrawal of any kind was made from them by Bhupathi from the day he disappeared. Same was the case with the credit cards. Sonia contacted the respective companies and applied for the cancellation of the credit cards. This was done not only to prevent someone from misusing them, but also to force Bhupathi out of his rat hole.

As a routine procedure, Puran Singh had circulated all the finger prints dusted from the car, to the police departments all over the country. Even this delivered no results. Bhupathi did not have any police record anywhere.

Despite the ensuing frustration, Puran Singh's intuition repeatedly pointed at a particular incident that Sonia narrated to him.

It was around midnight a few days before Bhupathi's disappearance. Sonia was sitting at the dining table along with Bhupathi. Vimal was already in bed. Sonia was watching the television and Bhupathi was working on his laptop. Bhupathi's cell phone rang. It was a long distance call. Sonia picked it up.

"Hello!"

"Can I talk to Mr. Bhupathi?" It was a gruff but deliberately polite male voice. The man spoke in English with a thick south Indian accent.

"Who is it?" "Friend!"

Sonia looked at Bhupathi who frowned and took the phone from her. As he did so, he inadvertently pressed the loudspeaker button.

"Bhupathi here!"

"Inna Aiyarey! Sowkyamma?" (Hey Aiyar how do you do?) the caller said in Tamil.

On hearing the word Aiyar, Swarna chuckled but stopped abruptly when she saw that Bhupathi had tensed up. Bhupathi switched the loudspeaker off.

"Who is it?"

Sonia could not hear the other man's voice, but going by Bhupathi's reaction, she suspected that the fellow and let out a volley of cuss words. Bhupathi closed his eyes and tried to interrupt the caller but failed repeatedly. A few minutes later Bhupathi took the cell away from his ears. A horrified Sonia stared at Bhupathi's face but could make out nothing.

"What happened?" Sonia asked after he switched off the phone.

Bhupathi stared at the table. Sonia got up and hugged him. Beads of sweat appeared on Bhupathis' forehead.

"Tell me! What happened?" Sonia whined. Bhupathi put his arm around her.

"Nothing!" He rasped. "An old disgruntled punk is trying to get even." Then Bhoopathi smiled at Sonia.

"Don't get upset baby. Business rivalry is common."

Sonia wanted to believe him, but her instincts suggested otherwise.

Bhupathi was a smooth operator. His reputation was impeccable and in the past so many years, there had been no untoward incidences in his professional or personal life. Then how could someone suddenly spring up from nowhere and use such colorful language on a low profile business man?

Sonia said that the man had a gruff voice. Normally business men are polite and articulate. Was Bhupathi in some way involved with unsavory elements?

Why did the man address Bhupathi as Aiyar? And why did the adage upset him? The more Puran Singh thought about this the more intrigued he got. It was very important to find Bhupathi—"dead or alive."

Trilokchand had mentioned that Bhupathi was brought up in a small town called Gokulpet near Chennai. To find the elusive Bhupathi Puran Singh had to begin at his roots.

During one of the regular police conferences that Puran Singh attended, he had met an Inspector from Chennai by the name of Jacob Janardhanan. Tall, very thin and cerebral looking, Jacob was a decade senior to Puran Singh and a legend of sorts in the department. They had exchanged notes and Puran Singh was impressed by Jacob's erudition, intelligence and incredible sixth sense. Puran had consistently improved himself keeping Jacob as an idol. The two had met again when Jacob came to Gwalior in search of a killer.

Now as he recalled the incident, Puran Singh was bemused. That case was a lot similar to the one that he had in his hand now. History was repeating itself. That time Jacob approached him for help. Now Puran was going to ask for a favor.

"Jacob!"

Puran was hearing the mellow voice after a long time "Sir! Inspector Puran Singh here."

"Wow! Buddy! Is it snowing in Gwalior?" It was Jacob's trademark question.

"No idea! I am in Indore!"

"Indore? You have been transferred?" Puran Singh told the story in short.

"Bhupathi? Sounds like a South Indian name!" "It indeed is."

"Haah!"

"And that is why I called you!"

"Tell me brother" Another trademark expression from Jacob.

"I need some information from an orphanage in Gokulpet."

"Done" Jacob assured him.

Except when it was absolutely necessary, Jacob did not delegate important work to his subordinates. He believed that to get the desired result one needed first hand information. Jacob was more of an intellectual and an analyst than a cop doing his beat.

Jacob had worked in Gokulpet and he knew the place and the people there. Next afternoon he took his jeep and drove to the town reaching that place at around six in the evening. Instead of dropping in at the main police station he drove directly to the orphanage.

Swami Siddhananda Ashram as the orphanage was called was situated at the southern end of the township. It was established by a saint whose name it bore, and was currently being run by a trust. There were around thirty kids of different ages in the Asharm now. Jacob met the in charge of the Ashram one Mr. Pranatharthiharan. Pranatha was around thirty five, of medium build, with a thickly bearded face and kind eyes.

Jacob explained his problem to the man.

"We are searching for a missing man called Bhupathi. The only clue we have is that he was brought up in your orphanage. I feel that your assistance would go a long way in tracking him."

"Sure Sir." Pranatha said. "Thanks to the computer we have a complete data base of all the kids who grew up here in the past fifty years."

"Excellent."

Pranatha went through the files and folders which had been arranged both chronologically and alphabetically. There were several names that began with the letter "B". These included a couple of Bhupathis too. But they were boys who had joined the Ashram in the past decade. Going by Jacob's description, Bhupathi must have passed out at least twenty years back.

Pranatha scanned the names carefully and then clicked at one. Immediately a page opened. Pranatha studied it for a few seconds and then said:

"Sir, please take a look at this." He turned the monitor slightly towards Jacob.

Jacob looked at the scanned photograph of a sixteen year old, at the right side top corner of what looked like a bio-data. Two black brooding eyes stared back at him from a long saturnine face framed by a thick mop of curly black hair. Jacob read the entries on the sheet.

Name: Bhupalan
Father's name: Late Dhanapalan
Mother's name: Mallika
Date of Birth: 31st October 1963
Date of joining: 9th July 1967
Date of leaving: 16th August 1979

Jacob sighed.

"I think he is our man." He mused." But I am not sure. I would be grateful to you if you give me a copy of this sheet. I shall sign an acknowledgement."

Pranatha nodded thoughtfully and took a printout.

"Yes! This is my husband." Sonia sighed.

"Sure?" "Yes!"

Puran Singh looked at the sheet that Jacob had faxed him. "Did you know that he had changed his name?"

"No he never mentioned that to me." Sonia said.

Despite a momentary elation at his own intuition Puran Singh kept a poker face. Bhupathi's story seemed more interesting than it appeared. Intriguingly, though the man had changed his identity for the world yet when Trilokchand asked him about his antecedents, Bhupathi had been honest enough to admit that he was an orphan.

But who was Aiyar? Rather why was Bhupathi addressed that way? Was it a nickname or that guy's surname? According to Jacob who was a Tamilian himself, Aiyar was a caste of Tamil Brahmins and Bhupalan alias Bhupathi could not be an Aiyar.

And why was Bhupathi upset when he heard it?

After leaving Sonia, Puran Singh put himself in the elusive Bhupathi's shoes and tried to put the pieces together.

An intelligent young man relocates himself thousands of kilometers away from his home town, establishes himself as a business man, gets married, raises a family, settles down and leads a smooth life till out of the blue, his past catches up with him.

What would he do?

Evidently Bhupathi had not taken the fateful phone call lightly. And for some reason he chose to take on the lam.

What could be the reason?

Bhupathi wanted to protect his wife and child, without revealing his true identity to them. With his family safe and secure though distraught, Bhupathi could take on the forces which threatened his existence. Puran Singh marveled at the man's ingenuity. Despite the advertisements in the media, no one had come forward with any clue about his whereabouts.

Puran was a busy cop. He had his hands full with various cases and problems. He also realized that he had reached a dead end in the case and that there was nothing else to do but wait for some interesting development. After requesting Jacob to be on the lookout for some bit of information which could lead them somewhere, Puran Singh went back to his routine work.

At around the same time when Puran Singh was pondering over the strange case, a man in his mid thirties was enjoying his drink in a worn out, over stuffed go down in the southern outskirts of Delhi. It was horribly cold and the guy sat on his bed with a thick quilt protecting him from the chilly piercing breeze that wafted into the room through the gaps in the closed windows and shutters. It was 1 AM.

After completing his nefarious errands for the night, the man had returned to his hideout with a full bottle of rum and some snacks to go with it. He had cooked his supper in the evening before leaving for work, and now he was on his second peg. The solitary party would go on till 3 AM when the guy would at last have his food and then go to bed. This was a routine with him. Like all guys of his ilk this man was a night bird.

He gulped down the peg in one go and grimaced. The liquor had a soothing effect on his sore throat. He was new to the Delhi winter, having arrived there just a year back. Without wasting much time the fellow popped a hand full of salted peanuts and made another large peg.

The sudden piercing sound of his cell phone startled him. He cursed and picked it up before it could ring again.

"Hello!"

"Any news about Aiyar?" It was the same gruff voice that had caused such a commotion in the Bhupathi household.

"Nothing yet" The man replied.

There was a deep sigh at the other end.

"We are trying to track him down. Our guys are already on the job." The man assured.

"You better be fast!" The voice on the other side was visibly irritated. "Before the cook or the cops catch up with him."

"Okay!"

The phone went dead.

The receiver of the call was Manickam, a short, dark, wiry man in his mid thirties. And the caller was a notorious gangster who the Tamilnadu police knew as "Orukan" Murugesan. The adage "Orukan" meant "One eyed". Murugesan had lost his left eye in an ancient gang war.

As he stared at his cell phone, Manickam ground his teeth and swore at no one in particular. If only Murugesan hadn't been his boss, Manickam would have strangled the scumbag. The punk always messed up things and tossed them over to underlings like him to clean up.

After years of tracking and losing trails, Murugesan had pinned down Bhupathi. After that he should have moved cautiously.

He should have used his own outfit to nab the guy and squirrel him away. Instead, Murugesan's elation and over confidence got the better of him and he had made that stupid phone call which alerted the quarry. Now Bhupathi was nowhere in sight and Murugesan was making life miserable for his associates.

Neither Puran Singh nor Jacob would have guessed that the man they were tracing was hiding from forces that were far swifter than the powerful but slow moving police department. They were also equally vicious and savage.

All successful cops have their own stable of informers, members of the underworld who provide tips about other hoods. Some do this for rewards in cash or in kind. Others help the department just to be in the good books of the law or to get even with foes who they cannot confront personally. And then there are those who are either disillusioned or disgruntled with their lives and start ratting about the more successful hoods.

Babu belonged to the third category.

Fifty five year old, soft bodied, nondescript looking Babu was a retired small time hood who had neither the physical nor the mental prowess to reach any respectable position in the underworld. Starting as a pickpocket at the age of twelve, Babu had spent almost half of his life behind the bars. Even when he was out, he was either a petty thief who often got caught and thrashed by the public or worked at the bottom of the rung of some criminal outfit. There was almost none who Babu liked or trusted, and that included the police, the public and the guys from his own line of operation.

Jacob knew Babu. The fellow had "Dropped in" several times at various police stations where Jacob had been posted. Jacob found that he was beyond repair and that only by tickling the fellow's raw nerve could one get something out of him. A couple of years back, Jacob had decided to cultivate this man with a dual purpose.

First of all as a man who had been a hood for donkey's years, Babu could inadvertently give some clue which could be far more priceless than the bum himself reckoned.

The other reason was more noble. Jacob was a nice man. He knew that Babu had got a raw deal in life. At least in his twilight years, the guy could do something useful for the society and die with pride.

One evening Babu came to Jacob's police station like all history sheeters on parole, to sign the register. Except for a few bored looking constables, the station was empty. After Babu completed his formalities, Jacob called him to his cabin. While Jacob kept writing on his pad, Babu entered and stood staring at the floor.

"How are you Babu?" Jacob continued to write. "I have not done anything." Babu whined.

"But I heard differently!" Jacob said without looking at him.

Fear, Anger and Frustration rose within the aging hood. He did not reply but braced himself for a night in the lockup. Jacob knew what was coming. Babu had gone too far to expect anything good from any one least of all a cop. It pained Jacob. But he had to do this to put the guy off guard.

Jacob took out a twenty rupee note from his pocket.

"Go to the nearby tea shop." Jacob said handing over the note to Babu

"Have a cup of tea and snacks and wait for me. I shall come in an hour."

A shocked Babu took the money and walked away like a zombie. Jacob sighed and looked at the ceiling.

That evening in a dilapidated go down in the outskirts of the city, Jacob spent quality time with Babu. He had purchased a bottle of country brew and snacks of Babu's choice, and thrown an impromptu party. After the initial wariness, Babu took a few pegs and opened up. As they talked shop Jacob prepared himself for the evening. He knew that when the liquor loosened Babu's tongue the first gush would bring forth unprintable trash from the lips of the guy who had been bottling up his feelings for ages. For the next one hour, Babu raved and ranted at no one in particular. Jacob listened patiently. When he was six pegs down, Babu stopped abruptly and began crying. It was rain after the thunderstorm. He wailed and sobbed so bitterly that for once Jacob feared that the fellow may collapse.

Totally drunk and exhausted, Babu finally stopped. Jacob dropped the man near the slum where he lived.

A week later Jacob got the call that he was waiting for. Babu requested for an appointment.

After apologizing for his misdemeanor, Babu admitted that Jacob was the first person he had genuinely admired. Babu offered to be of service to him, regardless of the returns. Jacob posted him as his observer in the underworld.

"Just be a silent spectator. Don't make any move that would arouse suspicion. Unless and until it is most important, don't call me. We shall meet every week at the same place where we met the first time."

This was three years back.

Babu would give a report of whatever he had observed. After the initial teething trouble, Babu picked up the art of being an informer. The fellow had a remarkable memory. Thanks to his long and continuous career in crime, Babu could trace the history of several hoods. The guy was acquainted with almost three fourths of the "Faces" in the underworld. At the fag end of his life, Babu was shaping up as an asset of sorts for Jacob.

Right from their first meeting, Jacob taped every word Babu said. Back at home, Jacob would listen to the monologue several times to fish out something useful. Even if most of the information was worthless, Jacob did not ignore it. He believed that even a small piece of information could be useful in solving some cold case. Meticulously he fed all the tapes to his laptop and created a huge folder before destroying the tapes.

Jacob had also prepared a file which contained every intriguing term, or alias, or name that Babu mentioned, along with an entry of the source from which it had been recorded. This file was protected with a password, and was in a folder in Jacob's laptop.

When Puran Singh mentioned the word "Aiyar" Jacob had picked up his ears. He had heard the name from Babu. Jacob searched for the word in the file and found that it was mentioned in a particular tape. Jacob checked the date and found that it was a few days before Puran Singh filled him in about the case. Jacob listened to the conversation again.

"Two days back I met THE COOK. I and he go back a long way. The punk has become a big shot now."

"The Cook?" It was Jacob's voice.

"Yes!"

"Hope you are not talking about the Gokulpet guy."

"Same guy, You know him?"

"Never met him but I have heard about him."

"He should have been dead by now. But call it devil's luck, or his lawyer's genius, the fellow got life and is out now, resurfaced a few days back."

"What did he say?"

"Nothing special, Just mentioned that he had to meet "Aiyar"? "Aiyar?"

"Not the one that you are thinking about. It is a nick name for someone from his outfit."

Jacob listened to the tape several times and went into a brown study.

After a few hours he put a call to Babu and arranged for an urgent meeting. "Remember Irumban?" Jacob asked a few minutes after the two met.

"Of course!"

"Can we find him?"

"I shall try! I know where he hangs out!"

Two days later Babu reported that Irumban had not been seen by any one for the past couple of weeks. Jacob feared this. He suspected that Irumban and the guy

Aiyar had at last met and vanished together for good. Till now it wasn't clear what a hardcore gangster had to do with a soft spoken businessman.

On a hunch Jacob asked Babu to probe further and find out if he could get some clue. All the while he cautioned the old man to be careful. Jacob's sixth sense pointed towards a far more dangerous situation than it seemed.

AND THEN JACOB GOT THE CALL HE WAS WAITING FOR.

Immediately Jacob took charge and left for Gokulpet from where he took a posse' of policemen and proceeded towards the village.

Beginning as a push cart vendor selling vegetables and fruits in Gokulpet, Dhanapalan learnt business the hard way. A school dropout, he was forced to work at an early age to make both ends meet. Being a single proprietor, Dhanapalan had to take care of every aspect of his miniscule business.

After months of scouting around, shouting, haggling, reasoning and fighting with other guys of his ilk, and with the big fat wholesalers, Dhanapalan ultimately found one big dealer who took pity on the young man and assured him a cart full of goods every day.

Seven days a week, Dhanapalan would get up at 3 in the morning and go to the wholesale market. From there he would load his cart with goods, and bring them to the streets where he would hawk them. Dhanapalan had to be a good purchaser, a good seller and above all, a good calculator to survive in his business.

Dhanapalan persevered and picked up the skill to compute complex arithmetical problems without the help of pen and paper. He had to calculate the amount that he owed or paid to the dealer including the interest rates there on, and arrive at a figure which would be the cost of each ounce of vegetable that he hawked per day. He would quickly add the overheads which included the cost of food, tea, snacks etc that he would be consuming that day and compute the sales price after adding a small profit margin. All this had to be done before he began his rounds.

While selling the goods, he had to avoid missing even one penny of his meager earnings. And for this he had to use arithmetic again. In the evenings he would count his daily earnings. After setting aside the amount repayable to the wholesaler, and a bit for his personal expenses, he let out the rest as petty loan to other traders. Here too he had to be good with figures to compute the right interest.

With a savagely tightened belt, Dhanapalan saved enough to pay for a tiny bunk shop in one of the localities. Dhanapalan became a shopkeeper. Then he married a young woman named Mallika who worked as a maid in several houses in that locality.

Bhupalan arrived a year later.

Sitting in his shop, Dhanapalan used to watch neatly dressed young men and women going by chartered buses or on their own vehicles to various factories and organizations situated at an industrial township in the outskirts of the city. Dhanapalan wanted to see his son in their shoes. He had great plans for him. He wanted to educate the boy and get him a respectable job in the government or in some big organization.

Mallika continued to work as a maid. She and Dhanapalan wanted to save as much as possible for the future of their only child. Bhupalan grew up under the indulgent eyes of his doting parents like any other normal kid—innocent, playful and mischievous.

Years of deprivation began taking their toll on Dhanapalan. Though he was financially better off now, Dhanapalan's health began failing him. He was often tired, his body ached and he ran high temperature frequently. Being a tough guy Dhanapalan did not change his Spartan habits. He still continued to get up early and work late.

One evening Mallika was preparing the evening supper. Two year old Bhupalan was playing with his toys in a corner. A young man from the neighborhood came and knocked at the slightly opened door. Bhupalan toddled out and stared at the guy whose name was Vinayakan.

"Mamma home?" Vinayakan asked.

"Hmm" The two year old lisped and called his mother.

Mallika came out wiping her hands. Vinakyak said something to her. The next moment Mallika let out a wail that brought the neighbors rushing to their door step. Mallika picked up the scared and crying Bhupalan and ran towards the shop which was a furlong from their house.

Dhanapalan lay slumped on the counter with his hands hanging limply. He was dead.

It seemed like the end of the road for Mallika. She was alone, illiterate, with a small child to take care of and a long life ahead. People did help, financially and otherwise, but with the passage of time, everyone got back to his or her business, and she was left fending for herself. And then Vinayakan returned.

Vinayakan, a bachelor had been with Mallika through thick and thin. He was also a friend of Dhanapalan. He helped Mallika run the shop for some time but when they found that she lacked the required business acumen he helped her sell it off. Then he went even further. With the best wishes of the neighbors, Vinayakan married Mallika and brought her and Bhupalan to his house.

Vinayakan was a jack of all trades. He was an auto driver, a plumber and an electrician rolled in one. He was always on demand and earned reasonably well. He also had good contacts with resourceful people.

Bhupalan was three years old when Vinayakan put him in a school which was run by Swami Siddhananda ashram. Vinayakan was kind and affectionate to both Mallika and Bhupalan and he worked hard to raise his family.

When Bhupalan was four years old, Vinayakan got a three year assignment to work as an electrician cum plumber in the Andamans. The salary was lucrative and anyone who Vinayakan consulted, advised him to take it up. By now Mallika was pregnant again.

After a lot of brain storming, and looking at the matter from all angles, Vinayakan and Mallika decided that they should leave for Andamans, leaving the young Bhupalan in the custody of the Ashram. The kid would not only be safe there but would also get the right upbringing and education. Initially the Ashram was wary of taking such a small child in its fold but after considering the situation they accepted the boy.

Bhupalan was only four but his tender brain grasped the situation better than an adult would imagine. The kid realized that all was not well in the family and that after losing his father, it was time to let his mother go as well. Numb with depression and shock, the kid shed silent tears as his mother hugged and kissed him and promised to take him back with her soon. Vinayakan gave him a box of chocolates and sweetmeats and told him to study well and be a brave lad. As the two left the boy at the gate of the ashram, and got into an auto, Bhupalan's tender instincts told him that they would never return.

On a rebound, the child shut himself up into a tiny world of its own. Even at that impressionable age, Bhupalan began looking inward. What he found within fascinated him. While the other kids (who were equally unfortunate but more adjusting), looked for comfort and distraction outside, Bhupalan spent all his free time sitting alone and brooding. And gradually he found solace in his text books.

By the time he completed his primary school, Bhupalan had proved that he was a brilliant student. He always stood among the top three in his class, and was blessed with a phenomenal mathematical acumen. The kid was a wizard with figures. A loner by nature, Bhupalan spent all his leisure hours, studying and solving complex mathematical puzzles. The ashram management found in him a worthy pupil.

When he was fourteen years old, Bhupalan came across some old news papers which were stacked in one corner in the library. Leafing through them casually Bhupalan found something that caught his eye. In one of the last pages of the newspaper, Bhupalan saw several columns with names and complex figures mentioned side by side. Bhupalan asked one of the administrators, what it was.

The man told him that it was a list of companies with their share prices. He explained the table to the inquisitive boy. Bhupalan was hooked. He had found a new hobby.

Now whenever he found time, Bhupalan would pore over the charts in the old newspapers. He also took notes meticulously. His keen analytical mind kept thinking about business and commerce and he lapped up whatever information he got on these matters. In spite of being a brilliant student, Bhupalan opted to drop out of the school after completing his matriculation. As he bore a good character and was a conscientious boy, the authorities allowed him to leave and fend for himself in the big bad world. They also assured him that the ashram would be his home for as long as he wanted.

Bhupalan's intuition was right. Mallika never returned.

As a consummate reader, Bhupalan used to wait early in the morning for the newspaper boy to deliver the daily supply at the Ashram. Before the others got up, Bhupalan would scan them and then make an in depth study of the share market columns in the evenings and late nights. It was not surprising that when he decided to start earning, he accosted the same delivery boy. After a couple of chats with the guy, Bhupalan joined the band wagon.

Like his father Bhupalan would now would get up at three in the morning and reach the spot where the delivery guys took their daily load. Bhupalan was assigned to a locality in the city. The ashram gave him an old bicycle to cart his goods. Bhupalan worked diligently and when he received his first payment he was on cloud nine. It was a pittance but still Bhupalan deposited ten percent of the earnings in the Ashram's donation box.

After the first month Bhupalan realized that his work was over by eight in the morning. Now he had nothing much to do except go back to the ashram and while away his time doing odd jobs. He wanted to earn more. And he began looking out for opportunities.

Once he hit the streets, Bhupalan began meeting new faces, new people and new friends. He found that some of the delivery boys were busier than the others. Bhupalan was intrigued. He gravitated towards them and found out that these guys were doing several part time jobs besides throwing newspaper missiles at doorsteps. One of these jobs was to deliver paper and polythene bags to various shops in the city.

Bhupalan befriended the group that handled this job and got an assignment to deliver bags at a particular locality. Paradoxically it was the same one that Bhupalan was born in. And the crowning glory was that his first delivery took him to the same shop that his father Dhanapalan had opened several years back.

Rasaiah the man who had purchased the shop from Mallika had toiled hard and developed the business. From a tiny bunk shop it had now grown into a wholesale grocery cum vegetable mart. It was the biggest in the locality and was forever crowded.

At the rate of 5 Naya Paise per bag, Bhupalan earned Rs. 10/—per day from this delivery of 4 packets of 50 bags each at the shop every day. This was pittance compared to what the shopkeeper made by selling his goods, but Rasaiah helped the boy by recommending him to other shops in the city and very soon Bhupalan was making a neat 50 Rs. per day from this business. Bhupalan continued to work, save and donate a percentage of his earnings to the Ashram. Meanwhile he also learnt a lot about commerce through experience and through the books and newspapers that he pored over regularly.

Making money became Bhupalan's sole aim.

Rasaiah knew that Bhupalan was Dhanapalan's son. He developed a soft corner for the young man. Whenever Bhupalan came to his shop Rasaiah would smile at him, inquire about his welfare and offer him tea and snacks. And in return Bhupalan would run errands for the old man.

Rasaiah's regular customers used to buy provisions on a monthly basis running up long complicated bills. Rasaiah or his cashier would write down the items in long sheets of paper and compute the aggregate amount meticulously. One day as usual the cashier was writing down the figures dictated by the salesman. Bhupalan was standing there and watching the proceedings. As soon as the salesman stopped, Bhupalan came up with the aggregate figure. The shocked crowd of customers and staff looked at him.

"What?" A bemused Rasaiah asked.

"Seven hundred and Twenty Rupees and Eighty Paise" Bhupalan repeated.

Rasaiah chuckled. The salesman beamed. Rasaiah looked at the cashier. "Have you written down the list?" he asked.

"Yes Sir."

"Okay total it up!"

The veteran cashier did the math and came up with the total after a few minutes. "Seven Hundred and Twenty Rupees and Eighty Paise" He rasped.

The crowd gave an impromptu applause. The cashier smiled. "Son I need you!" Rasaiah quipped.

"Any time Sir." Bhupalan replied.

Once Bhupalan exhibited his mathematical wizardry, Rasaiah, gauged his IQ. The boy was brilliant. Besides his natural advantages, Bhupalan had a gluttonous appetite for knowledge which he had diverted towards commercial subjects. Rasaiah began thinking about how to put the boy's talents to maximum use.

A few weeks later Rasaiah took Bhupalan to Parthipan.

"This boy is my find, but I feel that you can use him better." Rasaiah told him.

Rasaiah's elder brother Parthipan owned a hardware shop at the other side of the town. Unlike Rasaiah, Parthipan was a slightly shady character who had made his first pile through nefarious dealings. Later, Parthipan had retired from the rackets and set up this hardware shop. Still he was a "Face" in the underworld and had maintained his contacts with guys who where once his associates in crime. He also ran a poker club in one of the flats a furlong away from his shop.

Parthipan asked Bhupalan a few questions and then belted out a string of complex figures. Even as Parthipan dictated them, a man nearby wrote them down. As soon as Parthipan finished, Bhupalan gave him the final figure. The other man computed his figures and stared at Bhupalan. The two aggregates had tallied. There was a reason for the bewilderment. Not only were the amounts in four figures but Bhupalan had to add, subtract, multiply and divide them simultaneously. As Parthipan stared at Bhupalan quizzically, Rasaiah preened at his discovery.

A week later Parthipan and Bhupalan went to the poker club. At 9 am, It was already full. Bhupalan would learn later that the place was seldom empty. People used to play all days and all nights with some die hard addicts going on a binge that stretched up to forty eight hours.

The flat consisted of one hall and two rooms. The hall had six tables and the rooms had four each. There was a medium sized kitchen plus two wash rooms. There was a small Balcony in the front and a service verandah at the back. The counter was at the west end of the hall. Tea, coffee and cigarettes were served free of cost to the players.

It was a twenty four hour club and the staff worked in eight hour shifts. Two men in the kitchen, One man for each table, Two guys in the counter and a couple of professional masseurs who served the players whenever the guys complained of back ache.

Every one nodded at Parthipan when he entered. As arranged before, Bhupalan went near the counter and took a stool. There was no idle chatting or frivolous talk. Every one minded his business.

There were no women in the club.

A poker game took 5 minutes to culminate. With the club running 24 hours a day, each table witnessed 288 games a day. And there were 14 tables in all. So the total number of games in a day in the club was 4032. And the club made Rs. 5/—per game.

For Bhupalan this was an easy calculation. But once he arrived at the daily take, he had to compute the daily net profit after deducting the per day wages of the workers, the overheads, plus the kick backs to the authorities and other muscle. After arriving at the figure he had to compute the weekly, fortnightly and monthly figures without using pen and paper.

Exactly 15 minutes after he stepped into the club, Bhupalan gave the figures to Parthipan. Parthipan went out and made a call to his bookkeeper. When he returned a few minutes later, he went straight to the counter, opened the drawer, took out a bundle of notes and tossed them at Bhupalan.

"Aiyarrey you are incredible" He dead panned.

Parthipan had addressed Bhupalan as "Aiyar" because of his slender build, studious look and amazing intelligence.

The nickname stuck.

Within months of his joining Parthipan, Bhupalan's income had increased manifolds. He still studied the share prices, saved money and began investing in them. He also educated Parthipan on this new line of business. Whenever they got time, the two would discuss business matters. Bhupalan fed him a lot of information that he had gleaned from newspapers and periodicals over the years. Parthipan was astonished by the young man's erudition.

Six months later, Parthipan called Bhupalan to his house.

"Go to Chennai!" He suggested. "That is the best place for a guy of your intelligence and aims. I shall give you a phone number. Call and ask for 'The cook.' Arrange a meeting with him. He will tell you what to do."

Bhupalan obeyed Parthipan's orders to the tee. He called on the given number, talked to 'The Cook' and the latter asked him to meet him at a graveyard, on the same day at midnight.

Five foot nothing, rock solid at 100 kilos, with a long rectangular head, tiny piggish eyes, and heavily muscled long arms, Irumban 'The cook' was in his late thirties when Bhupalan set his eyes on him for the first time.

He was called the cook because that is what he was for the civilized world. Irumban was a cook par excellence. He could cook both vegetarian and non vegetarian south Indian dishes with amazing skill, and was seldom unemployed. But he preferred to work only in select restaurants and hotels, because of a valid reason.

Despite his incredible culinary skills that would have provided him with enough income to survive, Irumaban was a consummate criminal. He was not only one of the best safe crackers in the Chennai underworld, but also a stone killer. He was a respected member of one of the most powerful criminal outfits in the city—The Rajasuryan gang.

Opposites attract. Irumban took an instant liking for this tall slender, brooding young man who had been referred to him as Aiyar by his own mentor Parthipan from Gokulpet.

Irumban belonged to Gokulpet, and had the ear of his current boss Raja Suryan. Further he was strong and menacing enough to protect Bhupalan from any danger.

"Where are you staying?" Irumban asked Bhupalan after the preliminaries were over.

"Anna asked me to book a room in a mansion in Triplicane." By "Anna" Bhupalan meant Parthipan.

"Anna and Aiyar" Irumban smiled inwardly. He knew why Parthipan had sent Bhupalan to that mansion. Parthipan was a silent partner in that building. This way he could keep an eye on Bhupalan besides protecting the boy from the wrong guys.

"Very good, hang on there! Take a look around the city. You may be here for a long time. I shall get in touch with you a week from today."

Bhupalan nodded deferentially and left.

Parthipan had pondered over the matter for months before sending Bhupalan to Irumban. As a retired gangster, Parthipan knew the demands and problems of the underworld like the back of his hand. One of the major hurdles that the underworld faced besides the law and the rival gangs was the proper investment of its ill gotten gains. Criminals were by nature greedy, ruthless and distrustful. And they were always on the lookout for someone who could help them without being one of them. Bhupalan could be an asset to any criminal outfit. He was young, intelligent, honest, hardworking and straight forward.

The Chennai underworld had divided the city into four broad divisions—The North, the South, the West and the Central. The Bay of Bengal took up the east side of the city and was considered as common property. In each division there were several gangs, which reported to the top man of that division. This chief was in turn elected by a commission which consisted of the best brain in the business and which had been in existence for around half a century. Members came and went but the commission remained. The chiefs of each division were also members of the commission.

The chief or don of each division was responsible for the welfare, control, and protection of his area and its inhabitants both inside and outside the law. Small skirmishes within his jurisdiction were handled by him and his decision was accepted and respected by all. There was no interference from outsiders as long as things went smoothly. It was only when the matters got out of hand that the chief of a division approached the commission for negotiations and rulings. The decision of the commission was final.

Tall, thin, with a dark long face, sharp features, and a thick mane of snow white hair combed straight back, Chaukacheri Rajasuryan looked more like a respectable business man than the Don of Central Chennai that he actually was.

Rajasuryan, an erstwhile associate of Parthipan was in his late forties. Pursued by the law, the two had fled their home town Tuticorin as teenagers and had landed in Chennai, through the sea route.

After bumming around for a few weeks, they struck up friendship with another young man who in turn introduced them to a local slumlord called Koti. Koti was at that time in the midst of a losing turf war with another gang and was desperately in need of extra fire power. On meeting the duo, Koti was delighted. Within days of their first meeting, Rajasuryan and Parthipan were in the thick of the bloody battle, breaking heads and bones for their boss.

The fights ended a week later when the local chieftain, worried about the deteriorating situation in his area, ordered a sit down. Koti and his rival went to the meet with their guys and Rajasuryan and Parthipan attended it. After a lot of yelling and shouting it was found that the whole problem started when one of Koti's men had thrashed a member of the rival gang in a drunken brawl. Under the eagle eye of the chieftain the two slumlords embraced each other and called off the war. Every one heaved a sigh of relief, but the two who benefited most by this whole episode were Rajasuryan and Parthipan.

Koti took them in his fold and got them a boat to start a living as fishermen. As respectable members of the gang they received help from other members. The duo found that though these guys were young, tough and brave, they lacked the foresight to apply their talent in making money.

Gradually the duo managed to have the ears of their boss Koti. Though a totally illiterate guy himself, Koti was intelligent enough to listen to good advice regardless of who ever gave it. Raja Suryan and Parthipan convinced him that he could make more money for everyone without tainting his reputation, if he went along with them. Koti agreed.

Koti and his gang hailed from the fishermen community. With the help of the duo, the gang planned out a distribution system for the sea food that was brought every evening. Rajasuryan persuaded the fishermen to sell all their goods to Koti's gang at a reasonable price. Parthipan arranged for the transport and distribution in the wholesale market. From there the stock was parceled out to retailers who sold them to the public as shop keepers, vendors and travelling salesmen.

Koti's community benefitted at every stage of the business. The day for each family began with some of the members going into the sea to get fresh catch. Meanwhile, the existing stock was sold to the Koti gang. Women in the family took care of the cleaning, processing and packing of the fish. Thanks to Parthipan the guys purchased fish carts, small vans and lorries to transport the goods to the wholesale market. This gave employment to several other guys.

Though the wholesalers were big business men, they employed guys from the fishermen community to handle the stuff. Here too Koti's guys made their money in the form of wages, and commission.

And finally the same stock was sold to retailers who again were Koti's guys.

Thus, within a year the gang had infiltrated the complete sea food market in their area.

Koti was a reasonable guy. He acknowledged the duo's contribution and rewarded them handsomely. The grateful duo then trained him in the art of loan sharking. Koti was making thousands every month thanks to this new line of business. Taking the duo's advice, he ploughed the extra money back into the industry. He loaned out his savings to those who wanted to buy or repair boats, nets, fish carts, shops etc. This way all the money remained in the community.

Two years after they joined Koti, Rajasuryan and Parthipan took his permission and relocated to a place called Triplicane which was just a few kilometers away from Koti's stronghold.

Rajasuryan and Parthipan did not return to Tuticorin. As teenagers on the run for some minor misdemeanor, they did not attract much attention from the department. Slowly the duo carved a niche in the Chennai underworld thanks to their resourcefulness and Koti's muscle. They began as gamblers running poker digs at various flats in the locality. From there got into loan sharking, unions, providing hired muscle, and taking "important contracts" for the underworld.

Eight years after the duo set their feet on Chennai soil, Parthipan contacted his family back in Tuticorin. By now he had been written off as dead by his kith and kin. When they realized that he was alive and kicking they were delighted. His mother came to Chennai and met the two. By this time Rajasuryan and Parthipan had made enough to construct a small mansion in Triplicane. This building served as their office cum residence.

After a lot of running around, Parthipan's mother arranged for an alliance for her eldest son. The girl was the only daughter of a prosperous hardware dealer in Gokulpet. Parthipan married her and came into a flourishing business. He retired from the rackets and settled down in Gokulpet. His younger brother

Rasaiah arrived there a year later. By now Parthipan was a proud father of a girl child.

Though he had handed over all the rackets to Rajasuryan, Parthipan still maintained contacts with him. By now Koti had grown old and with increase in prosperity, he and his cronies began drifting away from crime. But Rajasuryan did not give up. He was an ambitious young man and he wanted to reach the top in his field.

Left alone in Chennai, Rajasuryan found it difficult to run his growing establishment. He had the brains and the people who could carry out his plans which did not involve much risk. But in the line that he was Rajasuryan also needed muscle. There were a lot of predators who were waiting for him to drop his guard so that they could pounce and grab whatever he and Parthipan had built over the years.

Then Irumban came.

Irumban had started his career at the ripe old age of Twelve. He hailed from a village near Gokulpet and had come to the town looking for a job. Even at that age, he was blessed with phenomenal physical strength. After some time he landed a job as an errand boy in a small tea stall. After a few months he came across a man who sold homemade snacks. Irumban joined him and slowly developed culinary skills. Now the two would cook the snacks at that man's shack and sell them in the market on a cycle rickshaw. After some years, thanks to the intervention of a patronizing local politician, Irumban's partner got a small place outside the municipality building where he opened a snack bar.

Irumban was seventeen when his partner who was a few years older, got married. His wife began frequenting the shop to give her husband a helping hand. With her arrival, Irumban found himself in the streets again.

Irumban was born tough. In spite of the deprivation that followed his unemployment, he refused to go back to his village. The ex-partner was kind enough to feed him free of cost every now and then. After some time Irumban landed a job as a laborer in a transport company which carted iron scrap. It was there that his parallel career began.

Some of the laborers in the company belonged to an area which was controlled by the Gokulpet underworld. Looking at Irumban's physique and awesome physical prowess, these guys invited him to their locality. After the preliminary introductions, the local chief put Irumban under the apprenticeship of a professional burglar.

Irumban was a quick study. Just as he had learnt cooking a few years back, he also learnt how to open locks, crack safes, open windows, climb and scale walls, walk like a cat and run like a cheetah.

Irumban's mentor was a brilliant planner and organizer. His outfit consisted of guys with different talents. Everyone knew his part of the job. Some of the guys who were excellent observers would hit the streets and give a feed back to the boss about shops, offices, and houses which could be likely targets for a hit. The boss would study the information and then select one of the targets. The second set of guys would then case the joint. Casing meant that these guys would give a complete report of the location of the target, how many people frequented the place, what were the timings, when it was safest to hit, how to break in and get out, etc. Once this blueprint was through, the third set would go and find out what was worth burgling in the target, where it was kept what was the security system and so on. For this, the third group also employed informers who worked in the fringe of the underworld. These informers were blissfully unaware of who the actual boss was.

After getting all the information, the boss would contact the fences and inform them that he would be coming to them with a consignment. Once he had the okay from them the boss would lay out a plan to hit the target.

It was then that Irumban's role began. Irumban, His boss and another guy who was tiny in size and could wriggle in and out of the smallest of space, would go to the spot. Irumban and the boss would use a jimmy or a rod or any other instrument that suit the need of the moment to lift the shutter, open a window or create a small passage. The tiny guy would then worm himself in and open the door. They would then pick the locks & crack the safes. The loot would then be divided into three, with the tiny guy carrying the smallest and Irumban the heaviest parcel Once they were safely back at their hide out, they would dump the loot in a go down. Everyone would go home and lie low for a few days. Then the boss would contact the fence and arrange for a meeting. The loot would change hands and the fence would pay the price agreed upon. Once the boss got hold of the cash, he would take his cut and distribute the proceeds. Irumban got his share too. Everyone was happy.

The gang did a few well planned jobs in the next few years, and Irumban made a pile. Then one day the boss fell ill and took to bed.

Gloating over their newfound success, and free from the controlling hand of their boss, some of the members of the gang decided to strike out on their own. They had the muscle and the manpower but lacked in the brains department. Within a span of three months the fellows struck the sleepy town with a spate of robberies and chain snatchings.

There was a huge public outcry and the cops got the brunt of the heat. Accusing them of being hand in glove with the gangsters the media threatened a national exposure.

Frustrated and furious at this sudden commotion, the department cracked down on the Gokulpet gangland. Boiling with rage the cops went berserk and arrested, tortured, shot and killed several gangsters.

Irumban was in trouble again. Fortunately for him, he was a new comer in the underworld and few knew him. He was extremely low profile and had not been a part of the reckless campaign that the gang had indulged in. And to cap it all, he had taken a long deserved break and gone to his home village when the cops struck.

Meanwhile Partihpan had settled down as a respectable business man in Gokulpet. Thanks to his resourceful father-in-law, he started as an agent for hardware goods and then opened his own shop. Simultaneously he also put his past experience to good use and started a poker club.

Parthipan had followed the events in Gokulpet, and was intrigued by the whole matter. He and Rajasuryan continued to exchange notes and they wondered how the hoods in Gokulpet could be so fool hardy. Rajasuryan had his contacts in the Chennai Police department and thus he used to get a lot of information from the grapevine.

Even as his family was euphoric over Irumban's visit, the young man was shocked by the developments in Gokulpet. Most of his associates were shot and the balance was behind bars. Irumban panicked. It would not be long before the law learnt about him and the cops began breathing down his neck. Irumban's folks believed that he had made his money the hard way. Though poor, they were simple hard working people, and any blot on their collective character would have shattered them. Irumban decided that he would rather die than have the department at his door step.

Irumban's ex partner, the same guy who ran a snack shop, belonged to a village a few kilometers away from Irumban's home. Despite his paranoia, Irumban recalled that the man used to visit his village every Thursday.

One Thursday night, Irumban packed his bag with the barest of necessities, and left his home. He had already given a substantial part of his ill gotten gains to his father. Now he decided that he would not visit them until the heat had died down.

Irumban reached his partner's house early Friday morning. After listening to Irumban's woes the partner flared up and harangued him for a few minutes. Finally he calmed down. After all Irumban was a friend and he needed help. The partner asked him to stay put there and returned to Gokulpet.

Through his contacts the partner learnt about Parthipan. He met him and begged for help. Parthipan listened coolly and gave him a message. Two days later Irumban was in the headquarters of Rajasuryan's outfit in Chennai.

Faced with a gloomy future that could end either with a bullet on his head, or a long haul in a prison, Irumban tough guy that he was, broke to pieces when he met Rajasuryan and Parthipanin Chennai. The duo listened to his whole story patiently. They could make out that he was telling them the truth. Irumban was amazingly strong, young, a skilled cook and above all desperately in need of help. Such guys could be blindly loyal to anyone who offered him a second chance.

Rajasuryan recruited him.

For the next one year, Irumban worked in a restaurant run by the outfit at Wallajah Pet, a small town around hundred kilometers west of Chennai. Within weeks of his joining the restaurant, the clientele increased two folds, thanks to his Biryani and the spicy gravy that he served with it. Irumban loved cooking and was always experimenting on new recipes. Soon the restaurant had to start a full fledged door delivery service, to cater to the locality.

By then the heat had died down in Gokulpet. The robberies and chain snatchings stopped and the public heaved a sigh of relief. The press forgot its animosity and even praised the department for its efficiency. In the milieu Irumban was completely forgotten. Irumban sent money to his parents through the same partner friend who had bailed him out a year back.

Wallajah pet was a common territory, shared by all the four divisions of the Chennai underworld. The Chennai hoods did brisk business there in partnership with the local guys. Regardless of the division to which a Chennai hood belonged, he was free to enter into joint ventures and partnerships with gangsters who belonged to other divisions. As long as money kept flowing everyone was happy. The politicians and cops in Wallajah pet preferred to look the other way because the Chennai dons had deeper pockets and the payoffs from them were far more substantial than the pittance that the officials would have received locally.

Vallam was a small township in the outskirts of Wallajahpet. It had several tiny, small and middle sized workshops and factories that catered to the nearby Industrial town ship of Ranipet.

Being an industrial area Vallam was known for its rough and violent inhabitants. Brawls, fights, knifings, and muggings were a way of life in Vallam. Every household had its share of weapons and their users, and the law seldom interfered when gangs clashed regularly in the dark alleys. Decent people avoided traveling through the town after dusk. The people were so wild and vicious that the town provided muscle to other criminal outfits in the surrounding areas.

The Vallam underworld was ruled by two brothers.

Murugesan, Bhadra and Sethu were three brothers and they belonged to this town. Their ancestors hailed from Nagarkoil a town in the south of Tamilnadu. Blacksmiths by trade, they had relocated to this town several decades back. Now the family ran the oldest blacksmith workshop in Vallam.

Dark, thin, around five foot nine, Murugesan was the eldest of the three brothers. He had fought his way up the gangland ladder with the assistance of his middle brother the shorter and powerfully built Bhadra. The third and youngest brother Sethu managed the family business. During one of the skirmishes with another mob Murugeasn had lost his left eye.

Murugesan and Bhadra were regular history sheeters. Cases were registered against them in various police stations in the district. They had been arrested several times for assault, battery, robbery, attempted murder and murder, but neither had ever been convicted due to lack of evidence or witnesses.

Murugesan was cunning, greedy and a good organizer. Bhadra was an out and out muscle head known for his violence and murderous rage. Thanks to Bhadra and his crowd of equally rough guys Murugesan was able to terrorize Vallam. Content with his shop, Sethu the youngest brother shied away from the rackets. Like Murugesan, Sethu was slight in build and had an uncanny resemblance to his eldest brother.

The hotel where Irumban worked was owned by an old friend of Rajasuryan, a guy called Annamalai. He was of around Rajasuryan's age and a fringe member of the outfit. One of the men from the Rajasuryan group was based in Walajahpet and he provided protection to Annamalai and his hotel. In return Annamalai sent him weekly pay offs besides sweets and savories during festival time. As Annamalai was never even remotely involved in the rackets, he had no police record.

Despite knowing about this, the greedy Murugesan had an eye on Annamalai's hotel. The place was at a prime location in the city and the business was brisk. Murugesan had contacts with one of the gangs operating in the northern division of Chennai. The two outfits were waiting for an opportunity to muscle into Rajasuryan's territory in Wallajah pet.

To begin with Bhadra and his guys began frequenting the hotel. Annamalai saw them but kept mum because the fellows came as patrons, enjoyed the food, and paid the bills correctly. However being a cautious man, Annamalai tipped off Rajasuryan's contact, who in turn informed Rajasuryan about the matter.

Rajasuryan knew Murugesan and had a nodding acquaintance with him. The two had met each other in some meetings. Rajasuryan assured all protection to Annamalai.

Rajasuryan used to make regular trips to other parts of Tamilnadu, to look up his business, meet his associates and contacts and discuss important issues. A year after Irumban landed in Wallajah pet, Raja Suryan visited the town. Irumban gave him an emotional welcome, and praised him effusively for his timely help. For Irumban, Rajasuryan was the knight in shining armor who gave him a new lease of life. Being a simple man, Irumban swore undying loyalty to him. Rajasuryan feasted on Irumban's best dishes and joked that he would take the guy to Chennai and keep him as his special chef. Irumban hoped that this should happen ASAP.

When he heard that Rajasuryan was in Wallajah pet, Murugesan was delighted. This was the right time to talk directly with the boss and cut down the underlings like Annamalai.

Loaded with gifts and flowers, Murugesan met Rajasuryan at the big man's abode in a mansion at the outskirts of Wallajah pet. Rajasuryan deserved due respect from hoods like Murugesan. But unlike uptight dons, Rajasuryan was a decent man. He received Murugesan and his men courteously and played the perfect host. But Murugesan being what he was mistook this hospitality.

Over drinks and snacks Murugesn broached the subject. He "informed" Rajasuryan conspiratorially that Wallajahpet, and all the surrounding areas including the industrial township were up for grabs and that he Murugesan was planning to muscle in.

Before this could sink in, he fired another salvo. Murugesan "offered" to be Rajasuryan's man in this campaign, promising the old man a weekly take several times over what he was making now. The only thing that Murugesan wanted in return was absolute non interference from the Chennai bigwigs including Rajasuryan himself. Without saying it in so many words, Murugesan made it clear that he wanted to be the undisputed king of the whole district.

Despite marveling at the hood's impetuousness, Rajasuryan was aghast at the foolhardiness of the offer. The district was stiff with muscle and power wielded by numerous gangs which owed allegiance to various bigger gangs in Chennai and other parts of Tamilnadu. Rajasuryan would not dream of taking on all of them to support this illiterate oaf who along with his savage brother had been terrorizing the people of Vallam for years.

Seething within at Murugesan's audacity, Rajssuryan talked to him like a teacher to an idiot child. He told him that things were not as simple as they seemed. Rajasuryan enlightened the stupid guy that if the Chennai underworld got even a whiff of Murugesan's fond reveries, they would come after him so hard that the avaricious little lout would not know what hit him.

A suitably chastened Murugesan returned home to nurse his wounds. Though Rajsuryan had been as mild as it could be possible under the circumstances, Murugesan could not stomach the fact that he had been belittled in front of his own underlings by the wise old man. After pondering over the matter, Rajasuryan decided not to tip off the Chennai underworld. He however asked his own contact man to take the necessary precautions and avoid Murugesan. Rajasuryan returned to Chennai with a huge packet of savories specially made for him by Irumban.

Nothing happened for the next few months.

It was a rainy November night in Wallajahpet. Annamalai's eatery was jam packed thanks to Irumban's fish pakora and steaming hot tea. At eleven in the night the last customers began trickling away. The drizzle combined with a breeze, had brought the temperature down. Irumban washed down his supper with country liquor. He was a regular drinker and could enjoya full bottle every evening and still stay sober. After supper, he kept sipping the remaining brew while washing the dishes, and cleaning the kitchen. Then he closed the shop.

As he knelt down to lock the shutter, Irumban stiffened. From the corner of his left eye he spotted a shadow at the end of the street. Unaware of this Annamalai lit a cigarette and went near his motorbike.

Suddenly someone stepped out of the bushes and pounced on Annamalai. Totally unprepared for this sudden attack, Annamalai let out a cry and began grappling with the fellow. But the attacker was younger, more powerful and fully prepared. He caught hold of Annamalai by the throat and pulled out a long knife.

Lunging from the place where he crouched, Irumban was on the fellow in a moment. Instinctively the intruder swung the knife at Irumban. In one swift move, Irumban ducked the knife and landed a solid kick on the fellow's groin. The villain let out a gasp and toppled over. But by then two more guys had joined the scuffle.

With incredible strength Irumban tossed Annamalai across the ground, towards the shop. A stunned Annamalai landed on his back and stayed there. Now the two attackers ran for Irumban's throat. Irumban headed a fellow on his face and the guy went down.

The third guy was as powerful as Irumban. He punched him so hard that a surprised Irumban grunted and landed on the bushes. Before the attacker could land another blow, Irumban sprung up and lunged at the fellow head first.

As a shivering Annamalai looked on, Irumban and Bhadra clashed with each other like enraged bulls. Both were short, very powerful and of around the same age. Kicking and punching the two fought for their dear lives. Both knew that even one slip could be fatal.

Suddenly Bhadra was on top of Irumban. Grinning through his bloodied face, he caught hold of Irumban's neck and began squeezing.

Visions of his childhood passed in front of Irumban's glazed eyes. His face got motley and he gasped for breath. There was a sudden dull thud and Bhadra's head jerked backward. Annamalai and thrown a brick at him and it had landed. Bhadra's grip loosened.

A desperate Irumban butted Bhadra between his legs, with as much strength as he could muster. Bhadra made a gurgling sound and fell back. Irumban flayed his hands frantically and caught something. Still half conscious, he gripped the object and swung it at Bhadra.

The first attacker's long knife went through Bhadra's left rib and tore his heart.

On hearing about Bhadra's macabre end the jubilant Vallam cops blessed the hand that struck the ogre down. At the same time they braced themselves for the backlash that could follow.

The Wallajah cops took the remaining two attackers to the hospital and put them under arrest. Bhadra's body was handed over to Murugesan with a stern warning that if he acted funny, the whole department would pounce on him like hungry wolves. Wallajah pet cops were already fed up with the capers of their own hoods and they did not want any more trouble from the Vallam guys.

The two accomplices were released when the cops found that they were casual laborers who had been hired by Bhadra at the last moment. The guys were poor and had no police record. The cops took pity on them, pooled in some money and gave it to the fellows to help them go straight.

Thanks to the two nincompoops, Murugesan found himself in the midst of problems. Not only was his brother dead, but the cops were after him to find out why Bhadra had started the fight in the first place. Both Murugesan and Bhadra were uncouth thugs and no cop liked them. This was the best time to squeeze the flab out of the oaf.

Because he had taken on a man like Rajasuryan, his own associates in the Chennai underworld dropped him like a hot brick. The department waited for a few weeks and then tossed Murugesan in the can for some old gangland rubout.

With the timely intervention from Rajasuryan, Annamalai and Irumban lay holed up in one of the outfit's hideouts. Annamalai thanked Irumban for saving his life. The hotel in Wallajah pet was closed down for the time being.

Annamalai was a good business man. He was intelligent, hardworking and above all trustworthy. The hotel that he ran in Wallajah pet was inherited by him from his father.

Rajasuryan had been pondering over a matter that worries every hood who has a substantial income from the rackets. How to plough the money back into the market and launder it without attracting unwanted attention? For this Rajasuryan wanted a "front", a man who he could entrust with his funds and expect him to invest it properly. Besides possessing the required business acumen, it was perennial that the man should not have a police record.

Rajasuryan decided to use Annamalai as his "front".

The Wallajahpet hotel was sold away and Annamalai relocated to Chennai. Rajasuryan bought him a small eatery in Triplicane. After the necessary renovation, Annamalai and Irumban were back in business.

Besides laundering Rajasuryan's money through the eatery, Annamalai also let out the extra funds in the market to the vegetable, grocery, milk, egg, fish and meat suppliers. Slowly Annamalai created a wide network for his loan sharking operation. Because the money circulated in the food market, where most of the borrowers were below the tax bracket, Rajasuryan's wealth got laundered faster than he could even make it.

Once things cooled down, Irumban took a vacation and he went to his home town loaded with cash and gifts. On the way he also met Parthipan and expressed his gratitude to him. Rajasuryan had already informed Parthipan about Irumban's exploits in Wallajah Pet. He had also hinted that he intended to groom Irumban to be his right hand man.

Murugesan was released three years later. By then he had made quite a few powerful contacts with hoods from various parts of the state. These guys in turn had their own associates in the Chennai underworld. Through their good offices Murugesan came in touch with some of the hardest guys from the southern division of Chennai underworld.

Though Rajasuryan learnt about Murugesan's release through the grapevine, he wasn't much worried. Rajasuryan thought that as Murugesan's old contacts from North Chennai had cold shouldered the guy, Murugesan would retire with a small piece of action in Vallam.

He would regret this presumption in the months to come.

Annamalai kept a mistress in a place called Vannandurai in the south of Chennai. Her name was Ponni and she had been his keep even when he was in Wallajah pet. She too belonged to that town but had settled down in Chennai after her marriage to a driver. A few years after the marriage, her poor husband had died in an accident. Annamalai, had gallantly come to her rescue and settled her along with her daughter Rani in a comfortable pad in that southern part of Chennai. He kept supplying her with funds and her child went to a respectable school.

It was the month of October. In this month, Tamilians celebrate a festival called Ayudhapuja which in other parts of the country is called Dussehra. On that day Tamilians from all walks of life, worship their tools and instruments and decorate them with flowers, and vermillion. They also invite their relatives and friends to the puja. Annamalai invited Ponni and Rani to his puja in the eatery.

The hotel, and the utensils were well decorated and the puja went off well. Rajasuryan came with his family. Irumban and Annamalai completed the formalities and Annamalai distributed Prasadam. After the puja everyone had a sumptuous supper cooked by Irumban and his assistants.

After seeing the guests off, Annamalai left in his car for Vennandurai with Ponni and Rani. On Ponni's insistence, Annamalai decided to stay overnight. After Rani was put to bed, Ponni joined Annamalai in the other bed room, with a bottle of rum and a plate of sliced fruit. They made love till 1 am and then fell asleep.

It was around 3 in the morning when Ponni heard some noise. She turned around sleepily and felt that side of the bed where Annamalai slept. It was empty. A half asleep Ponni thought that Annamalai had gone to the washroom.

Then she heard a gurgling sound and a commotion that sounded like a scuffle. In an instant she was wide awake. She jerked around and peered into the darkness.

Annmalai was struggling to break free from the clutches of a thick set man. Another man stood in front of him. Before Ponni could make out what was going on, the other man pulled out a huge sword hidden under is shirt at the back of his neck. In one swift move he slashed across Annamalai's chest. Annmalai's legs swung into the air, but the guy was prepared for this. He turned to his right, taking the kick on his left thigh.

All this was happening in the large verandah outside the house.

The burly guy lifted Annamalai and threw him across the floor. Annamalai landed with a thud and rolled to a corner. In a moment Ponni was on the assailants.

And then she found that they wore masks.

Cursing furiously Ponni lunged at the thickset man. Instinctively the fellow turned around and ducked as Ponni clawed for his face. She lost balance and crashed on the other guy.

The other guy was slight but extremely powerful. He caught Ponni by her throat and tossed her back so hard that Ponni flew into the house, crash landed on the hard floor, let out a sobbing yell and fainted.

By now Annamalai was trying to get up. The slight guy swung the sword across Annamalai's throat.

A few minutes later when Ponni came to her senses, all was quiet again. She groaned, got up and went to the verandah.

A writhing Annmalai lay on the floor bleeding like a pig. Ponni let out an ear piercing wail and threw herself on him. She tried to take his head and place it in her lap. A thick gush of blood soaked her sari.

By the time the neighbors rushed out to help, Annamalai had given up the ghost. From the description that Ponni gave, the cops suspected a gangland killing.

Their intuition was further confirmed when they learnt of Annamalai's identity.

The locality was shocked by the ghastly incident. Underworld grapevine went on an overdrive.

The southern division of Chennai underworld moved fast. The commission was informed that the powers that be in the southern division had nothing to do with the killing. This speedy denial from their part was very important to avoid a full scale gang war, as the man who was killed, belonged to the Central division. A hasty meeting was called and attended by big wigs from all the divisions. Rajasuryan accepted the condolences graciously and assured the guys that he did not blame anyone for this tragedy. The southern division assured all possible help to track down the killers. Rajasuryan thanked them for their offer. Every one heaved a sigh of relief.

Through the good offices of the southern division, Rajasuryan made sure that Ponni and Rani were not troubled by the law and the public. As Annamalai was a bachelor and had no relatives to call his own, Rajasuryan arranged for his wealth to be invested properly. Ponni and Rani were declared as nominees for Annamalai's property. The two continued to live in the same house.

Annmalai's sudden demise was a body blow for Rajasuryan. The fellow was an astute business man and had made Rajasuryan quite rich over the years. With him gone, Rajasuryan not only lost a good money launderer but he also lost track of the money loaned out in the market.

Now Irumban proved his worth.

Irumban contacted all the guys who dealt regularly with Annamalai and asked them to report to him. He prepared an almost accurate list of guys who owed money to Rajasuryan. A few weeks after Annamalai's demise the well oiled loan sharking business was in operation again.

Rajasuryan was delighted. He rewarded Irumban by making him in charge of the eatery as well as the money lending business.

However Rajasuryan still wanted someone who could have the business acumen of Annamalai and the loyalty of Irumban, someone who could make money for him and his outfit, in more legitimate ways. Rajasuryan craved for respectability.

And then he remembered Parthipan.

It was Parhipan who had given Irumban to Rajasuryan. Rajasuryan asked him to look out for the right guy to act as a front for the outfit. Knowing the business well, Parthipan needed someone who was intelligent, a quick study, willing to make money and dedicated to his bosses.

Parthipan chose Bhupalan.

After making sure that Bhupalan was comfortably ensconced in his new surroundings, Irumban went to meet Rajasuryan. Parthipan had already given a detailed account about Bhupalan to the old man. Irumban confirmed it.

"He is a young kid." Irumban said earnestly "Looks quite intelligent and educated. And further he has been recommended by Anna."

"Why is he called Aiyar?" Rajasuryan smiled.

"The boy is slender and delicate." Irumban chuckled "And looks like one who has spent more time in a library than in the market."

Rajasuryan nodded gravely. "Call him to your place tonight."

The restaurant was a two storey building with a large rectangular hall in each floor. The kitchen was at the far end of the ground floor hall. There was a counter at the entrance and wash rooms in each floor. With two rows of eight tables in each floor, at a time the restaurant could seat 128 persons. There was a partition in the first floor, just above the kitchen, which was sealed by a thick wooden wall. The average customer wouldn't know that there was a full fledged apartment behind the wall, which served as an office. Entrance to this office was through a wrought iron ladder which stood at a dark corner in the north east of the kitchen.

Bhupalan arrived at the restaurant at around 9 pm. A waiter accosted him and seated him at a place near the kitchen. He then served him water and coffee. Presently Irumban joined him.

Unknown to anyone except Irumban, Rajasuryan studied Bhupalan who was facing him, from the first floor office. Irumban kept up a conversation with the young man and Rajasuryan's eyes did not miss anything. Bhupalan was all ears as Irumban talked and explained things to him.

"Did you take a look around?" Irumban asked him.

"Yes sir! I went to the stock exchange today." Bhupalan said politely.

"What is it?"

"Sir it is the place where shares and debentures of various companies are traded. It's a share market."

"How did you know about it?"

Rajasuryan was listening to every word through a microphone that was attached to the bottom of the table.

"Sir that is my favorite subject" Bhupalan said excitedly. "I live on business news. I have always wanted to be an investor. Even when I was in Gokulpet, I knew about this exchange."

Irumban smiled and nodded. He then ordered for some snacks for the boy. Bhupalan began eating.

"Would you like to use your talent for me?" Irumban asked him.

"Sir! Anna has sent me to work for you." Bhupalan said.

"Good! Good! Enjoy your snacks. We shall talk about it." Irumban excused himself and went in.

Later that night Rajasuryan complimented on Irumban's handling the boy. He told him that from now on Irumban would be Bhupalan's handler. Rajasuryan did not want anyone in the outfit to know about Bhupalan. At the same time he also made sure that Bhupalan did not know anyone except Irumban. This way it was safe for all.

Despite the Wallajah pet fight, Irumban had no police record. The first thing that Bhupalan did was to open a bank account jointly in his and Irumban's name. Bhupalan would operate the account and Irumban would have access to all the bank statements. For the first six months the duo kept depositing money in the account. Meanwhile Bhupalan contacted a broker and opened an account with him. He also spent long hours studying the share market, the business journals, and books on commerce.

Six months later Bhupalan made his first investment. He purchased blue chips worth 50 thousand rupees and registered them in the joint names of Bhupalan and Irumban. The registration expenses were paid in cash. Rajasuryan beamed when he saw the share certificates.

Slowly through this business, Bhupalan began transferring shares and debentures in the names of Rajasuryan's wife and children. Rajasuryan was a fair man. He ensured that Bhupalan also handled the finances of other guys in the outfit, including Irumban. The Rajasuryan group got legitimately wealthy with each passing day. At the same time, Bhupalan received a hefty commission which he ploughed back into the share market. He also donated a fair amount to his orphanage as charity.

Two years after Bhupalan joined the group, he was the treasurer for the whole outfit. Rajasuryan was now a millionaire, and every one in his outfit was financially sound and independent. Because it was engineered by Rajasuryan and Irumban, everyone was grateful to them. And like all self contained guys, the hoods never bothered to ask, who the whiz kid behind all this was. Rajasuryan encouraged them to set up their own shops, establishments and businesses. Guys became shop keepers, travel agents, local transporters, auto rickshaw and taxi owners and travelling salesmen.

Bhupalan was on cloud nine. His favorite hobby was now his full time occupation too. He delved deeper and deeper into the market and started learning about the next step in speculation—Commodities and futures.

Investors in commodities usually speculated on only those items that they felt comfortable with. It was not like in shares where the speculators traded in all sorts of scrips basing their judgment solely on the share prices.

Through the good offices of the broker, Bhupalan contacted those who speculated in steel in Chennai. He met them, made friends, moved in their circle and collected endless information. Once he was comfortable with the trade, Bhupalan jumped into the fray with his own money, to get a feel of the ground. Initially he took some time to break even, but then in one of the transactions he came up with a tidy profit. Bhupalan contacted Irumban.

Irumban was extra special for Bhupalan. Over the years the two had come close to each other. Bhupalan considered him a father figure. Though he had made Rajasuryan and his gang rich, Bhupalan did not know anyone in the outfit, other than Irumban. Irumban was his only contact to the wider network Bhupalan worked for.

Irumban listened to Bhupalan and gave him the go ahead. With extraordinary care and meticulousness, Bhupalan entered the commodities and futures line, and invested the outfit money. Six months later he received a tip that if he went bullish on steel now, and if he could hold on to the investment for a month, he could at least double its equity. After consulting Irumban, Bhupathi took the risk.

The D day came. Thanks to a sudden upsurge in the market, steel prices soared to dizzy heights. When Bhupalan reported the profit that the outfit had made, Rajsuryan almost fell off the chair. One master stroke from Bhupalan had transformed several guys in the Rajasuryan outfit, including Irumban into millionaires.

Rajsuryan asked Irumban to give a hefty bonus along with the usual commission to Bhupalan. He further arranged for a paid holiday for him to Kodaikanal. A delighted but shy Bhupalan requested Irumban to accompany him, and got a guffaw in return.

Once they had made their pile the other guys from the outfit pulled away their investments from Bhupalan's account. They had established their own businesses and wanted to concentrate in developing them. Rajasuryan too, took a major share of his money and invested it in gold and jewelry to make his family secure. Having been a hood all his life, he knew the uncertainties of his line. Only Irumban and Bhupalan concentrated in speculation.

Now Rajasuryan decided to pay a few old debts.

Rajasuryan had not forgotten Annmalai's murder and he had no intentions of letting it go unlamented.

"Revenge is a dish that is sweetest when eaten cold."

Recalling this proverb, Rajasuryan had decided to lay low for the time being to secure his own financial position before striking back. He suspected that despite their vehement denial, some bigwigs in the southern division of Chennai underworld were involved in the murder, and that any hasty move from his side could result in a turf war.

Meanwhile Murugesan who had dealt the death blow to Annamalai that fateful night, wondered whether Rajasuryan had developed a yellow streak. Murgesan wasn't as stupid as he looked. He had all the cunning that makes one a successful hood. The fellow who had been a party to the murder was a low level thug called Dilli Babu from Velachery, a suburb in the south of Chennai. Dilli Babu's chieftain a notorious hood called Sudalai had lent him to Murugesan for this job.

One of Rajasuryan's best spies went to work and came up with the dope on Sudalai. The fellow was quite high up in the southern division and had taken this job because Murugesan had been referred to Sudalai by his own cousin from Palayankottai prison.

Rajasuryan called a meeting with the heavyweights in the southern division. It was held in a bar cum restaurant owned by one of the top hoods in a place called Saidapet. With cold fury Rajasuryan confronted Sudalai and asked him why he had interfered in a matter that did not concern him. This was a sensitive situation and the other hoods knew that Rajasuryan was on the right side.

A haughty Sudalai retorted that Murugesan was an old friend. He had lost a brother and it was only natural that he wanted his pound of flesh. Sudalai waxed eloquent about bloody revenges being normal in their line of business.

The wily Rajasuryan got the drift. Sudalai, big as he was, had no guts to stand up to Rajasuryan on his own, especially when he was on the wrong side of the court. There were quite a few crooks in the Chennai underworld who could benefit from gang wars. Not only did this get rid of bad blood but there was a lot of money to be made in the ensuing tension. These guys had silently backed Sudalai and had told him to stand his ground in the event of a showdown.

"Okay!" Rajsuryan said slowly "Our friend here did what he did and I don't want to get into any trouble with you guys. The problem was between me and Murugesan. Annamalai was killed in your territory, yet I kept my word and did not bear any ill will against you." Rajasuryan paused for effect. There was pin drop silence and everyone was all ears.

"But let me declare right here and now that I am going to go after that gentleman from Vallam. If you guys still think that there is anything wrong in my decision, let us go to the commission." Rajasuryan leaned back on his chair and cold eyed the gathering.

The word "commission" had its desired effect. There was dead silence. Going to the commission invited endless troubles. Their ruling was final and there was no appeal against it, even if they ruled in favor of Rajasuryan and put a hit on Sudalai and Dilli Babu. The two punks had indeed crossed the line.

Presently the head of the southern division spoke.

"Mr. Rajasuryan, we are your friends and we appreciate your stand. But do we need to go to the commission for matters that could be sorted out among ourselves?" Here he stopped and looked at the others who nodded vigorously to second his opinion.

"Let me assure you on behalf of my friends here that you have all our goodwill and sympathies and that we shall not interfere in your personal matters unless requested by you." There was another round of vigorous nods and friendly grunts.

Rajasuryan thanked them and left. But he was under no hallucination. He knew that many hoods envied his sudden prosperity and wondered how he, a hood just like them had become a legitimate businessman over night. He knew that from now on every move from his side would be observed by these guys. And this was a problem.

Murugesan sat in a closed room with one of Sudalai's most trusted lieutenants. He had just been informed of the minutes of the meeting. Beads of sweat appeared on his long dark face.

"I knew!" Murugeasn hissed "I knew that that blighter would not forget me in a hurry. The fag waited for so long to come after me."

"You should consider yourself lucky" The other guy said "That you got to know about it even before it began."

"Yeah! Thanks!" Murugesan grunted.

"Now I have to make my own arrangements. Bhadra is dead and the hoods who were at my beck and call when he was alive, vanished after my brother went to his maker." He added bitterly.

A week later Murugesan and a couple of his cronies went to the nearby industrial township of Ranipet to collect some money from a scrap dealer who operated from a godown. It was after midnight and the scrap dealer received them at his office which was in one of the corners of the go down. While Murugesan and his cronies counted the money, the scrap dealer went inside to get some drinks and snacks for an impromptu party.

The godown had rows after rows of bundles stacked up to ceiling height, with scrap material. The dealer was a big guy in his line of business. He had the contract for purchase of scrap from almost half the factories in the area and he made a hefty profit disposing off the material which he used to get at dirt cheap price. Murugesan had been toying with the idea of getting into a full fledged partnership with this guy.

Noiselessly, three fellows materialized from among the rows of bundles and headed towards the office. Murugesan and his guys were sitting, with their backs towards the door.

The three intruders stopped a few steps away from the door. They then drew their sickles, took a deep breath and simultaneously plunged the swords into the back of the three chairs.

Murugesan's men were pinned to the chair in an instant. One guy died without as much as a gasp. The other let out a yell and his feet flew up the air hitting the table and toppling it over.

But Murugesan was lucky. The third sword got stuck against an inch thick metal board which was packed into the cushion at the back of his chair. Murugesan leapt and did a complete somersault, landing on his back across the table. Immediately he dived into the room where the dealer was placing the drinks and the snacks on the tray.

One of the attackers followed Murugesan and confronted the two inside the room. The scarp dealer threw the tray at the fellow and It landed flush on the villain's face. Murugesan ran and plunged headlong through the window into a dirty ditch. The scrap dealer followed him, and the two ran as fast as their legs could carry them.

After running a few furlongs the two parted ways and went in different directions. Murugesan reached the main road where he got into an auto rickshaw whose driver knew him. Murugesan went to the guy's house, washed, changed his clothes took some cash from the guy and boarded a bus to Vellore. From there he contacted his friends. The next morning he was in a truck bound for Pudukkottai, a township in the south of Tamilnadu.

Rajasuryan got a call in the wee hours of the morning. The killers told him what happened. That the two hoods were killed but Murugesan had escaped. They also told him that the scarp dealer saw one of the assailants but they did not kill him because it would be against the laws of the underworld. Rajsuryan nodded gravely and instructed the trio to lie low for some time, before going back to their home town Nagarkoil.

Blissfully unaware of what was going on around him, Bhupalan continued to make money for himself and Irumban. He also gave the necessary tips to Rajasuryan and his men who invested accordingly and got richer day by day.

After spending a few weeks in Pudukkottai, Murugesan went further south and joined some of his old contacts in Rameshwaram. These guys were heavily into gun running and they took Murugesan in their fold. Murugesan worked with them, made his money and dreamt of sending Rajasuryan to hell.

Murugesan was far more cunning and curious than Rajasuryan had credited him with. Over a period of time he had meticulously collected the dope on Rajasuryan. When he learnt that his outfit was heavily into speculation and that the Rajasuryan hoods had heaped a pile through that complex business Murugesan went through the ceiling.

Murugesan knew that with the possible exception of a couple of guys, all others in the outfit were as illiterate and boorish as Murugesan himself. Even those who knew their three "R" s weren't adept enough to delve deep into the murky waters of commodities and futures. Murugesan wondered who the brain behind this sudden affluence was. Here he was running from the law and the outlaws, and there the punks were living it up as respectable shopkeepers. Night and day he pondered over this and suffered endless migraines.

Rajasuryan was blessed with two daughters. One was already married and the second was ready to tie the nuptial knot. Because he had no sons, Rajasuryan had invested in gold and jewelry so that his wife and daughters could live happily, once he was gone.

Rajasuryan's elder son-in-law belonged to a family of landlords from a place called Thiruvaroor. He was also a practicing lawyer. That man looked out for a suitable groom for Rajasuryan's younger daughter and found a boy from a decent well educated family. This boy had done his electrical engineering and was working in a large construction company in UAE. Every year the boy used to come to India on annual vacation. This time when he did so, Rajasuryan's son-in-law informed Rajasuryan. After a few telephonic conversations, the boy's family invited Rajasuryan to their house in Mannargudi. Rajasuryan and his wife went their accompanied by their elder daughter and son-in-law.

They liked the well educated and cultured boy. When the young man saw Rajasuryan's younger daughter's photograph and agreed to marry her, gifts were exchanged, and Rajasuryan invited them to his house in Chennai to complete the formalities. On the evening before Rajsuryan's return to Chennai, his son-in law hosted a dinner at his house.

The atmosphere was serene and pleasant and everyone enjoyed a hearty meal. It was around midnight when Rajasuryan went to the backyard to wash his hands.

A volley of machine gun bullets fired from behind a small grove of mango trees sieved the old man's chest. By the time the others rushed out to see what had happened, Rajasuryan was dead.

Panic descended on the Chennai underworld. This was no ordinary slaying. A senior member of the underworld had been killed by a rival from another part of the state presumably with the help of his contacts in the Chennai underworld. Rajasuryan was not only a respected figure in the gangland, but his underlings were known for their fierce loyalty towards their boss who had always been kind and generous to them.

Ironically If Rajasuryan had been alive, he could have exercised a restraining hand over his more volatile subordinates. But with him gone, all hell broke loose.

This was the first time that firearms had been used in a Chennai gang war. And this opened a can of worms. Within weeks after Rajasuryan's funeral, his men struck with a vengeance. The outfit had a considerable war chest thanks to Bhupalan's financial wizardry.

Hot blooded, angry and vindictive as they were, the other guys in the outfit were no match to one man among them who literally worshipped Rajasuryan. He owed everything that he had to the old man, without whose timely intervention this guy would have been rotting in a prison cell, or in a paupers' grave.

He Was Irumban.

The first thing that Irumban did after learning of Rajasuryan's death was to withdraw fifty percent of his investments in Bhupalan's business. Then he asked the boy to vanish without a trace. Hence forth the two would communicate with each other only through Parthipan.

Irumban purchased the necessary hardware both in the form of sickles and fire arms, and went out looking for Rajasuryan's killers. The first two casualties were Sudalai and Dilli Babu from the southern division, who had helped bump off Annamalai.

Retaliation for their killing was immediate and before long the whole city was caught in a full scale gang war.

The crimson water shed had begun.

In the six months that followed Rajasuryan's death, the cops in Chennai and the surrounding areas, were busy sweeping corpses. In a way it was sweet justice.

The department always welcomed such periodic draining of bad blood as long as it did not affect the common man.

Murugesan realized that he had finally met his match. Irumban was like a mad elephant on a rampage. The fellow somehow managed to get the right tip about some hood or the other, and he never missed a hit. As his cronies fell one after the other Murugesan got worried. He was several hundred miles away from his home ground and this incapacitated him.

And the worst thing was that Irumban was not aware of this.

Irumban knew that Murugesan, was tall, slender, one eyed and that he wore dark glasses even at night. Unlike other sober guys in the gangland, Murugesan was a flashy dresser always attired in bright colored shirts over white pants, and black leather slippers.

One evening, Irumban got an anonymous tip that Murugesan would be coming to a place called Sriperumbadur in his red colored bike to collect some money from a hardware shop. Irumban knew that Murugesan had a lot of dealings with people in that line of business. Without wasting a moment, Irumban took his bike and rushed to the spot.

The road from Wallajah pet to Sriperumbadur was a highway which did not have much traffic especially on a chilly December evening. Irumban stopped his bike at a lonely spot and waited for his quarry. To make things doubly sure, he called the informer and confirmed that Murugesan would indeed be arriving at the spot within an hour.

It was twilight when Irumban spotted the bike with its lone rider, cruising towards him from the opposite direction. Irumban placed his bike in a slanting position, and crouched behind it, balancing his high powered rifle over the seat of the bike. When the other bike came a hundred meters from where he crouched, Irumban stared hard at the rider. He was slight, wore dark glasses, and was dressed in a multicolored half shirt.

Irumban stiffened, took careful aim, and squeezed the trigger. The first bullet hit the rider on his belly, and the second hit the front wheel of the bike. The man was travelling at 80 kilometers per hour. The sudden impact jolted him out of the bike and threw him several feet away. The poor guy plunged headlong into a ditch where his head hit a huge granite rock.

Thanks to the uncanny resemblance between the two, Murugesan's youngest brother Sethu, sacrificed his life for the sake of his prodigal brother.

Sethu was a straight guy and had no police record. Irumban had at last done what the law feared most—killed an innocent man. Two days after the killing, Irumban went with his lawyer to the district court and surrendered.

Now Irumban was safely behind bars, and the police could not interrogate him. On the contrary they had to take extra precautions to protect him as he was a prize catch and his life was in imminent danger. Irumban's lawyer pulled the necessary strings and had him spirited away to an undisclosed place where he would remain till the trial began. Shortly after Irumban's arrest, the gang war stopped.

Sethu's murder and Irumban's arrest turned Bhupalan's life topsy turvy. Without wasting any time, Parthipan arranged for Bhupalan's disappearance from Tamilnadu.

And Bhupalan landed in Indore as Bhupathi.

Like all frustrated punks Orukkan Murugesan was exceedingly sore at everyone except himself for what had happened to him. He cursed God and the Satan alike and comforted his bruised ego by assuring himself that both his brothers would have been alive if only he were by their side.

And the person he hated most was Irumban. He had killed both his brothers and Murugesan refused to take this as a coincidence. He also turned his blind eye to the fact that Irumban had dutifully surrendered after killing the innocent Sethu.

Murugesan developed persecution mania.

The more he thought about the matter, the more Murugesan wondered about Irumban's resourcefulness. And with that he got into a vicious cycle of despairing ideas, frustrating fears, and fits of rage. He was convinced that he had lost the war because of the wealth of the Rajasuryan outfit. They had used their money to get the information, the arms and the ammunition.

This was in fact true. If only the outfit hadn't been financially sound enough, it would not have survived the onslaught by the Chennai Underworld after the death of Sudalai and Dilli Babu.

It seemed like the end of the road for Murugesan. He had scored the scalps of Annmalai and Rajasuryan at a cost far above any one would have paid. He had lost his two brothers, his stronghold in Vallam, and above all his goodwill in the Chennai underworld which was cursing him for their situation.

The department and the judiciary felt that Irumban's trial in an open court would mean endless trouble. Cases like this would take several years, and with each passing day the security could get more and more lax. Underworld had a vengeful memory and the hoods could strike any time during the course of the endless proceedings.

Irumban was tried for the murder of Sethu by an in camera court and sentenced to life. His lawyer pulled the necessary strings and had Irumban transferred to a maximum security prison in another state.

Helped by his gun running cronies Murugesan picked up his life bit by bit. He set up shop in Tuticorin and formed his own gang. Tenaciously he renewed his contacts in the Chennai underworld and recruited young and fresh muscle.

With Irumban safely behind bars, Murugesan could play his cards more freely. Through the good offices of his Chennai cadre, he got a fleet of sharp and intelligent youngsters who infiltrated Rajasuryan's erstwhile gang as delivery boys, helping hands, and salesmen in the shops and establishments of the retired hoods. Painstakingly these boys won over their bosses over the next few years, through sheer hard work and honesty. As instructed by their underworld employers, these boys kept their eyes and ears open and reported everything that they saw and heard, to their underworld bosses.

At last, after scavenging through tons of worthless information, Murugesan hit pay dirt.

One of the hoods called Kandaswamy who had made his pile in the Bhupalan windfall had gone into commodity speculation.

And as luck could have it, his driver cum man Friday was Gajendran, one of Murugesan's guys.

One night Gajendran was driving his employer Kandswamy home after a long drinking session in a seedy bar. Kandswamy had downed a full bottle of old monk rum and was in an expansive mood. He took Gajendran into confidence and started blabbering shop. Gajendran was all ears. Kandswamy went into a fond reverie and told Gajendran about how he was a small time hood turned travel agent who had hit big time. Kandaswamy talked about Rajasuryan reverentially and then the monologue changed course.

On hearing the name Irumban, Gajendran got alert.

"Raja Saar and Irumban Thambi were great guys." Kandaswamy said fondly. Gajendran nodded submissively.

"Gajendran you came to me a little late. If you had been with me at that time, you would have been driving your own car by now."

"Is it Saar?" Gajendran smiled.

"Yes sonny! Irumban had someone who was a genius. I never saw that fellow but once or twice I heard Raja Saar and Irumban mention the name 'Aiyar'. It is that guy who made me so rich through the same game that I am trying to get into now."

"Saar Aiyar is not a name!"

"Ha! Ha! Ha!" Kandaswamy laughed "Aiyar was the code name of that genius. He was from Gokulpet."

"Gokulpet?"

"That is right. Parthipan gave him to Raja saar."

With amazing control Gajendran kept a straight face and dropped Kandaswami home. Then he contacted his man in the underworld.

Murugesan was stunned. He had always suspected that the Rajasuryan gang had found a golden goose but never believed that his intuition could be so true.

Irumban belonged to Gokulpet. This Murugesan knew. He also knew about Parthipan. Now he had to dig out the guy who they called Aiyar.

The alert Gajendran got a hefty bonus with an instruction to remain glued to Kandaswamy. Meanwhile Murugesan asked his Chennai guys to get the dope on Parthipan from Gokulpet.

A month later Gajendran confirmed that neither Kandaswamy nor any of his erstwhile cronies had ever seen or met Aiyar, The only two persons in the outfit who knew this elusive character were Irumban and Rajasuryan. With Rajasuryan dead and Irumban in prison there was none to identify Aiyar for Murugesan.

However there was a silver lining. The Chennai hoods got a tip from the Gokulpet underworld that several years back Parthipan patronized a young guy who was a wizard with figures. The Gokulpet underworld also gave an almost accurate physical description of Bhupalan.

Murugesan went on an all out search for Bhupalan because he suspected that the guy still had some of the outfit cash with him. Murugesan wanted to lay his dirty hands on that pile.

It was not easy. The guy had vanished without a trace. And Parthipan had settled down in Singapore.

Several years passed before Murugesan struck gold again. By that time he was a big shot in the Tamilnadu underworld with his tentacles spread far and wide.

Irumban completed his sentence and was released after 14 years. Meanwhile he had kept in touch with Parthipan's younger brother Rasaiah. Irumban genuinely cared for Bhupalan and did not want to disturb the boy any more. Bhupalan had sent a hefty amount of Irumban's money to his family through Parthipan, and Irumaban had called it quits.

One of the Chennai gangsters got involved in a bloody battle in another state. The skirmish left 2 dead and several injured. One of the wounded was the Chennai guy. He was arrested, treated for his wounds and tossed in the can.

There he found Irumban a month before the latter's release. After the initial wariness the two got friendly. Irumban realized that this guy was too young to be a part of the underworld during Irumban's period. When Irumban hinted on his plans after the release this guy tipped off the Chennai underworld.

But Irumban was smarter than Murugesan thought. Even before his men could close in on him, he escaped. Rasaiah arranged for a passport for Irumban and sent him to Parthipan in Singapore.

Murugesan was left with just one consolation prize—Rasaiah.

With both Parthipan and Irumban out of sight, Murugesan's crooked brain went on an overdrive. He thought that logically speaking the guy they called Aiyar should be with his mentors. After all he was a genuine earner and no hood would let go of such a prize catch. Murugesan planted his own informers in Gokulpet and told them to keep an eye on Rasaiah.

Murugesan's men infiltrated Rasaiah's wide spread establishment and began collecting information. Rasaiah was an independent guy and had no truck whatsoever with his elder brother in business matters. He was a straight arrow, a devout family man, and his life revolved around his shops and his palatial house in the outskirts of the city.

Rasaiah had come a long way over the years. Besides owning a string of grocery and vegetable shops in the city, he was also the proprietor of one of the biggest shopping malls in Gokulpet. He was also the distributor of south Indian goods in north and north Indian goods in Tamilnadu, through the good offices of Bhupathi.

Rasaiah had his office at the first floor of his shopping mall. Every day he would get up at 7 AM take a bath and do his puja. Then he would have his breakfast and leave for work at 9 AM in his chauffer driven car. On the way he would get down at a temple and pay his obeisance. Then he would do the rounds of his various shops before reaching the mall at 11 AM. The driver would then leave to bring his lunch from home. Rasaiah seldom took hotel food.

After lunch, Rasaiah would stay in the office till 4 PM and then leave for his business meetings. He would again take a tour of his other shops and return to the mall at 7 PM and stay there till it closed at 9 PM. Then it was back home where he would have his supper, spend some time with his family, and go to bed at 11 PM. This was Rasaiah's daily routine six days a week.

Monday was the weekly off for the mall. And so it was for Rasaiah too. Instead of roaming around with his family and friends, Rasaiah would spend the whole day sitting in his private apartments in his house chatting over the phone, reading spiritual books and taking a well earned rest.

So methodically monotonous was Rasaiah's daily routine that Murugesan's men could not find anything interesting or intriguing in his life style. Still they hung on patiently hoping for a breakthrough.

Whereas the south Indian products were transported directly from their main source to Indore, the goods from north were stored in a huge go down before being dispatched to their ultimate destination in various parts of Tamilnadu. This go down was in the transport area of Gokulpet, and was owned by Rasaiah. It was an automatic and well oiled operation and Rasaiah seldom went there for supervision or inspection.

One of Murugesan's men worked there as a loader.

One evening this man called Segar, was sipping a cup of tea and smoking a bidi after a day of hard labor. He and the other workers had unloaded a huge consignment of ground nuts and were waiting for their payment. It was around 7PM. Whereas Segar was standing around 200 meters away from the godown, a group of workers chatted under a tree near the entrance.

Suddenly Segar sensed a commotion in the crowd of workers. The guys had stood up, dusted themselves and stopped talking. Segar's eyes followed the direction where the guys were looking.

A long car came towards the godown from the main road and stopped opposite the tree. Presently Rasaiah got out from the back seat. Segar tossed the bidi away.

The door on the other side opened and a man stepped out. He was younger than Rasaiah and was dressed in a white shirt and dark pants. Segar stiffened.

The man was tall, dark, slender and curly haired.

Rasaiah and that man went into the go down. Segar sauntered up casually to the door of the godown and gave a sidelong glance. On seeing Rasaiah the godown clerk stood up in reverence. Rasaiah and the man nodded at him and went inside. Segar knew that there was no office at the back of the godown.

It was time to report the matter to Murugesan.

"Did you see the guy clearly?" Murugesan rasped.

"Yes!" Segar said.

"He was tall, dark and slender . . ." "and curly haired . . ." Segar said.

Murugesan let out a deep sigh. "Old guy?" Murugesan asked.

"Not very . . . . younger than Rasaiah Sar, must be around 40."

Murugesan nodded thoughtfully. Segar said that the goods had arrived from somewhere north, and had been unloaded in the morning and afternoon. Rasaiah had come to the Godown with his companion in the evening. Segar also said that though such consignments were frequent, neither Rasiah nor his mysterious visitor had ever visited the godown before.

One thing was certain. This man was in some way connected with the goods. According to Segar the two spent a lot of time inside the godown. And it was the young man who was pointing at the rows and rows of gunny bags and explaining something to Rasaiah who nodded frequently in return. That meant that this man was not the customer but the supplier of the goods.

What Murugesan did not know was that Rasaiah was toying with the idea of getting into the edible oil business. Bhupathi worked with the north Indian traders. This time he had struck a deal with a rich groundnut farmer from Maharasthra a state in the western part of India. Because it was the first consignment from that farmer and that too for Rasaiah, Bhupathi had taken a detour from his regular business trip and come to Gokulpet to inspect the goods.

Not that Murugesan cared. He had got what he wanted. This fellow who bore a striking resemblance to the man they called Aiyar, was actually Rasaiah's associate. Things were at last falling in place. And Murugesan did not waste any time.

A few days later In the wee hours of a stuffy night Murugesan's men picked the lock of the Godown, entered and studied the documents of the groundnut consignment. They got the address of the farmer and the transport company. But both belonged to a small town in deep Maharasthra. With the help of a guy who spoke Hindi in south Indian accent, Murugesan contacted the farmer over phone and told him that he wanted the address of his agent in South India. The unsuspecting farmer gave Bhupathi's cell number to the delighted Murugesan.

And then an over confident Murugesan, preening at his own brilliance, made the fateful phone call that resulted in Bhupathi's disappearance.

As soon as Bhupathi got the call from Murugesan, he realized that his cover was blown. Bhupathi knew that Irumban had been released and that he was in Singapore.

Though he had been kept away from the outfit by Irumban, Bhupalan was no fool. He knew who Irumban was and what he did. Not that it bothered him. He was an orphan any way, and was happy doing what he liked most—making money.

However Bhupalan genuinely cared for Irumban and considered him a father figure. Irumban was illiterate and Bhupalan did not want the man to lose out on anything. Though he worked diligently as the treasurer of the complete outfit, Bhupalan gave extra special care to Irumban's money. After Rajasuryan and the other guys withdrew their capital to strike out on their own, Bhupalan applied all his intelligence and focus on making Irumban wealthy.

This did not stop even after Irumban went to prison and Bhupalan relocated to Indore. Bhupalan still had a chunk of Irumban's money with him. Now that he was on his own in a new city, Bhupalan went into a full fledged career as a legitimate business man.

It was Parthipan's foresight that made Bhupalan change his name to Bhupathi. Bhupalan and Irumban had a joint account in a bank. Though it was operated by Bhupalan alone, yet the fact remained that Irumban was a joint holder. Irumban was gaining notoriety day by day after Rajasuryan's death, and Parthipan suspected that some day or the other some inquisitive auditor may dive deep into the bank records and come up with dirty linen. Not that there was any fear from the law. Bhupalan was a straight guy and had no police record. But the underworld was a different ball game all together. They could take this route and track down Bhupalan.

Before leaving Chennai for good, Bhupalan withdrew all the cash from the bank account over a period of few weeks and closed it. He left a considerable amount of Irumban's share with Parthipan, and then opened another account as Bhupathi in a different bank in Gokulpet with the help of Rasaiah. On reaching Indore he opened two separate accounts with the help of this new account—one in the same bank's Indore branch and one in another bank. In one account he deposited his cash and in the other one he deposited the balance amount of Irumban's money.

From then on, unknown to anyone except himself, Bhupathi made Irumban a sleeping partner in all his ventures. He operated both the accounts, paid the taxes diligently and deposited the profits equally in both accounts. When he went into speculation he invested the money in such a way that gradually Irumban's share of income went directly to Irumban's account. Bhupathi decided that when Irumban came out of prison, Bhupathi would hand over his share to him.

But Irumban went straight to Singapore after his release, and refused to have any contact with Bhupathi. Though it upset him, Bhupathi knew that there must be some reason for Irumban's decision. Even Rasaiah discouraged Bhupathi from contacting him unless and until it was absolutely necessary. Bhupathi wanted to tell Rasaiah that he still had Irumban's money with him but got tongue tied at the last moment. Not because he distrusted Rasaiah but because he feared that there could still be some unsavory elements on the prowl. These guys could eves drop on the matter and come after him and Irumban.

Bhupathi did not know how correct his intuition was.

Murugesan's call sent Bhupathi scuttling for cover. This sudden attack from an unknown flank threatened to bare him in front of the two persons Bhupathi cared for most, Sonia and Vimal. Bhupathi could not imagine how they would take it if they found that he had a shady past. Besides this, in case of a direct confrontation with this man who, Bhupathi had never seen before, all hell could break loose. Bhupathi shuddered at the very thought of this eventuality.

Bhupathi did not know who the caller was except that he was in some way connected to the Tamilnadu underworld. Nor did he try to find out how the guy got his cell number. However after pondering over the matter for a few hours, Bhupathi deduced that the call had come a month after Bhupathi met Rasaiah for the first time after several years. Bhupathi rightly suspected a leak somewhere at that end.

Bhupathi had opened four savings accounts for Sonia. He had also taken several fixed deposits in the names of his wife and son and the interest from these deposits was credited directly into these bank accounts. Sonia operated it independently and owned a couple of credit cards too. Bhupathi also had credit cards against these accounts but he seldom used them. Bhupathi had made Sonia financially independent.

But none in the family knew about the existence of the Gokulpet account and the two bank accounts that Bhupathi had opened after coming to Indore. He alone operated them and that too mostly online.

As the call was a long distance one, Bhupathi knew that the caller had made sure that he had the right man, before coming to confront him. There was no time to lose. Two days after the call, Bhupathi packed his suitcase, and left. As he went on business trips very often, Sonia did not suspect anything more so because there was nothing in his behavior or body language which could point to something untoward.

Rasaiah had once given Parthipan's phone number to Bhupathi with a request that Bhupathi should use it only during emergency. Parthipan was now an old man content to be with his daughter's family. Though he had brought Irumban over, the two lived separately. Irumban worked as a cook in one of the restaurants in Singapore. Cooking was his favorite job and he was happy doing that.

When the emergency arose, Bhupathi called Parthipan albeit reluctantly. Parthipan listened to Bhupathi and took his cell number. A few hours later Irumban called him. Bhupathi told him about the phone call and asked him if they could meet in Singapore. Irumban baulked and said that it would be better if they met in Chennai. Irumban did not want his past to create further trouble for him in this foreign country.

Bhupathi took his car and drove out of the city. He hit the highway and headed north. The distance between Indore and Gwalior is 486 kilometers and Bhupathi reached that town on the same day at around 10 PM. He had come to Gwalior several times before and he knew the place well. He parked the car in the mango grove and checked into a hotel near the railway station. He signed the register as Mr. Dhanapalan which was actually his late father's name. As it was a small hotel, and he had arrived there at midnight that too in the winter, the person in charge was not inclined to inspect his credentials. Even if he had done so, he could not have suspected anything because Bhupathi had a fake driving license in that name.

Bhupathi had always been a cautious man.

Next afternoon, he took a train to Delhi and checked into a hotel using the same fake driving license. There he lay low for some time. He suspected that his car would have been found and that the resultant chaos would obstruct his further plans. Further, he did not know where the call had come from. Let alone seeing Murugesan Bhupathi did not even know the name of the man. Whoever he was, he spoke Tamil but that did not mean that the fellow was in Tamilnadu. He could be anywhere. Bhupathi placed a call to Singapore and found that it would take some time for Irumban to come to India.

Bhupathi was in a catch 22 situation. He worried about his family constantly but was unable to contact Sonia because he knew that the cops would swoop upon him immediately. And when they did, he would have to explain his disappearance and he did not know how Sonia would take it when she came to know about his past. Sitting in his room, Bhupathi shed copious tears and prayed that everything should end well. After a few days Bhupathi decided to make his move.

Bhupathi took a flight and landed in Hyderabad. From there he travelled by bus to various towns and villages in Andhra Pradesh. He visited some temples, did some sightseeing and avoided his business contacts. After some days he reached the Karnataka border and from there he took a bus to Bangalore. After spending some days there, when he got the message that Irumaban had at last got a leave, Bhupathi took a Volvo from Bangalore, reaching Chennai early morning.

For the past few years, Bhupathi had been a regular visitor to Chennai. His past was already behind him and the city had gone more and more cosmopolitan over the years. Bhupathi checked into the same hotel in the outskirts of the town where he stayed regularly.

Then he sent a message to Irumban that he had arrived.

Irumban took the flight to Chennai and proceeded directly to his village. His parents were dead and the other relatives had relocated to other places. Irumban's ancestral home was now at his disposal and he had been maintaining it with the help of a care taker.

Old habits die hard. Unable to control himself, Irumban went to Chennai the same evening.

As a member of the Rajasuryan outfit, Irumban used to hang out in an ancient bar during free time. Over rum and soda, he would while away his time swapping stories with other members of the Chennai underworld. This kept him abreast of the happenings in the gangland besides an insight into the minds of guys of his ilk.

That evening when Irumban peeped in, he found none of the old faces. He took a table in a corner and ordered his drink. At around 11 Am, an old coot entered. Irumban screwed his eyes and peered at the fellow. The face looked familiar but irumban could not place him. One of the patrons passed a comment and the old man retorted acidly. Then Irumban realized that he was Babu a small time hood and freeloader who used to get drunk at other people's expense. Irumban called that guy over for a drink.

After the initial pleasantries they talked shop for some time. Babu guzzled like a fish and spun his yarn. Irumban knew that Babu was a washed out pickpocket who loved to talk big. But he humored him because the guy knew something or the other about every hood worth his charge sheet. Irumban caught up on news that he had missed for so many years. Little did he suspect that a lot of water had flown down the Coovam river since he went to prison, and that Babu was now a full fledged police rat.

Babu on the other hand had honed his singing skills well. Though he was stunned on spotting Irumban in the bar, he kept a poker face and played the fool to perfection. Babu had been the favorite clown for hoods down the years, and this had helped him in maintaining the façade of a harmless dimwit.

All through the conversation, Babu hadn't addressed Irumban by his name even once. He knew that Murugesan's men were crawling all over and that if they smelled something fishy it was curtains for the duo.

And this worried him.

Babu hated violence of any kind and was averse to getting caught in a cross fire at the fag end of his life. After downing several pegs, Babu suggested that they should leave the bar. Irumban got the drift, settled the bill and the two walked out.

Irumban offered to drop Babu back home and they hailed a, Auto. On the way Irumban mentioned casually that he had settled down in Singapore and was doing well. He also dropped a hint that he had come to Chennai to meet a guy who went by the name of Aiyar. Though drunk, Babu remembered this information and ratted in his next meeting with Jacob.

It was a tearful reunion for Bhupathi and Irumban when they met after a very long time. For Bhupathi, Irumban was the father who he had lost at the age of two. He embraced the old man and shed copious tears that washed away all his bottled up emotions. Irumban was moved by this open show of genuine affection. It was rare for a man like him to be loved so much by another. Even he felt a lump in his throat and could not speak for a few minutes. Then, tough guy that he was he came back to his normal self and told Bhupalan that they should immediately depart for Irumban's village. Bhupalan agreed and they left in a car lent to Bhupathi by one of his old business associates.

As Bhupathi drove the two exchanged notes about their individual lives. A chronic bachelor himself, Irumban was glad to know that his protégé had married and raised a family beside doing quite well in his chosen profession. Bhupathi told him how Irumban was a sleeping partner in all his ventures and Irumban was amused.

Segar the Murugesan plant in Rasaiah's godown, lived in a village a couple of furlongs away from Gokulpet. When he was out of work, he used to hang at a tiny market place near his village. Everyone knew Segar in that area and he would spend hours chatting, sipping tea, smoking and waiting for something to come up. Whenever he had some cash he would wind up his evenings with country brew that was sold in a wine shop in one corner of the market place.

It was around nine in the evening when Segar sauntered up to the shop with a hundred rupee note. He purchased a bottle of arrack and then walked towards the small bunk shop which sold fish fry and other such snacks. Segar ordered his dish and went to a corner for a smoke.

As he lit up he saw a dark colored Maruti 800 stop a hundred meters away. Two men got down from the front seat. One of them walked towards the wine shop.

The other younger fellow stretched himself, and gulped a mouthful of water from a plastic bottle.

Segar's heart stopped for a moment and then started racing. The man was the same guy who Segar had seen in the company of Rasaiah at the go down that fateful evening.

Segar did not recognize the other man. Nevertheless he observed him from the corner of his eye. The man was very short and built like a retired professional boxer. He was around fifty years of age but still possessed a threatening mien and looked like he had seen harder times. He was dressed in a white half shirt and white dhoti and could have passed for a bodyguard of some local politician. The man went to the wine shop, and purchased 2 beers and a full bottle of rum. But instead of coming to the snack shop, he turned away and went back to the car. A moment later they roared away.

All this happened in a matter of few minutes. Segar trotted to a public telephone booth and placed a call.

Holding his expensive cell phone Murugesan sat pole axed on his red colored leather revolving chair. His contact had just then passed on the message that Segar had spotted the curly haired man proceeding towards west of Gokulpet in a car along with another man that Segar could not place.

But Murugesan knew who he was. He also knew why the two were going in that direction and where.

After decades of painstaking search and endless dead ends, Murugesan had got so used to the frustration and heart burn that when at last he saw the light at the other end of the tunnel he did not know what to do. The two most wanted guys in his hit list had appeared at the same time and were grinning at his face.

Waves of excitement, greed, pain, sorrow, and anger struck his psyche repeatedly and Murugesan could not make out which sensation was more powerful than the other. The more he thought about it the more his single eye strained out of its socket.

"Irumban!" Murugesan thundered at last "Welcome to Hell!"

It was time to payback some old debts. As the faces of his two slain brothers Bhadra and Sethu drifted through his subconscious, Murugesan got ready for the final assault.

Immediately after Segar tipped off the outfit about Bhupathi, one of the local guys was sent to the house. This local was an expert burglar. Before Bhupathi and Irumban reached home this fellow removed the screws of a side window, big enough to let a normal sized guy inside the house. Then he informed Murugesan and vanished.

Irumban and Bhupathi reached the village house at around eleven in the night. They had deliberately taken a circuitous route lest they came across any unpleasant surprise at this juncture. As Bhupathi placed the drinks on the dining table, Irumban went inside the house and returned with some vegetables, fruits, pickles, and sides of meat from the fridge and prepared the side dishes.

A zero watt bulb illuminated the large hall in which Bhupathi and Irumban sat and sipped their drinks. Bhupathi gave him a detailed account of his life after he left Gokulpet. When he mentioned the sum that Irumban had made as a silent partner of Bhupathi's ventures, Irumban shook his head in disbelief. Of all the persons that Bhupathi had worked for Irumban had been the largest beneficiary.

"I am a bachelor!" Irumban said in his gruff voice. "And my needs are meager. Further, you have already paid back my investments several times over. What I suggest is that you let the amount lie in the account as it is. Whenever I need it I shall let you know and you can send it to me through Rasaiah."

Bhupathi nodded demurely. He had already told Irumban about the reason for his sudden urge to meet him. He had also told him about his suspicion that the leak could have been from Rasaiah's end. But Irumban soothed his frayed nerves and assured him that if he took the necessary precautions, Bhupathy could transfer the money safely through Rasaiah. As it would be online there should not be any problems.

"However" Irumban cautioned him "Avoid meeting Rasiah in person."

Whereas Bhupathi had sipped only a glass of beer Irumban had polished of half of the rum. Irumban was a regular drinker and he knew how to hold his drink. Bhupathi laid down on the couch in the hall and Irumban took a cold water bath before going to bed in the room at the back of the house.

After this meeting Bhupathi was a contented man. His confusion was over and he had gained Irumban's trust again. And after the beer and the heavy snacks that Irumban had served, the only thing he looked forward to was a dreamless slumber. As soon as he fell on the couch, Bhupathi was fast asleep.

It was around 3 AM when Murugesan and his men came in a black Maruthi Omni and stopped under a huge banyan tree a furlong from Irumban's village. They were 4 in number. 3 handpicked guys from Murugesan/s outfit and, Murugesan himself. The 3 guys had made their bones in the underworld by participating in several gangland skirmishes and were at ease in any violent situation. All of them were properly tooled up and combat ready. Murugesan did not want to take any chances with Irumban. They proceeded on foot, each going in a different direction. They all reached the house at almost the same time. One guy went to the back of the house, the other two approached from the flanks and Murugesan himself went to the front.

Murugesan went near the window, removed the grill, placed it on the ground noiselessly, and hoisted himself up. Deftly he placed his right knee on the base of the window and jumped in. As he was wearing tennis shoes, he landed on the floor like a cat. He straightened himself up and peered into the darkness.

A powerful beam of torch light hit his eyes with such sudden force that Murugesan winced and staggered back. An invisible foot tapped his right ankle and he tripped and fell. The torch light followed his face all the time. Murugesan brought up his right palm to shade his eyes.

"Good morning Murugesan!" A soft yet deep voice said "Is this a surprise visit?" With a click in the background, the hall was lit up by a fluorescent light. A stunned Murugesan stared at the benign face of Inspector Jacob Janardhanan. Another police man stood behind him his revolver drawn and pointed at Murugesan's head. Before Murugesan could make a move, Powerful arms hoisted him up and turned him around.

Neither Murugesan nor Irumban had ever seen each other before. But the hood recognized the short thickset elderly man immediately. Murugesan snarled and threw a solid punch at Irumban. It could have been easy for Irumban to duck it but he let it land as a compensation for Sethu's death.

It was quite a shot. Irumban was amazed at the brutal strength of the wiry fellow. But before either of them reacted, cops came from nowhere and surrounded them. Irumban was cooperative but Murugesan cussed, kicked and fought till a cop tapped him at the back of his head and threw him on the couch which was now vacant.

Moments later other cops trooped in holding Murugesan's other goons by their scruffs. Murugesan glared with anger, fear and frustration.

"Quite a party is it?" Jacob chuckled as all the hoods were handcuffed and chained together.

And then Murugesan looked behind Irumban.

Bhupathi stepped in from the darkness and stood behind Irumban. Jacob looked at him and then turned towards Murugesan:

"Come on Murugesan! He has come all the way to meet you. Won't you say hello for old times' sake?"

"Who is he?" Murugesan growled. At that instant Jacob turned towards Bhupathi.

"Hear that Bhupathi?"

A wide eyed Bhupathi looked at Murugesan "Sir this is the man who called me on my cell phone that night."

"Sure?"

"Yes Sir! There is no mistake. I can never forget this voice."

Half an hour later, the whole group left the house and proceeded to the nearest police station. Whereas Murugesan and his guys came in a police van along with the other cops, Bhupathi, Jacob and Irumban went by Bhupathi's car with Jacob on the wheel.

Though Irumban had left for Singapore after his release, he had kept in touch with one of the top cops who had helped him during his stay in the prison. This officer named Krishnamurthi was now retired and lived a peaceful life in a Chennai suburb. Before starting from Singapore, Irumban informed this gentleman about his plans.

This was an insurance against something untoward that could happen to him during his stay in Chennai. Irumban was more worried about Bhupathi than about himself. As a retired hood who had no contacts in the present underworld, Irumban desperately needed protection for himself and his companion. And what better way to ensure that than to inform a genuine retired cop about his plans? Irumban knew that Krishnamurthy would understand the situation and act accordingly.

Jacob had done a thorough study of irumban's file and had learnt about Krishnamurthi's role in Irumban's life. He contacted him to get some information about the case.

Krishnamurthi told him that whereas he was aware of Irumban's plans to come to Chennai, he had no idea about anyone called Bhupathi. Krishnamurthy assured all possible help to Jacob and promised to keep him posted. And as promised, Krishnamurthi informed Jacob when Irumban called him over phone. Krishnamurthi said that Irumban had not mentioned anything about Bhupathi but had suggested that he may be spending some time at his village to sort out some personal matters. Krishnamurthi also gave the address of Irumban's house to Jacob.

This was the information that sent Jacob on an overdrive. Jacob's men began casing Irumban's house a day before Irumban and Bhupathi landed there. Next night the team caught the local Murugesan man red handed while he was removing the screws from window of the house. From him they learnt that Murugesan was expected to hit the place that night. This confirmed the fact that Irumban would be arriving there. The burglar was ordered to make the call to

Murugesan confirming that all was well at Irumban's place. Then he was locked up in the police station.

Meanwhile when Segar spotted Bhupathi and Irumban at the market place, Irumban observed him too. Having been a hood all his life, Irumban smelt something fishy about the man. Immediately he sent a message to Krishnamurthi who in turn assured him that the cops were already all around his house and that he had nothing to worry. A relieved Irumban reached his house and went about his work as if nothing had happened. Though Bhupathi was blissfully unaware of anything, Irumban felt the presence of the cops around the house. While Bhupathi was in the hall, Irumban quietly went in and opened the back door. Then he went back with food items and joined Bhupathi.

Jacob and a few cops entered the house noiselessly and settled down for a long wait. Meanwhile other cops waited for Murugesan and his men to arrive.

When the Murugesan gang came, each from a different direction, the cops surprised the three fellows and nabbed them so fast that none was able to alert Murugesan. And Murugesan landed into the house through the same window and received a rousing welcome.

"What are you going to charge me with?" Murugesan jeered at Jacob. "You pounced on me before I could do something!"

The whole team had trooped into the small village police station and Jacob and Murugesan were now sitting face to face. Irumban and a visibly scared and tearful Bhupathi were taken to an adjacent room where they recorded their statements to a young and kind looking female inspector. The other goons were tossed into the same lockup where the cat burglar was waiting for them.

"Come on Murugesan!" Jacob smiled "Professional ethics demand that an ace gangster should respect a cop especially when the cop has been more efficient than the press and the public gives him credit for!"

"Sorry!" Murugesan sneered "No offence meant! But you have not answered my question."

"Well!" Jacob drawled "Breaking and entry to begin with!"

Murugesan scowled at him "What do you mean to begin with."

"Attempted burglary, possession of dangerous weapons with an intent to inflict bodily harm, attempted murder, and—" Jacob trailed away.

Murugesan felt a slow burn at the back of his ears. Sweat trickled down his side burns. Jacob's abrupt pause hinted at something ominous.

"And?" Murugesan parried

"Kidnap of Bhupathi!" Jacob spoke softly.

"Are you out of your mind?" Murugesan shouted. Two cops opened the door abruptly and peeped in.

"Manners, Murugesan, Manners!" Jacob said blandly. "I know how to make that charge stick. After all I have the "victim" as well as his "best friend" on my side. Further, the clowns that you brought along for this fool hardy caper would willingly testify against you to ensure a milder sentence for themselves."

By now Murugesan was sweating like a pig. He knew that Jacob had him by his most sensitive spot. He suddenly felt very tired. His shoulders hunched forward and he shook his head like a pendulum.

"Can I call my lawyer?" He asked in a hollow voice.

"Sure!" Jacob said kindly "Why not have some tea to boost your spirits before you make the call?"

As Murugesan sipped his tea, Jacob went out and called Inspector Puran Singh. Two days later, after the formalities were completed, Puran Singh took Bhupathi back to Indore. He and Jacob had tutored him well about what he had to say to the press. After an emotional reunion with Sonia and Vimal Bhupathi turned towards the local press reporters:

"I had been kidnapped on the highway by some unsavory elements and taken to Chennai. They also took my car and parked it in Gwalior to mislead the department. These men were not after my money, but they wanted to misuse my business acumen and my contacts in the market for their nefarious ends. It was thanks to the Gwalior, Indore and Chennai police department that I was rescued from their clutches without much harm. I and my family express our gratitude to Inspector Puran Singh and Inspector Jacob Janardhanan for saving my life."

As Bhupathi, Sonia and Vimal drove back home in the same car that he had abandoned in Gwalior, Bhupathi went into a brown study. As a voracious reader of business matters, Bhupathi had come across the biographies of several famous business men and industrialists. One of them had mentioned that every human being is born in a particular orbit and he strives all his life to pull himself out of it and jump into another one. Some of the ambitious ones keep changing their orbits till they reach a position where they feel that they have finally arrived.

Bhupalan was born with both his parents alive.

The first change in his orbit happened when his father died and his mother left him in an orphanage.

The second jump was when he left the orphanage and began earning.

The third was when he met Rasiah who in turn introduced him to Parthipan.

The fourth one was when Irumban took him in his fold and Bhupalan became a front for Rajasuryan's gang.

The fifth one saw Bhupalan become Bhupathi and start afresh as a legitimate businessman in a new city several thousand kilometers away from his home.

The sixth one was when Bhupathi got married and raised a family.

The running around should have stopped there. But Bhupalan alias Bhupathi had to work out some more Karma.

The seventh jump was inevitable because of Murugesan's phone call and forced him to flee from his peaceful existence into the same vortex of intrigue and violence from where he had escaped several years back.

And now he was back after tying up some loose ends.

If only Dhanpalan had not developed his arithmetical skills to survive in the market, he would not have transferred the same skills to his son.

If Rasaiah had not bought the tiny shop that Dhanapalan had left with his wife, he would not have had a soft corner for Bhupalan.

It was because of that that Bhupalan used to hang around the shop.

It was Bhupalan's extraordinary arithmetical wizardry which made Rasaiah to introduce him to Parthipan.

His father's talent and his tiny shop helped Bhupalan reach his present position, though the route was circuitous and at time vicious.

And when he went on a flight after the call from Murugesan, Bhupathi used his father's name to book his hotel rooms and tickets, to reach Chennai safely into the powerful arms of Irumban.

Alive, Dhanapalan could not see his dreams of educating and helping his son settle down cum true.

But dead, Dhanpalan had helped his son reach his final orbit.